HERE ARE THE
YOUNG MEN

To Binh Nguyen

HERE ARE THE YOUNG MEN

ROB DOYLE

THE LILLIPUT PRESS | DUBLIN

First published 2014 by
THE LILLIPUT PRESS
62–63 Sitric Road, Arbour Hill,
Dublin 7, Ireland
www.lilliputpress.ie

Acknowledgments
Thanks are due to the following people for invaluable
support of various kinds: Binh Nguyen; Antoinette
and Jimmy Doyle; Jamie Coleman; Alice Zeniter and
Dave Lordan; the staff at The Lilliput Press, especially
Antony Farrell, Fiona Dunne, Daniel Caffrey, Kitty
Lyddon and Nicole Flattery; and all my early readers.

A CIP record for this title is available
from The British Library.

10 9 8 7 6 5 4 3 2 1

ISBN 978 1 84351 619 4

Set in 10.5 on 15 pt Caslon with
Akzidenz Grotesk titling by Marsha Swan
Printed in Spain by GraphyCems

A Perversion of the Course of Justice

A confession without confessing. Admission without consequence.

Guilty. It's all true. We did these things.

I'm sorry.

Crucial details have been smudged: we're sorry and we don't want to be punished.

The boy's name, for instance. If I told you, and you're from Dublin, and you're of a certain age, you'd probably remember.

I'm sorry – I mean, I want to be.

This is all true. We did these things. This is all reality.

PART ONE

REALITY

For whom was one to bother, and to what end?

—E.M. Cioran, *The Trouble With Being Born*

1 | Matthew

If it's not broken – I chanted silently in rhythm to our steps – then break it. If it's broken, don't fix it. If it's fixed, break it again, break it more, wreck it. Wreck everything, and for no reason whatsoever …

We came to a stop.

Cocker drained his can of Coke and threw it on the ground. It rattled for a bit and then was still. We looked at it, the empty can. A breeze blew in across the grey stones of the beach, gusting the can a few feet along the seafront walkway.

'Give us a light,' I said.

Cocker lit my cigarette. Then he pulled up his hood and shivered. 'Poppers would be good,' he said.

I didn't respond.

He drew on his cigarette. After a moment he said again, 'It'd be good if we had some poppers.'

'But we don't,' I replied.

He said nothing.

Those two tall, red and white towers were on the horizon, kind of hazy in the cold morning light. There was some sun but it was a greyish day. I didn't mind. I liked grey days. So did Cocker. He told me that once, while we were on top of the hill in Killiney, looking out at the sea. Fucking freezing up there, it'd been. We'd had poppers that time, and two daddy-naggins of a type of vodka called 'The Count: Big Force!' that we'd bought at an offo out there but I'd never seen again.

'What do ye want to do?' said Cocker after a while.

'Yer ma.'

We walked along the seafront a little, though not because we were going anywhere. It was the force of inertia that moved us. That was a concept I'd picked up in one of Mr Ryan's science classes. It was sort of poetic.

The wind was picking up again, not that strong but cold, bracing. I shivered, pulled my bomber jacket close around my neck, focusing my eyes on the warm glowing dot of ember and ash at the end of my cigarette, lovely against the grey, like a telly in a window down some rainy street.

'There's nothin to do,' I muttered. But there was a sudden gust and my words were lost. It was better that way, I reckoned. What use was there in drawing attention to these things?

The red and white towers loomed in the distance. The Poolbeg Towers, wasn't that what they were called? I didn't even know what they were for.

'What are the towers for?' I asked Cocker.

'What towers?'

'The fuckin Poolbeg Towers. The two towers up there in front of ye. What are they for?'

'Industry, maybe,' said Cocker vaguely, looking elsewhere.

A while later he said, 'So here we are then, our first taste of freedom.' He gave a low whistle.

I'd thought I'd be more excited. We'd finished the last exam of our Leaving Cert, and now school, Irish, physics, and all the rest of it was behind us for good. I just craved a packet of crisps – salt and vinegar.

'Rez and Kearney will be finished soon,' said Cocker.

'And Jen,' I said.

We sat on a deserted pier and watched the foamy grey sea spewing driftwood and six-pack rings on to stones that were dark from the wet; shiny whenever the sun cut through the murk. We'd arranged to meet the others in Killiney later, so we could all get fucked and finally pay a visit to Bono. I lit another cigarette. Cocker was trying to smoke one through his nose, just for a laugh. I saw a ship in the distance. A seagull flew into a wind that pushed hard against it, so that it hung stationary in mid-air.

Cocker watched the bird for a while, hanging in the sky. 'Why do ye think yer man killed himself?' he said. He was talking about Stephen Horrigan again – the fella who'd been found hanging in our school on the last day of classes, a couple of weeks ago. A former pupil, he was. Some fifth year had found him when he entered his classroom that morning. Horrigan was swinging in the doorframe, his eyes bulging and staring right at you. The rumour was that he was on a boner. By the end of the day there were drawings of him all over the school, on blackboards, desks, everywhere. I wished I'd seen him, though not much.

'Who knows,' I said.

But Cocker was insistent, really thinking hard about it. 'But, like, what if that's it, though, that's what's in store for us?' he said. 'I mean, like, maybe he did it that way as a sort of warnin or whatever. Like to say, "Youse lads will be finished school in just a week or two, and look, here's the way it goes after that, this is the fuckin final destination or whatever." Ye know what I mean? Like a warnin.'

'Ah, I don't know, Cocker. Maybe he had other problems that ye don't know about. There's probably more to it than just that the world is rubbish.'

'Yeah,' Cocker muttered, unconvinced. After a while he said, 'Suicide,' and then whistled, reverting to his usual, unworried manner. 'It's a strange, strange thing.'

I let those fairly pointless words fade away. I looked out along the grey murky coastline, towards Bray.

―――――――――

Around one o'clock I perked up and said: 'Let's get a couple of naggins and get fuckin wasted!' Wasted was my new favourite word for fucked. Later I would start to use annihilated, or mangled, or destroyed. But for now, wasted was the word.

Once the idea – the inevitable idea – had been expressed, there would be no satisfaction at all until we got our hands on some alcohol and started getting wrecked, even earlier than we'd intended. Everything felt empty, drained, horribly boring. I needed a high, something to make it less oppressive.

'We'll have to go into the town and find someone to buy it for us,' said Cocker with a businesslike air. He had been trying to skim stones on the waves. All of them had plopped into the foam on first contact and vanished.

We couldn't buy the vodka ourselves because we were still in our school uniforms. Otherwise, we might have been okay. I had just turned seventeen, and looked seventeen. Cocker had turned seventeen just before me, but with the height of him he could pass for eighteen, or maybe not.

'C'mon then,' I said. We got up and walked towards the town. Cocker started humming the bassline from 'She's Lost Control' into the cold wind. We talked about the coming weekend. The plan was to get fucked on the Sunday night, not to mention the Saturday and Friday. Primal Scream were playing in the Olympia on Sunday. We were planning to try E for the first time. No doubt all our mas and das would soon be hassling us to go and get jobs. We'd be mad not to have one mental weekend first.

'Go on and call yer man,' said Cocker. 'See if he really can get us some of these happy love pills.' We were supposed to be cynical about ecstasy because of our punk-rock attitude, but curiosity was winning the day.

'Okay.' I took a crumpled scrap of paper from my pocket and unfurled it. _SCAG_, it said, followed by a phone number I'd gotten from Rez's older cousin, Patrick. 'Scag'll sort yis out,' he'd said.

Cocker watched as I took out my phone. I dialled the number.

Half an hour later, having arranged to pick up the E in a couple of days, and then gone and bought a litre of cheap vodka, we left the leafy little suburb with the posh oul ones, walked back to the seafront, and sat on the pier. It was still deserted, windswept. A big fat rat scuttled up from the rocks down the side of the pier and vanished down a black crack. I imagined all the rats having some kind of meeting down there, like in a cartoon. In my mind all the rats spoke in Cockney gangster accents.

Cocker opened the bottle and poured a shot into the lid. He drained it and grimaced. Then I did the same.

We were running along the beach, roaring and waving our hands in the air. There was no one else around, but we wouldn't have cared if there had been. I felt free, blissful. Anger flooded my nerves and limbs like the Rapture. I looked towards the city, blurry and over-heated in pale afternoon drunkenness. That city, it was full of cunts. I stopped running and planted my feet apart and raised my two middle fingers towards the low coastal skyline.

'CUNTS!' I roared.

Later we took the DART the rest of the way to Killiney. I was on a great buzz and I thought Cocker was too. But when there was only one stop to go, he fell quiet, closed his eyes and leaned forward. 'Hang on, Cocker,' I said. 'We're almost there. Seriously, just hold on another couple of seconds …'

We were moments away from the station when he puked across the floor. People turned to look. I hid my eyes but my shoulders were shaking with giggles. There weren't too many people in the carriage, but one oul one was sitting on her own in the back seat. She saw Cocker puking but then she fixed her gaze straight ahead, looking all serious and dignified. She pretended nothing was happening; no doubt she thought we were a threat, a violent urban menace. 'Cocker ye nutcase,' I said through the laughter as we stumbled off the train. 'You're such a fuckin lightweight.' Cocker still heaved with nausea, but already he was seeing the funny side.

Out on Killiney beach we could see Rez and Kearney near the edge of the sea. I whistled to them and waved but Kearney didn't notice because he was pacing about, waving his arms, in the middle of one of his rants. Rez was looking at the sea, with his sunglasses on and an inward expression, like he was only half listening. He was always like that, these days. When he heard my whistle he turned and smiled, absently.

I could hear what Kearney was saying as we came up behind him: 'Ye have to start shootin loads of Proddy fuckers in the street in front of their families and everything. Then ye have to plant bombs in shoppin centres and all, and shoot yer way out if the RUC get wind of ye. And when yer comin up to the end of the game, it switches over to England, ye have to start takin the war to the Brits, like fuckin bombin pubs and trams and all that. The RUC have started torturin and decapitatin Catholics on the six o'clock news on the BBC and all, so it fuckin … deviates from history a little bit. And the last mission, listen to this, the last fuckin mission is ye have to assassinate the queen. And fuckin Prince Charles and the young princes as well. It's a sniper-and-bomber co-ordinated job, ye have to –'

Rez was making a here-we-go-again face for me and Cocker. Now he turned and said, 'But are ye takin the piss, Kearney?'

Kearney frowned. Only now did he notice me and Cocker. 'No. What do ye mean?' he said.

'They made a game about the IRA? And ye have to plant bombs in shoppin centres and kill the fuckin queen? Are ye jokin or what?'

'No. Jesus, Rez, were ye even listenin? It's not a real game, this is a game that *I* want to invent. *Provos!* it's called. Were ye even fuckin listenin?'

I laughed.

'It'll be a great fuckin game,' Kearney went on, flashing me his alligator grin. He turned back to Rez. 'But come on and make us another one of those spliffs. We deserve it after all those exams. The amount of study we put in!'

We laughed at that.

We finished the vodka and then Rez took another bottle from his tattered, heavily grafittied schoolbag. When Cocker and Kearney were off howling at these two girls who were walking past, Rez took a swig, passed me the bottle and said, 'Did ye notice it?'

'What?' I said.

'Kearney's accent. Like I was sayin to ye before. Have ye not noticed? It's not like a real accent any more. It's like a caricature of an accent, like he's doin an impression of someone doin an impression of an Irish accent. Someone from fuckin Sweden.'

I grinned and wiped my lips with my hand. 'I don't know. He still just sounds like Kearney to me. You're just smokin too much. You're such a weirdo, Rez.'

I was about to ask him how he'd done in the final exam, but my phone beeped in my pocket. I took it out and read the message. It was from Jen: '*Hi am on the way. Hope u did well, c u in 10 xx.*'

I wondered if she'd sent it to all the lads. I looked around; none of them were taking out their phones. She had only sent it to me. I put the phone away.

On his hunkers in the sand, looking out at the waves, Rez lit a cigarette. Then he swigged on the vodka and swung the bottle in front of him, tracing the horizon. 'I love it out here. Seriously. That's the best thing about Dublin, you're never that far from the sea. All exiles are drawn to the sea – I read that somewhere.'

I watched Kearney in the distance. Cocker had come lurching over, cheerful again after the vomiting. 'Yer always readin books, Rez,' he said. 'Yer mad, ye are. Who ever learned anything from a book?'

'That's a good point, Cocker. I'll have to rethink my whole entire outlook on things, now that you've told me that,' said Rez.

'But this thing about the sea, it doesn't work for us,' I said. 'How can we be exiles if we're in our own country?'

Rez shrugged. 'Well, ye can be an exile in your own body, or in your own family, or in your own fuckin century, so why can't ye be an exile in your own country where ye were born?'

'Ye can be an exile in yer own arse,' said Cocker. He cackled and fell backwards to land with a thump on the damp sand.

But now Rez was warming to his theme. 'Are ye seriously tellin me ye don't feel like that here?' he asked me.

I shrugged. 'I suppose.'

'I mean, what does it really mean to you to be Irish? I mean, like, growin up in the suburbs, which may as well be anywhere, and watchin American films and English telly and English football, and everyone you're supposed to look up to, all they go on about is cars and mortgages, and these are supposed to be the most important things in life. The property ladder. Jesus. And now we're expected to race out there and join in the fun? No thanks. I mean, at least we feel depressed about what we're seein around us.'

'Yeah,' I said. I'd heard it a hundred times. I murmured something about the consumer wasteland and threw a stone into the sea.

Really, I was thinking of Jen. I lit a cigarette and sat down, scanning the grey horizon, the waves.

Just then I heard a call and we looked around: Jen, walking towards us along the beach, waving. She was smiling and her dark-red hair was swept up in the wind.

When she reached us she said, 'So here we are on the other side. It's all over. We made it. We're free. So how did it go?'

We made vague noises.

'I see,' she said, raising an eyebrow. Jen was the only one among us who'd done any real study.

After a while we went down to where there are caves cut into the bottom of the cliffs. We found a quiet spot and sat down on our jackets, putting the bottle and some cans on the ground beside us. Rez got a spliff together. While we were smoking, Jen asked, 'So guys, have yis worked out what yis're all goin to do now that the Leavin Cert is over?'

There were various mumbles, nothing in particular.

'Have you?' I asked her.

She shrugged. 'Yeah. I mean I'm still plannin to go to college, but probably not straight away. In the meantime I know I can always work with my dad for a while, if I want to. I know he'd pay me well and I wouldn't have to do that much work. But I really don't know if I want to work for *daddy*.' She said the word in a piss-taking kind of way, which I liked. 'I think I'm goin to go travellin, maybe. Before college. Maybe at the end of the summer. I'm thinkin of takin a year out.'

'Oh yeah? Where are ye goin to go?' asked Cocker. 'I'd love to go to Spain. They're mad fuckers over there. The way they smoke, they make us look like a bunch of ponces. I knew this Spanish guy last summer, he was a mate of me brother's, and I swear to Jaysus, he made me feel like a fuckin pioneer. He'd light up a bong first thing in the mornin and wouldn't move away from it, even to eat his breakfast, until the middle of the afternoon. He clung to the bong like it was his fuckin baby infant. If he had to leave his gaff at all, even just to go down to the shop for munchies, he'd roll about four joints, just in case. Or, as he said it, "just if case-ed". Fuckin hell, now he was a *real* stoner.'

We were all laughing away. Cocker was probably exaggerating, if not making the whole thing up, but it didn't really matter. Even if the stories Cocker told were total bullshit, and they usually were, the fact that he'd bother to lie like that at all was funny in itself.

Jen was smiling too but she seemed far away, looking out at the sea. While we were still chuckling about the Spanish dope fiend, she said: 'I don't really know where I want to go. Maybe Asia, or South America. Or Africa. I don't know. Somewhere really *different*. Where do people go? People travel these days, don't they? You don't have to be rich to do it, or –'

'But ye *are* rich,' I interrupted.

'– or some hardcore adventurer type. People go travellin all the time. But anyway, we'll see if I get into Trinity or UCD first of all.'

'How come ye want to go travellin?' asked Cocker. 'Doesn't Dublin do it for ye? It's the centre of the universe. Don't forget Gay Byrne lives here, and didn't Celine Dion play the RDS only last week? What more could ye want, Jen?'

'Dublin is just so fuckin *dull*,' she said. 'I mean, I love you lads, and Louise, and Gráinne and Michelle, and some of the others. But most people here, they hardly seem to be alive at all, do ye know what I mean?'

'That's just what I was sayin to Matthew a few minutes ago,' said Rez.

'All the yuppies,' I said. 'They've taken over. We need to launch some kind of resistance.'

'An insurgency,' said Rez.

'Yeah, with roadside bombs and IEDs and stuff,' said Kearney. 'And a war on knackers as well. *Dawn of the Dead*, it'll be like.'

'It's not even that they're yuppies or whatever,' Jen said. 'That's everywhere. They're just … I don't know, spiritless or something.

They've no real curiosity for life, they just want it the usual way. I'd be bored out of my mind if I stayed here. Don't yis feel the same, ever?'

'Yeah, I do,' I said.

We all fell silent, thinking our own thoughts. After a minute or two Rez said, 'What about you, Cocker, what's your plans?' He'd put on his dark glasses again, despite the cloudy sky.

Cocker took the spliff that Kearney passed him, pondering the question. 'I haven't really got any idea. If I get enough points I'll study sound engineering, but I probably won't. I wasn't exactly at home burnin the fuckin midnight oil, was I? Haha. Porin over the books, like? I doubt I'll get enough points to get in anywhere.'

'That's the spirit, Cocker,' said Kearney.

'And what if ye don't get in anywhere?' I asked.

He shrugged. 'Work for a while, I suppose.'

'In Dunnes Stores where ye are now?'

'Why not? It's not exactly a long-term plan or anything. One place is as good as another.'

'As shite as another, ye mean.'

'That's exactly what I mean.'

'Stackin tins of beans and facin off on the jacks-roll aisle – Cocker, you're goin to be a credit to your parents, I'm tellin ye,' said Rez, chuckling.

'Yeah, I know. I can just see me ma flushin with pride when she goes to do the shoppin and meets her thirty-year-old son, fuckin moppin the floor over by the meat counter.'

Stoned off my head, I got the giggles at the image of a shabbier, older Cocker, ruddy as ever, in a Dunnes Stores T-shirt with some oul one asking him where the tampons were.

'And you, Connelly?' asked Cocker when my giggling subsided.

'Well, I'm still hopin I'll be able to get into college,' I said. I had applied to study English in the few colleges in Dublin where you could do it. English meant literature; that was alright. Books weren't bad. I wasn't into them as much as Rez, but they were more interesting than studying business, for example. Business wasn't interesting at all. In fact I despised it. Besides, the reason I wanted to go to college didn't have much to do with the pursuit of knowledge; I wanted to go because it seemed like the only alternative was to work, and I hated work. I'd had part-time jobs before and it was a load of shit. The idea of working full-time filled me with horror.

'Ye mean ye seriously reckon you'll get in when ye never lifted a finger to study for the exams?' Cocker asked.

'I'll get enough marks,' I said. 'I'm one clever bastard.'

'We'll see about that,' said Cocker, grinning.

The wind picked up. The sea was getting choppier.

'The future,' said Rez out of nowhere, somberly. We were silent for a while, the Irish Sea crashing cold against the cliffs. I was on a nice buzz and it was making me sentimental. I started feeling sad about everything, kind of nostalgic, and then anxious for what was coming next – real life, as everyone always called it.

I said to the others, 'We should all stick together, though. I mean, we should all keep in touch. Not just keep in touch, like ringin each other up and shakin hands when we meet and all that crap, like a bunch of yuppies, but stay *close*, stay as mates, like. Ye know what I mean?' I wanted to tell them that they were like a family to me or something, but I was afraid they were going to rip the piss out of me.

They didn't take the piss, though, not even Kearney. They didn't really say anything, just nodded and murmured softly, like they'd been thinking the same thing before I said it.

A while later, Rez had one of the sudden bursts of energy he was still capable of now and again. He pounced to his feet, dark glasses on like Lou Reed and a spliff dangling from his mouth, and announced, 'I know what we can do, lads! I've got it sussed. After we get the results we can all get our hands on a leprechaun suit each, and then we'll go into town and stand on Grafton Street and tell all the Yanks who come along that we're authentic fuckin Irish leprechauns. Can yis picture it? "Ah sure to be Jaysus, aren't we only a troupe of Irish leprechauns, innocently wanderin down this enchanted Grafton Street, but if yis'd like to throw a few of those silver American coins into me oul Paddy cap, sure it'd be no quare thing at all, at all. Sure aren't we only magic, us bleedin leprechauns, to be sure to be sure." ' He held the spliff out like a pipe and puffed on it with his brow furrowed. 'Jen, you can be Molly Malone.'

Cocker's eyes lit up. 'Did yis ever see the tits on Molly Malone, the one in town? Seriously, have a look next time you're in there. I always stare down at them until too many people are lookin at me. I can't help it, they're fuckin gorgeous. Ye can just tell she'd be total filth. Same as Miss Nolan.'

Jen was giggling. She looked up at me, sitting very close, her cheek resting on her knee. Her hair was curved like a wave. I looked away.

Jen went home around four o'clock, taking the DART the few stops back to Blackrock. We walked with her to the station. 'Give my regards to Lord Bono,' she said. 'Anyway, I'll see you guys on Saturday.' She flashed me a smile that was bright and sincere. My mind was warm and foggy with the drink. Jen is alright, I thought.

'Right,' said Cocker when Jen had gone, clapping his hands together. 'Are we ready to do this, or wha?'

We walked for twenty minutes before coming to Bono's house. Cocker knew the way. He had gotten the exact directions from his brother or someone, really keen on doing it, as we all were. Kearney remained quiet as we approached the coastal mansion. I wondered if he was building up to something. That was Kearney's style.

A wide gravel driveway led up to the black metallic gate. At the side there was one of those speakerphone things. 'Here we are,' said Rez when we reached the gate. 'The Bonosphere. This is as close as we can get without gettin shot by his lasers.'

'A-Bonomation,' I said.

We huddled around the electronic speaker and Rez pressed the button.

It beeped and a mildly distorted voice said, 'Yes?'

'Oh *hi*. Is Bono there, please?' said Cocker in a fake D4 accent.

'And who may I say is calling?'

'Oh we're just friends of the great man, friends and admirers, uh, don't you know.'

We sniggered and covered the sound with our sleeves, ducking away from the microphone.

'I'm afraid I'll need a name, sir.' The voice was deadpan, giving no sign of irritation. Maybe Bono's security guards were used to this kind of shit.

Now Cocker's accent was a posh English one, like the royal family: 'Oh well yes, please tell Mr Bono that this is his good friend Elton John.'

The grainy electronic voice had started politely but firmly telling us to get lost when Cocker leaned right into the speaker and shouted: 'BONO YE WANKER! YERRAN AN OUT-AND-OUT FUCKIN CUNT, DO YE KNOW THAT? YERRA TOTAL FUCKIN DISGRACE TO THE IRISH AND MOST OF ALL TO YERSELF, YER BAND IS SHITE AND I HOPE YE FUCK OFF AND DIE ...'

He paused, panting and out of breath, and I took over.

'YERRAN ABSOLUTE FUCKIN TOSSER, YE DON'T HAVE A CLUE WHAT YER TALKIN ABOUT AND YER FULL OF SHIT AS WELL, ALL THIS BOLLOCKS ABOUT AFRICA AND THE THIRD WORLD 'N' ALL ...'

Now I was the one who gasped for breath; Kearney shoved me aside and stuck his face into the speaker.

'CUNT! CUNT! FUCKIN GAY FAGGOT WANK-STAIN *BAS*TARD! FUCKIN *BAS*TARD! I FUCKIN *HATE* YE, I WANT YE TO FUCKIN *DIE*, YE FUCKIN *WANK*ER! I'LL COME IN THERE AND RAPE YER FUCKIN WIFE AND KILL YER FUCKIN

BABIES! I'LL TORTURE THE LITTLE SHIT-STAINS, I'LL STICK
ME FUCKIN COCK UP THEIR ARSES TILL IT PUSHES THEIR
BRAINS OUT THEIR LITTLE DEAD FUCKIN MOUTHS! I'LL
RIP THEIR LITTLE FUCKIN HEADS OFF AND I'LL STICK
THEM UP ME ARSE WHILE YER FUCKIN CUNT WIFE LOOKS
ON, THEN I'LL RAPE THAT SILLY LITTLE BITCH AND YE
CAN WATCH, YE TOTAL FUCKIN SPASTIC YE.'

Finally he had to stop and breathe. By now we had all backed
off; we looked at Kearney in astonishment. Where the fuck had all
that come from?

'Jesus, Kearney,' said Rez. 'That's goin too far, you're goin to get
us arrested.'

Kearney was bent over, squealing with laughter. 'Relax, Rez,' he
panted when he was able, hands on his knees and face all red.

'No I won't fuckin relax. Ye can't say all that stuff, that's too much.
Sayin you'll kill his children, for fuck's sake. C'mon, I'm gettin away
from here before the guards arrive.'

I was with Rez on that one. So was Cocker and so, finally, was
Kearney, racing after us as we scampered away, through clumps of
trees at the sides of the coastal roads, hurrying when we heard the
sound of sirens in the distance.

———————

Hours later, on the bus home, there was no more vodka and I was
feeling awful. It wasn't a hangover, just a sickening sense of emptiness, like there was a cold pit inside me and I was at the bottom,
looking up towards a distant skylight, shivering. I wanted to keep
getting fucked but there was no way. The lads were all heading home
and I had to as well.

Cocker got off the bus at his stop, muttering that he'd see me in
town on Saturday. I watched him walk away as the bus growled off
to take me the last few stops.

There was no one at home when I got there. I went to my room and fished out a porno magazine and had a wank; it was slow and long because I'd been drinking. The picture was of a woman on all fours, looking back over her shoulder into the camera. She had a pretty face. Before I came I felt a stab of sadness that I couldn't meet this girl, lie in bed with her and do all the things to her that I was thinking about doing while I pulled myself off; but talk to her as well, make her laugh and let her tell me kind things about myself.

When I had finished I slid the magazine under my bed, wiped myself off with some toilet paper, and then lay down and let a fog of doze wash over me, dragging me into oily oblivion as the night fell outside and the room grew colder.

2 | Kearney

Problems with Reality: Kearney Loves Death

Snapshot Number 1: Drink it in, Kearney!

– Big titted MILF has to whore herself to pay

– Fisted, fucked, and left for dead!

– Sexy fuck meat gets fucked so

– teen rape Asian anal frenzy

– Ebony cutie pounded in kitchen then forced to

– Filthy Euroslut Cindy gives great

– Clara fists herself in the back of a car. She spreads her pink

– horny Latina just loves the dick

– War and Peace – in her pussy!

– First-time teen slut sucks 2 black cocks and learns to love it!

– strap-on Sally made to bleed but begs for more

– Dildo Holocaust – the ANAL solution!

– 2 Cops pound there Massive Cocks into 4 ripe sluts and DP there tight assholes bloody red n Raw!!

– is a total freak who literally orgasms, she says, when you fuck her throat until she gags. Check out this

– Balkan bitch gets boned N stretched by

– Jane Pain says fuck her mouth til you rip the skin off her face

And so on and so on.

3 | Matthew

Dear Mr and Mrs Connelly,

We regret to inform you that Matthew has been forbidden from attending next Wednesday's graduation ceremony, due to his unacceptable behaviour and the lack of respect he has shown for the school, for his teachers and for his fellow pupils throughout the year. This will not affect your son's academic record with the school.

My da flung the letter down on the table and turned away in disgust. I said nothing. I sat there and waited for it to be over. My head was still in bits from all the vodka and spliff the day before. My ma looked on from behind him.

'What the hell is goin on with ye?' my da said.

We were in the kitchen. A pot was simmering and there was the smell of sizzling grease from fish fingers on the grill. I didn't answer.

'Well,' he demanded. 'What is it? Aren't ye happy? What a *fuckin* disgrace. We can't even see our own child graduatin. Do ye have any idea how humiliatin that is for us?'

I kept looking at the table, saying nothing. These were rhetorical questions. I wondered whether the lads had been barred as well. Surely they had: we were all as bad as each other.

'When that letter arrived this mornin the first thing I did was get on the phone to Mr Landerton,' my da went on. 'From what he says, ye've been lyin through yer teeth to us for months. He says he'd be very surprised if ye so much as passed the Leavin Cert. And he said it's a shame as well, cos ye used to be one of the brightest lads in your class, until ye started gettin all moody and actin the prick. What in the name of God is wrong with ye?'

I shrugged again, but sensed that if I kept doing that he might take it as a provocation. I said, 'I don't know. It's all … I don't know.'

'What's that supposed to mean? "I don't know." Can ye not even speak, is that the problem?'

My mother broke in: 'Leave him, will ye. Jumpin down his throat like that isn't goin to help anything, is it?'

'You hang on a minute. I was speakin to him, let me speak to him before ye go defendin him when he's not even answerin me properly!'

My mother had placed the lid of the pot at a slight tilt, so some of the heat escaped and it wouldn't boil over, and now she sat back down at the table with us. 'We're just worried about ye, Matthew, that's all,' she said softly. 'Ye always done well at school before. But now there's this. A whole year of it and then this. What's gone wrong with ye at all?'

I wanted to tell them that I was miserable and could they fix everything, like I was a child still. Instead I shook my head and looked intently at the surface of the table. 'I'm alright,' I said. 'Don't mind Landerton, I'm sure I did alright in the exams.' I started wondering if I could get away with smoking a spliff out the window of my room, or whether I'd have to 'go for a walk' as usual, smoke it out in the cold and the rain, then skulk back in and up to my room to listen to music and fuck around with lava lamps. Or maybe they would go out tonight because it was a Friday and I'd be able to smoke my joints freely, rob some vodka or Bacardi from their press, and get out the porno.

'Look at your sister,' my ma was saying. 'Never so much as a word from her teachers, unless they're singin her praises. Why couldn't ye have been more like her?'

I considered some nasty, sarcastic reply but I didn't have it in me. I kept looking at the table and shrugged limply.

My da started up again.

['Do ye not realize how lucky ye are? Ye don't, do ye. Look at all the opportunities that are out there, waitin for ye. This country has never had more money in it than it has now. Jesus, we used to be hardly any better off than a Third World country, and I don't even mean a long time ago. And now our economy is the envy of the bleedin world, and all you and your mates do is sit there mopin. I'll fuckin tell ye now – *I* envy *you*, and everyone else your age. Ye can sneer all ye like, but this Celtic Tiger they're talkin about, it's no joke. Ye just don't appreciate it cos ye don't remember what it was like before, when we had sweet fuck all. Back when I was eighteen, nineteen, Jaysus, I'd have given me right arm to have what all youse have. But ye don't lift a finger. Ye just can't see it, can ye.]

He looked like he was going to say more, but instead he just scowled and shook his head. I looked hard at the table.

'It's true, Matthew,' my ma said. I saw that she was nearly in tears and there was a feeling in me like a rising heat. But I hated them both.

'What the hell are ye goin to do with yer life?' my da said. 'I'll tell ye one thing, if ye really did make a balls of your Leavin Cert because ye were too busy dossin and feelin sorry for yourself, ye better not expect us to support ye. The way yer goin, ye might end up on the fuckin street. Have ye thought about that? I suppose ye'd expect someone else to sort it all out for ye if ye did. Just like me fuckin brother. What'll ye do for the summer? Have ye started lookin for a job yet?'

I scowled and said, 'I just did me last exam yesterday, how could I have had time to find a job?'

'Well ye better get lookin for one soon enough, cos ye needn't think ye'll be mopin around here all summer long.'

'What'll ye do if ye don't get into college?' my ma said desperately.

'I *will* get in,' I said, still not looking them in the eyes.

My da sighed in exasperation and clattered up from his chair. He hissed and muttered as he banged out of the room.

'Ye've just upset him,' said my ma. I looked at the table for a moment longer. Then I opened my mouth and was about to say something. Instead, I shook my head, exhaled sharply through my nose, stood up and went to my room.

I rolled a spliff and then I went out for a walk.

4 | Kearney

Snapshot Number 2: Typical schoolday

The alarm goes off and Kearney opens his eyes. A phrase is resounding in his mind: *Violence is my bread and butter*. Only half lucid, still embroiled in slaughter dreams, Kearney nods his head in grim acquiescence.

He eats his breakfast and leaves the house. On the bus into school, still irritable, and queasy from the food, he slaughters everyone onboard. This is routine. His expression is cold as deep space as gunfire tears through the upper deck, blasting out windows, ripping children in half amidst howls of terror. As the day's first visions of carnage stoke his mind into a semblance of alertness, Kearney exhales in relief. He needs this shit to make his bus journey interesting, to make it bearable.

At school he sits in class, more or less quietly, more or less obediently. Mr Landerton, then Maloney, then whoever, drones on about whatever the fuck it is – history, English, economics, Irish, biology – it all passes Kearney by while he stares at the back of the boy in front of him, or at the blackboard, lost to reveries of carnage and fucking. None of this shit is real for him; it is an alien world impinging on his reality, which is infinitely sexier. He perceives the *official* world through a kind of fog, dimly, and it nauseates him. He understands little of it and cares for less.

Just before the first break it starts to get too much. Kearney bites his lip and stabs his compass into the desk. He wants to fuck something, fuck anything. The equations on the blackboard mean so little to Kearney that he is overcome by a wild inner hilarity – what a wretched cosmos, what a hateful existence! He giggles until first the boys around him, then the entire class, are staring in astonishment. It is time, he thinks. Slowing his breathing, he closes his eyes for a moment; then he reaches down into his schoolbag for the two heavy, fully loaded handguns. Matthew, sitting innocently at his left-hand side, is the first to go. His brains, gore and bone shards spew a horizontal fount across the room. Then Kearney is on his feet, pumping round after round into the soft teenage flesh of his classmates: Kearney, the void at the centre of chaos.

And so on and so on.

5 | Matthew

On Saturday morning I went into town to meet Cocker and Jen. We met at the Central Bank, on the steps. The Goths were there as usual, a big gang of them, and the rockers in Slipknot hoodies and dyed hair. They were all the same. Some of the girls were nice, though. Most of the Goths had posh accents but they usually drank a lot. They smoked spliff as well, and probably even did other stuff, the kind of drugs that me and my friends didn't know where to find. I knew a few of the Goths and rockers from school. I said hello when I saw Aido, who had this scraggly yellow hair in curls. He was into Death Metal. I didn't like Death Metal at all. It made me want to die – too cold and hard.

Jen came last, getting off the bus from Blackrock. She smiled when she saw me and Cocker, stopping twenty yards away to wave at us with exaggerated emotion, like we were long-lost siblings reunited. I nodded at her, but sullenly. Cocker's greeting was brighter. Jen had been with Cocker before. They had kissed one night when we were drinking cans down the banks of the skinny

Dodder that flows through Tallaght like a fugitive sewer. She had been with Kearney as well, and Mick Mooney, and most of the lads I knew – everyone except me, basically. She had even been with the Cabbage. Mick Mooney said he'd shagged her and she had never confirmed or denied it; all the others said they'd fingered her, and Kearney said she'd given him a blowjob, though she did deny that. She said she'd only ever kissed Kearney, once while she was drunk. That was a good while ago; they didn't seem to talk that much, Jen and Kearney.

We wandered around Temple Bar for a while, killing time. We went into Purple Haze and Spindizzy Records, rifling through the punk section, looking at the DVDs. We went into the new head shop, but it was a load of bollocks because they sold this 'marijuana substitute' for a score a bag, and all it did was give you a headache and make you thirsty. Besides, it wasn't like real hash was exactly hard to come by, even if the stuff we got was always fairly shit.

We didn't buy any CDs because we didn't have much money, and we wanted to get drink later. We went down to Meeting House Square and smoked two of the spliffs that me and Cocker had brought, pre-rolled. The smell and taste of the hash was sickly, pungently sweet and not pleasant at all. But I sucked hard on the joint, and when the second one was half gone I felt panicky because there was nothing worse than that feeling of not having anything left and all you wanted to do was keep going. There were more joints for after, though, so it was okay.

It was kind of sunny that day, but cold like the autumn. When we were stoned, Cocker led us out of Temple Bar, across Dame Street and down a narrow side street. He ducked into a doorway and we followed, into a grimy stairwell that led upwards to a roof at the top of the city. There was nobody around to tell us to go back down. We stood up there and leaned against the wall, looking over at Trinity College, all stern and proud like some hostile alien fortress. Behind College Green and to the left was O'Connell Bridge and the Liffey, and then the whole of O'Connell Street, running up past Easons and Clerys and all the rest of it. There were big statues on that street but I'd never bothered to learn who they were. Jen probably knew. There were books in her house.

We were leaning against the low wall, alone up there. Jen was in the middle, with me and Cocker on either side. She leaned over and spat down. We watched it fall, spiralling out in widening arcs before landing on the path near a trendy-looking woman with spiky blonde hair and a shiny green jacket. Stoned, I thought of how there were so many people in this city who made me feel strange, different, alien, just by looking at them.

Jen and Cocker had shuffled closer to each other, and she was running the toe of her Converse runner up his calf. She was giggling a lot, and he wasn't laughing exactly but he had a smile on his face as he murmured to her, words that I couldn't hear.

Fuck them, I thought. But I looked at Jen's arse, round and trim in her close-fitting jeans, and was nauseous with stoned desire.

Jen had stepped back away from the edge and was doing a dance, flailing her arms about and closing her eyes. Cocker watched her and I pretended not to. 'Dublin's burning with boredom, now! Dublin's burning dial nine-nine-nine-nine-nine!' she chanted.

I started worrying that I wasn't stoned any more, or that I was still stoned but less so, which would mean it was all downhill from here. 'Let's smoke another joint,' I said, already fishing out my hash box from the back pocket of my jeans, where I had placed the row of pre-rolled spliffs.

'I'm still stoned,' said Cocker, but he didn't try any harder than that to dissuade me. I lit up, sucking hard on the spliff, constantly monitoring the progress of my buzz, anxious that because I'd already been stoned it would be hard to get back to that level again. Maybe it was time to start drinking.

I passed the spliff to Jen and she drew on it, letting smoke spill slowly from her nostrils. Then Cocker puffed on it meditatively, quietly. He smoked like he could take it or leave it – that made me feel inferior, chronically unsatisfied.

'Give us a blow-back,' I said to him when it was near the end. We cupped our hands and he brought his mouth close to mine, puffing out a cloud of smoke through the tunnel of our interlinked hands. It shot into my lungs and made me wheeze, my eyes watering.

Jen was laughing. 'Too much for ye, Matthew, was it?'

'Fuck off. You do it and see if you can not splutter,' I said when I had regained my composure.

'Fair enough,' she said, surprising me. Then Cocker was leaning over her, his forehead pressed against hers, their eyes close together, mouths nearly touching. They stayed pressed together for a long time. Then Jen inhaled and she drew back. Cocker's hands slid down to rest easily on her hips, lightly holding her belt. She held the smoke in, looked at me over Cocker's shoulder, smiled, and then carefully let the smoke flow from her nose, a swirling stream of wispy grey.

'There ye go,' she boasted, grinning. I shrugged and turned away, looking out over the city. It was nearly evening, the sun starting to disappear further on up the Liffey, towards the Four Courts. The sky was pink-splashed and streaked with high cloud. It was kind of beautiful. A chill arrived suddenly, an end-of-the-day, stoned sort of chill.

'Let's go down,' I said. 'We should go and get the drink.'

Walking slowly, giggling now and then but not saying much, we crossed the Liffey and headed up O'Connell Street. The buzz from the hash made everything warm, like the world was coated in a soft, amber light. Everything felt more vivid and more interesting than usual – the hash was like a tool to drain the banality out of life. I looked at people's faces as they streamed past me, fascinated; how strange they all were.

An anti-abortion group had gathered outside the GPO to protest. Their violent slogans were slashes of blood-red over long white sheets and boards.

ABORTION: THE SILENT HOLOCAUST. WILL YOU LOOK AWAY WHILE THEY SLAUGHTER THE DEFENCELESS? ABORTION IS THE MURDER OF THE INNOCENT

The protestors had set up a stall and, just as we were walking past, they unrolled a huge image of a bloody foetus, whose head was partially crushed and oozing green and dark-red matter. You could see that it was a human, a baby. 'Uugh,' said Jen, crinkling her nose in revulsion. 'They're not allowed show that, are they?' Up further, another group was protesting the invasion of Iraq, and claiming that the Irish had blood on their hands because they let the Yankee war planes stop over in Shannon. The fighting in Iraq was supposed to be finished already, only a couple of months after they'd gone in, back in March. But every day on telly there was slaughter and mayhem, and some said that the guerrilla war would go on for years and years. Kearney was gleeful at the prospect: according to him, anyone who protested was a wanker, because the fact was: people loved war and loved watching it on telly, and if we didn't have wars like Iraq and Afghanistan we'd all be bored senseless and turn on each other to get our fix of violence.

We walked on, to the end of the street and the big monument to whatever social hero it was, his arms outstretched, his face stern and domineering. Rez had gotten sick at the base of that statue one night, it was hilarious. I wondered where Rez was today: probably out somewhere with Julie. They didn't seem that close any more, though. Maybe he was out wandering around on his own again. Something was up with him. I thought of Stephen Horrigan and wondered if someone would find Rez like that some day, slung up by his belt, staring at you with dead, bulging eyes. That would be weird.

We turned on to Parnell Street, which is where some of the dodgier offos were to be found, and looked around for someone to buy us a daddy-naggin and eighteen cans of Dutch Gold.

A few hours later I was sitting on the couch in Jen's spacious living room out in Blackrock. *Xtrmntr* was playing loud on the stereo. The lights were low and the telly was jittery with late-night images. Kearney, who had come into town to meet us, was passed out on the floor. There was a joypad in his hand and dribble glistened under his lip. I watched him for a while. Then I opened the last of the cans and drank.

Jen's da had gone away for the weekend, and her alcoholic ma had long since moved out, so she had a free house tonight. But in the sitting room there were only me and Kearney. Jen had gone upstairs with Cocker more than an hour ago. I kept thinking I could hear noises from them, and put the music up louder to drown it out. It was hate music, fast and vicious, and I relished how it made me feel, the rage and power. I drank more and felt a surge of omnipotence, but then I heard the creaking from above and it was like there was nothing inside me.

I wished I had something to get high with. I got up and went into Jen's da's garage, not sure what I was looking for until I stood beside the red petrol container. I hesitated for a moment because it could kill your brain or whatever. Then something that fella Scag had said on the phone came back to me: *Do one thing every day that ye know yer goin to regret.* I unscrewed the cap, cupped my hands over the hole, lowered my face, and inhaled slow and deep on the fumes.

My brain hurtled and I let out a shriek of laughter, then fell backwards, crashing through toolboxes and shelves before slumping on the cold concrete floor. A spanner clattered down beside me and I laughed again, sprawled out on the ground. I saw a weird image in my head: a line of silent abortions, all floating serenely down a sewer, being washed out to sea. It was sort of poignant. When the buzz wore off I got up and went back into the living room and sat down on the couch, beside where Kearney was passed out.

The sky had started to pale outside the window. I wasn't ready to stop just yet. But I hated being there on my own, the only one still going. I wished Kearney would wake up. 'Kearney!' I called, kicking his shoulder. 'Kearney! Are ye awake?' He kept lying there, snoring into his armpit. I turned on the telly: Sky News. There was stuff about the insurgency and clips of soldiers returning fire from street corners and dusty alleyways, the camera shaking with the force of their guns. Nine Inch Nails was playing on the stereo, making the footage seem like an action film. Then I noticed that on the floor behind the telly there was a can of Dutch Gold that we had over-looked. I picked it up and cracked it open.

I drank the can slowly, because when it ended there wouldn't be any more, and I smoked many cigarettes as the sky continued to brighten and my thoughts swirled and blurred together and I could get no more satisfaction from the music. Then I passed out.

6 | Kearney

Snapshot Number 3: A selection of titles, notes and sketches culled from Kearney's sixth-year notebook

– *Jihad: the Age of Outrage*, a first-person shooter based on the War on Terror.

– *Sleeper Cell: The Enemy Within*, in which you play a young extremist, trying to climb the ladder to martyrdom.

– *Towelhead Onslaught*, a third-person shooter/fighter set among US commandos in Afghanistan. The climax takes place deep within the tunnel networks of the Tora Bora mountains, and involves a brutal fistfight with Osama Bin Laden himself.

– A historical saga called *Baader-Meinhoff: Operation Apocalypse*.

– A game called *Sexkrime* where you play a rapist in a squalid inner-city high-rise, and a related title, *Hatekrime*, where you play a member of a skinhead gang.

– *Pusher: City Business*, where you play a ruthless smack dealer.

– *Alcoholocaust*, merging autobiography and zombie-slaughter, an atmospheric first-person shooter set in Dublin.

– *Nigga B Real*, a *GTA*-style rape-'em-up where you play a crack-addicted gang-banger, betrayed by his ex-crew and now taking on the LAPD and the city's underworld single-handedly.

– *The London Cunt*, another *GTA*-influenced pimp-sim with bitch-slap elements and a roaming, free-world environment.

– *Slaughter High*, an RPG/first-person shooter comprised of lovingly detailed, Columbine-styled atrocities. Defiantly plotless.

– *Orgasm of Hate*, Kearney's 'baby', the project he felt most invested in, spiritually and intellectually. Though only sparse and enigmatic plot notes existed – the game seemed to involve some kind of Dublin-based, Fourth Reich genocide, possibly aimed at the homeless, the elderly and the itinerant community – Kearney felt sure that one day this game would make him the legend he knew he was born to be.

7 | Matthew

The next morning I was the first awake. I was still drunk, having slept only two or three hours on Jen's couch. I played the PlayStation and waited for the others to get up. Later, Jen cooked a fry-up. I didn't say much as we ate, ignoring Cocker but for a few muttered words. I wished someone would suggest we start drinking again. Instead I drank tonnes of coffee because it gave you a buzz as well. I had to take some Paracetamol, though, cos my head was killing me.

I told the others I'd see them that evening. Then I went into town to pick up the pills from Scag. I met him in a lane behind Dame Street. He looked around twenty years older than me, with a crewcut, black leather jacket, Doc Martens, and the All-Cops-Are-Bastards dots tattooed in uneven green ink across his knuckles. He looked like a serious punk. Or like he'd been a serious punk years before, but had evolved into some nameless, dangerous kind of outsider. I'd heard from Rez's cousin that Scag was a junkie. Or 'a former junkie who still liked to use', as he allegedly labelled himself. I noticed that Scag's black T-shirt had the word *Wittgenstein!* printed on it.

'So what's yer story, anyway?' he said, rolling a smoke after he'd given me the pills.

I didn't know what to say. I didn't have much of a story.

'Are ye a workin man?' he asked.

'No. Not at the moment. I've just finished school. That's why me and me mates are celebratin this weekend.'

'Good. Fair play to ye, Matthew. Long have I fuckin dreamt of the day when the workin classes refuse to work. Don't do it if ye know what's good for ye. There's nothin noble or dignified about workin, it's just degradation. Are ye gettin me, Matthew?'

'Yeah.'

'"Beware the eulogizers of work" – those are the words I've got painted on the wall above me bed, to remind meself of what's important. This is an age of bitterness and resentment, so make yerself at home. Do ye follow?'

'Yeah. So ye don't, like, work yourself then?'

He hissed, all indignant. 'I wouldn't work even if they paid me for it. Never get out of bed for less than ye got into it for, that's my way of lookin at it. There's a hundred solid reasons not to work. The big one for me is that it distracts me from me poetry.'

'Ye write poetry?'

'Of course I do. If this wasn't such a cretinized culture, all real men would be writin poetry. It used to be a sign of manliness – and now they'd have ye think it's effeminate! Can ye believe that, how far we've fuckin regressed?' He lit his smoke, took a puff, and added, 'Look out for me buke, Matthew, it's in a few of these shops around town. I had it printed meself. Blazin stuff it is. Poetry as nailbomb, poetry as napalm. Poetry to fondle your testicles. Decimation in the service of a higher ideal. It's good stuff, Matthew.'

'What's it called?'

'*Molesting Your Inner Child.* I'm tellin ye, there's more truth in a single page of it than you'll find in most of the bukes linin the shelves of Hodges bleedin Figgis. It's my ambition to say in ten sentences what other cunts say in whole bukes – what other cunts *don't* say in whole bukes, more like it.'

'I'll look out for it.'

'Ye will in yer bollocks,' he said with a chuckle. 'But go on ye mischievous cunt ye, enjoy those yokes and remember, the sacred and the ecstatic are your fuckin birthright. Don't let these Fianna Fáil pederasts tell ye otherwise. They wouldn't know God if she bent right down and sucked their balls.'

I nodded along as if I knew what he was on about. He told me to give him a call some time and we'd 'tear this city a new arsehole'. I said I would. Then I hurried off to meet my friends.

———

It was around six in the morning. The last pubs and clubs had long since closed and me, Cocker, Rez and Kearney were roaming the city. Jen had gone home earlier (she was the only one who hadn't taken a pill). We were still off our heads, watching the streets run pale with morning light. All was eerily, magically still. Had this been any other morning, people would have been going to work, the city coming to life, but today was a holy day.

'It's like *28 Days Later*,' said Rez as we approached Merrion Square.

'And we're the zombies,' added Cocker.

I rolled my jaw and watched Rez gazing about in blitzed wonder. He looked kind of beautiful in the light of dawn, sallow and gaunt, his hair slicked back in waves of grease and sweat. My mind was blasted, my ears still ringing hours after the gig.

We reached the gates of Merrion Square.

'It's closed,' said Rez.

We stood around for a while in aimless, contented silence. Rez made flicking movements with his fingers, engrossed in the motion and sensations. I looked up the street, towards the National Gallery.

This was a very Georgian part of Dublin, I had been led to believe, though I had no real idea what that meant, nor did I care.

Still the contented silence. Some birds were singing. Eventually Cocker said, 'Will we go somewhere else, then?'

'I suppose so,' I said. 'The park is closed.'

With that we started walking, heading up past Trinity, following the road around to Pearse Street Station.

Now Rez was at my side, going on about Quentin Tarantino.

'He's just the only relevant director, the only one. Every other film ye see is just totally obsolete, just completely dishonest. The thing with Tarantino is that he doesn't pretend there's a real world out there for his films to show us – there are only more films. And the "real world" is only a copy of films – Tarantino knows this. Ah, he's just amazin. But all these other directors, they keep tryin to make films about "real" people – as if they still exist! They just don't get it. I mean, like, ye see a guy in a film, and he's sittin in a doorway down some alley, wearin a dark coat and drinkin whiskey from a hip flask. And we're supposed to believe that what ye see is what ye get, and this character is doin all this in a *natural* way, and he's not even aware of the glamour of it, of how much it reminds ye of, like, fifty other films. Whereas in "real life" the camera is always on you. You're always in a film.'

He paused to inhale through his nostrils, tilting his face to the sunlight. 'That's the point of Tarantino – he's after givin up on reality. He knows that it disappeared back in the forties or whenever. He doesn't pretend we're still livin in that time when people had, like, emotional journeys and dramatic conflicts and, ye know, moral dilemmas. He's cut the crap.'

I grinned and nodded along, caught up in his enthusiasm. He looked happy, glad of an audience.

I noticed that we were by now surprisingly deep into the north-side. It was shabbier, dodgier than the city centre, and unfamiliar. There were some homeless people on the streets; alcos and junkies.

We ignored the alcos and looked at the ground when we passed the junkies, and hid our drink from all of them.

'Gis a smoke, lads,' demanded a junkie in a shrill whine, emerging suddenly from the doorway where he had been perched. I was nearest to him and he had seen the pack in my hands, so I gave him one. His skin was the colour of your fingers after you've smoked eighty cigarettes. 'Gis another one for later,' he demanded. I refused. 'Lads have yis got some change for a hostel,' he said. Nobody believed for a second that it was really a hostel he wanted and nobody was expected to.

'No, sorry,' said Rez, starting to walk away.

Cocker fished in his pocket for some coins, but Kearney shot him a disgusted look and said, 'Don't go givin anythin to that junkie cunt.' Cocker looked at then obeyed Kearney. We all turned to walk away.

'Girrup to fuck!' the junkie screeched after us. Now his grey, squinting face was scrunched up with hate. 'A few fuckin pence for a bleedin hostel, are yis tellin me yis don't have a few fuckin pence?'

'No,' me and Rez muttered, walking faster, heads down, tensing ourselves for an assault, possibly with syringes. I noticed that, to my side, Kearney was slowing down, like he was deciding on something.

The junkie kept screeching at us: 'Go on yis pack of cunts, yis fuckin liars. I can hear the fuckin coins rattlin in yisser pockets. I've got nothin, all I'm after is a bleedin hostel.' A wave of sentimentality flooded his voice on the last sentence, like he was suddenly believing his own spiel. He sounded close to tears.

Kearney came to a stop. 'Just leave it, Kearney,' I said.

Kearney turned and walked towards the junkie. I cursed. He was going to start something, and here we were in some dodgy part of the northside. Rez shouted at him but Kearney didn't turn around. The junkie watched as he approached. The junkie wasn't nervous; he knew the street people around here. We were the outsiders.

And then I heard Kearney's voice, soft and low, talking to the junkie – he was being friendly. He put his hand into his pocket, rooting for coins, keeping up his pleasant stream of chat. The junkie looked baffled. I started to giggle. 'Holy fuck,' said Cocker. Now Kearney, holding a fistful of coins in one hand to drop into the junkie's palm, raised the other and placed it on the junkie's shoulder. He patted him softly. 'I can't believe what I'm seein here, lads,' said Cocker.

That was when Kearney loafed him. He just lunged in and brought his forehead smashing down on the bridge of the junkie's nose. There was a loud moan and the junkie went down, ejaculating blood. As he crashed to his knees he put his hands to his face, wailing horribly. I roared. Kearney stood above the kneeling junkie for a moment, looking down at him, serious and intense. Then he lifted his heel to waist height, took careful aim, and brought it crashing down on the junkie's head. The junkie toppled over, his face hitting the ground, crying and gurgling through a mess of blood.

'Oh Jesus,' Cocker whined. 'Kearney ye prick! Leg it, lads!'

We were gone, not caring if Kearney was caught there and beaten to death by a horde of junkies and winos and scumbags.

———————

We didn't stop running till we were back near the river, down Marlborough Street where it was quiet. Kearney wasn't with us. 'He's probably gettin his head smashed into the path as we speak,' said Cocker.

'Good,' Rez muttered. 'I hope he is, he'd fuckin deserve it. I can't believe this. What an arsehole.' I had rarely seen Rez so angry. Fighting had never been our thing, despite the punk-rock attitude and the cynical agenda. In fact, we were against it.

'Jesus,' said Cocker, looking at me. 'Yer hands are shakin. Here, have a smoke.' I took the cigarette, sat down on the kerb and lit up.

'Jesus Christ,' Rez said every few moments, pacing up and down.

'Do ye think I should ring him?' said Cocker.

'What's the point, fuck him,' Rez replied.

A minute later, my phone beeped. I read the message: *'gone to dwaynes gaff. see yiz l8r. dat was MENtal!'*

I showed the others. 'He's an arsehole,' said Rez. 'He thinks we all find it hilarious.'

'His brother will appreciate the story,' said Cocker. 'I'd say that's why he's goin there.'

'Not to mention to keep gettin off his face,' I said. Kearney's brother, Dwayne, lived in a flat near the Black Church, not far into the northside. He'd been living there with his girlfriend until recently, but she had left him. Now he just got wrecked all the time, so said Kearney. The brother was a weirdo; Rez reckoned he was autistic. I'd met him a couple of times and you got the sense that he wasn't really there with you, even when you were talking with him. He laughed too harshly at things that weren't funny, and just stared into space when you made a real joke. Dwayne was about to head over to the States to work for the summer and Kearney hoped to follow as soon as he could.

'Jesus, that's after bringin me down,' said Rez. 'I'd never felt so good in me life, then he had to go and do that. Jesus. We should go somewhere we can sit down and drink the cans, and take the last pills as well.'

We decided to take them in a church, for a laugh. We went in just as Mass was starting and knelt down the back, behind the scattered oul ones and oul fellas, off our faces. All the oul ones looked like Yoda. The priest was old, but probably only half the age of most of his audience. We passed the cans between us and said 'Body of Christ' when putting the pills on our tongues. Then some oul one shrieked at us for drinking in the house of God and we fled.

It was turning into a sunny morning. We walked back down over O'Connell Bridge and into the grounds of Trinity College, where we found a quiet, grassy corner to finish our cans. Rez started rolling a spliff and we had a laugh about the scene in the church.

'That oul one probably thinks we're Satanists,' said Cocker.

'Beelzebub,' I said.

'As if we *gave* a bollocks about any of it, one way or the other,' said Rez with a chuckle.

'The Catholic Church,' said Cocker, sneering. 'Who'd bother to give a fuck about them any more? Bunch of paedos – all they want to do is ride the arses off little boys all day.'

My mind was fucked from the drugs and again I had the vision of thousands of little abortions, holding their hands to make a foetus chain and singing in harmony, flowing down the sewers and out to sea. It was deadly.

Rez said, 'Lads, what is the fuckin story with Kearney? Seriously. He's turnin into a scumbag. Remember when he used to always be dead quiet and shy? You'd have sworn he was an altar boy or something. Since when has he turned into a fuckin psychopath?'

'Maybe it's to do with his da,' I said.

'What do ye mean?'

'Just, ye know, the way he headed off to Thailand and married some young one basically the same age as Kearney.'

Rez looked unconvinced. 'Nah,' he said. 'I really doubt Kearney even cares about that. I'd say he's glad. That was just the card he played in school whenever they were about to kick him out. Lashin on the waterworks and then laughin as soon as they'd turned their backs.' He frowned, thinking for a moment. Then he laughed and said, 'That boy needs therapy.'

I said, 'Well I suppose we'll be seein him on Wednesday for the graduation. Or outside the graduation, more like it. There'll be no keepin him away. But ah, that's alright though. That's the kind of night ye actually want Kearney around on.'

They nodded. 'Yeah, he's a good soldier, no one can deny that about him,' said Cocker. 'Anyway, that junkie was a total knacker. Maybe next time he won't go screechin abuse at people in the street. So what are we goin to do at the ceremony? I can't wait. The fuckers will rue the day. It's goin to be like Baghdad.'

'A final fuck you,' said Rez, grinning.

'Our 9/11,' I added. That was a phrase we threw in anywhere we could. Cocker passed me a can and I gulped on it. 'What a night this has been,' I said. 'Welcome to the summer, lads.'

The sun cheerfully mounted the morning sky and we lay about, off our heads and laughing in the sunshine like it was all a big fucking Coke ad.

8 | Kearney

Snapshot Number 4: Kearney B Real!

Kearney finished off the whore in the pink miniskirt with a crack of a baseball bat to the skull, then shot her in the face for good measure. The name of this bloodied mess was Jen. Now an innocent bystander came strolling around the corner – it was Matthew! Seeing what was happening, Matthew let out a terrified yelp, turned on his heel and ran. Kearney walked after him, switching to the shotgun as he reached the street corner. He hoisted the gun to waist height and fired. A circular flash of blood coloured the murky middle distance. Still Matthew staggered on. His moan withered to a protracted, tearful gasping. Then Kearney switched to the assault rifle and wasted the cunt with a languid spray of gunfire.

That cleared the area of any other innocent bystanders. No one is innocent, thought Kearney, breaking into an easy jog to get himself out of these back alleys and shady laneways. He hijacked a Mercedes and shot the driver in the jaw. Then he cruised towards the city's main shopping district. He was supposed to be picking up a backstreet abortionist from a house in West Town and taking him to Eddie Fly's in Kingsland. Or was it that he was supposed to ferry a trunkful of coke to Sly Diamond the Mexican and then kill the greaser punk when he paid for the shit? He couldn't remember, cos he didn't give a fuck. Following the missions was good once in a while, a diversion. But most of the time Kearney preferred to just cruise and kill.

He broke the red lights as he arrived at the glitzy city-centre plaza, then pulled a handbraker and flattened an old man as he screeched to a halt. Onlookers screamed as Kearney emerged from the car, slow and deliberate, a man of steel. He hammered the combination to activate the Maximum Weapons Cheat – he had resisted it thus far, knowing that total overkill all the time could become monotonous. But now the moment was right: it was time to climax.

'Are yis ready, humans?' he bellowed across the plaza. 'Are yis ready for *me*, human race?'

He pulled out his rocket launcher and fired randomly. 'ALLAHU AKBAR!' he roared as the missile swooshed across the dark expanse of the plaza, tracing a horizontal plume of smoke. It slammed into the side of a building and Kearney, exultant yet sober, relishing every moment with cold intensity, saw his own face lit up in the orange flare of the explosion.

Cars were skidding on to the scene, unsure of which way to flee. Kearney launched a rocket into the side of a dark-green Mazda. It burst on impact, a thump of flame igniting the car behind, which also exploded a moment later. The cops were swarming in by now. Kearney took cover behind a burnt-out car and switched to sniper rifle. He picked off a few pigs as they ran for position, savouring the founts of blood that spouted from their neck wounds. He pinned a copper in the shoulder and he spun in the crosshair once, twice, slowing with each turn – lo and behold, it was Kearney's da! 'Ye fuckin paedo ye!' Kearney roared. Then he pulled the trigger and the pig's face vanished in a halo of dark gore.

'YOU ARE SURROUNDED! THERE IS NO ESCAPE! DROP YOUR WEAPONS OR YOU WILL BE KILLED!'

The voice came from the sky; they had set the cop chopper on him but Kearney got it in his sights with the rocket launcher and took it out with the first shot. The helicopter bled smoke and began to spin earthwards in drunken spirals. 'Fuck yis, humans!' screeched an ecstatic Kearney. The people below screamed and tried to run, but there was no way of knowing where the bird would fall. It crashed finally into the entranceway of a skyscraper at the side of the plaza, killing three innocent bystanders.

No one is innocent, insisted Kearney – and as he did a single crack of gunfire sounded behind him and his face exploded in a drenching of blood and gore. He had been shot through the back of the head by a lone copper who had stealthily taken position to his rear – it was Rez, the gay bastard! 'Ask me hole,' Kearney gurgled poignantly through a clot of facial tissue and splintered bone. Then he crashed face first on to the concrete.

Kearney saw his body from above, and as he spiralled into the night sky, keeping his gaze fixed on his own corpse and the carnage that surrounded it, he was informed of the following.

You have been FUCKED!

Kills (total): 316
Cops slaughtered: 32
Missions completed: 0
Depravity rating: 94%
Appraisal: Loose cannon/psychopath

Fallen Henry the Titan says: *You a mean motherfucker, kid, but you ain't never gonna climb to the top in this business – too goddamn crazy. Shit, you the kind of nigga we send in when the situation be really fucked up, to clean shit up when all hell be breakin loose. But you can't be trusted, man. Too goddamn crazy. Shit.*

Kearney's ma was calling him. She sounded angry, by which Kearney surmised that it was her third or fourth time to call.

'Joseph, I won't fuckin call ye again! Would ye come down here before this is cold!'

'Yeah, hang on will ye, I'm comin.'

She threw the plate on the table in front of him when he sat down, and called him a selfish bastard. She brought her own dinner into the living room on a tray to watch Judge Judy. She left the door open and Kearney was able to see the screen. Judge Judy was arrogantly presiding over the fate of some tubby black guy who was supposed to have stolen his girlfriend's dog or her daughter or something. It was all so fucking boring. What kind of crime was this? Where were the cracked neo-Nazi spree killers who unleashed Armageddon on high schools, or emptied Uzis into shopping-centre crowds? It was all so fucking boring. 'I'm innocent!' pleaded the tubby nig-nog. No one is innocent, mused Kearney philosophically.

He looked at his plate: beans, fish fingers and chips – the usual shite. He went to the fridge and poured himself a glass of milk, then sat back down. As he chewed the first mouthful, he observed his ma watching the telly. She was a fat, ugly slapper. To rectify this, Kearney stood up, walked into the sitting room and stood above her, blocking her view of the telly like a cruel eclipse. He switched to baseball bat, raised it behind his head, and brought it down in her face with a vicious swing. She was dead on the first smash, but he switched to pistol and shot her repeatedly in the face nonetheless, just for the craic.

Kearney finished his dinner, left the plate and empty glass on the table, and returned to his converted-attic bedroom.

9 | Rez

Problems with Reality: Rez and the Postmodern Condition

Rez watched himself having sex with Julie. Glancing down across their chests and stomachs he saw his erect penis, condom-wrapped, gliding in and out, in and out of her vagina. The erect penis didn't seem to be a part of him – it was like the baby creature in *Alien*.

They were in Julie's bedroom. It was Monday afternoon and Rez hadn't slept after his night with the lads. Everything was pitilessly visible in the daylight. They'd been having penetrative sex for five minutes. This was a reasonable time for Rez to allow himself to ejaculate and bring it to an end. But Julie hadn't come. He had to make her come.

He could hear himself panting and see the winces and grimaces he made – he couldn't tell whether these reactions were genuine, or just imitations of pornography, echoes of someone else's long-vanished pleasure. He closed his eyes and tried to focus on pure sensation: the sound of her breathing, the feel of her skin where it pressed against his own. But he couldn't dam the gush of his thoughts. He wondered whether he was even excited, whether there was any lust in this at all. He had an erection, therefore some excitation must have been taking place. But maybe the erection was a mechanical reaction to the gestures they were making that they'd picked up from films, telly, porno …

Julie still hadn't come. Rez wished it was all over. These noises they were making: who were they trying to convince? But he had to keep going. He had to make her come. Julie's face was bobbing up and down beneath him. She panted and rolled back her eyeballs but Rez couldn't blot out the sense that they were both alone, imprisoned in their separate minds. He kept seeing flickers in Julie of film-sex, responses downloaded from beautiful actresses. It was the over-eager way she contorted her body, the hyperbole in her whispered incitements and dirty words. He felt like he was having sex with a hologram. But he had to make her come.

They manoeuvred themselves through various positions. Rez was concentrating hard, trying fiercely to enjoy himself. Eventually Julie seemed to come; at least, she made a loud, prolonged warbling noise and went, 'Oh fuck!' Then she formed an O with her lips and began to take noisy breaths, in and out, as if recovering from a near-fatal pleasure. Rez's orgasm was imminent: it would all be over soon. Determined to enjoy these last few seconds at least – otherwise what was the point? – he urged himself to stop analysing and just be in the moment. But it was hopeless: he registered the mechanism of ejaculation taking place in his penis and testicles without the faintest tremble of pleasure. Miserably frustrated by his inability to stop thinking and just enjoy things like a normal human being, as he ejaculated he let out an anguished, gasping whine. Julie, mistaking it for a sound of pleasure, renewed her moany porno-noises. 'Yes, Rez! Oh yes, oh yes!' she cried, not looking into his eyes. Shuddering as the last spit of ejaculate squeezed into the condom, he groaned and slumped down into her shoulder. He buried his face in her neck and hair, and wished he never had to see anything ever again.

It wasn't only when he had sex that Rez saw it, but that was when it was most visible, and most excruciating. Sex, real sex, had a lot to live up to. Real life had a lot to live up to.

Rez worried. He worried that he was losing it, smoking too much dope and falling out of orbit with the world. For as long as he could remember, he'd had the sense that he wasn't as fully connected to reality as you were supposed to be. But he had always struggled to express the specifics of this condition, even to himself.

Recently, so much had fallen away, no longer trusted as being real: emotions, pleasure, music, art, even gestures and expressions. Nothing was simply itself; everything was a reflection of something else. Nothing was to be trusted.

Take Cocker, leaning against the wall the other day, smoking a cigarette – it was stylized, he had learned that from telly and films. Or Jen, raising an eyebrow and smiling as she walked away from Matthew one night – that was straight off the telly as well, prob-ably from *Sex and the City*, or *Friends*, or something. It was a cheap imitation; there was nothing genuinely enigmatic or seductive about it. Was there? Rez couldn't tell. He had begun looking around at the people in his life – his ma and da, Michael and Trisha, his friends, Julie – and seeing them more and more as unreal, sinister, holo-graphic entities, hardly human at all. Then, with rising unease, he had begun to look at himself in the same way. He had turned his gaze inward, but found no depth or substance, only froth and fever. There had arisen in him the weird and inchoate sense that he was a centreless chaos, becoming self-aware.

Whenever the anxiety threatened to engulf him, he would tell himself that surely the best way to deal with this was to try and talk to someone about it, to communicate what he was going through. Maybe even Julie could help him.

Later that afternoon the two of them took a DART out to Howth, to walk along the cliffs. It had turned into another dull, windy day. Fatigue weighed heavily on Rez. He wanted to sleep and sleep and not wake up for days.

As they walked away from the town, through the heather and scrub, high above the sea, he told Julie he had been barred from attending the graduation.

'What, even you?' Julie said.

'Yeah. They sent letters out to our parents. I mean, Foley likes me cos I read books, so I thought I'd be alright. But no, I'm barred as well. Me ma and da are goin mad.'

'But the school will be sorry they barred ye when they see how well ye do in the Leavin Cert ...'

He gave a cheerless laugh. 'I doubt it, Julie. Honestly, I think I've probably failed half the subjects. I know ye don't believe me, but ye'll see for yourself soon enough.'

Her voice was strained with anger. 'I don't see how you could fail, Rez. You're so smart ...'

'But I just ... I told ye, I just couldn't concentrate. All year. I ... there's too much goin on in me head.'

She pulled away, sick and tired of hearing it. He didn't blame her. He couldn't even say what he meant. An older guy with a moustache and a shaved head approached them on the trail. Rez happened to glance up at Julie as they passed him: she caught the guy's eye and smiled faintly, not realizing Rez was watching. Rez said nothing.

Julie suggested they stay for the sunset, and watch the darkness drift in over the Irish Sea. They sat on a perch and waited. Rez didn't want to be there. These days, situations like this always made him miserable. He wished there was a switch he could flick to turn his mind off, and he'd sit there and look at the darkening sky, untroubled by doubt or rumination.

'Isn't it gorgeous?' Julie murmured, lying back to enjoy the panorama of crashing waves, cliffs, and the dissolving day.

Rez sniffled. 'I don't know, is it?'

'What do ye mean? Of course it is. Just look at it.'

'I am lookin at it. It's just, I don't know if I can see it properly.'

'Is there something wrong with your eyes?'

'There's nothing wrong with me eyes. Well, there is and there isn't. I mean …'

He was determined to articulate what was in his head. Otherwise the isolation would suffocate him. He tried again.

'When ye look at it, are ye not just thinkin it's beautiful cos ye've seen so many pictures of sunsets in magazines and car ads and everywhere, and ye've been told that they're beautiful? Do ye know what I mean? Is it like an automatic thought, like ye look at it and ye think, "Ah, a sunset, it's beautiful," but really ye feel nothing? Or even worse, maybe what yer really admirin is yerself, sittin there and bein all cinematic, starrin in something like a film or a novel or whatever. Or like ye're sayin to yerself, "This is what an experience looks like," only ye've never really had one – just the experience of not experiencin anything at all. Ye know?'

Julie was shaking her head. Her voice was low, almost hostile. 'No, Rez. It's gorgeous.'

He shook his head. 'I don't think ye get what I'm sayin, I –'

'I do get what yer saying, but I don't agree. I look at the sunset, and the sea, and I like it. I think it's gorgeous. It's very simple, Rez.'

'Yeah,' he muttered, more unsure of himself than ever. Maybe it *was* just him, maybe his mind was fucked up. He felt terrible. He couldn't even enjoy a fucking sunset. Julie made everything so simple. That was why he liked her, he reflected. He drew her in and squeezed his body against hers. The evening was getting chilly. He kissed her cheek and she put an arm around his waist. He could feel her heat coming into him, protection from the chill that drifted in over the Irish Sea, cold and insidious as doubt, as questions.

He spoke into her ear. 'Julie, don't listen to me. I'm just … I just need to get me head clear, that's all. Don't mind me.'

She exhaled in frustration. 'But Rez, you're always like this now. What's wrong with you? You're not the way ye used to be. You're like a different person. How come we never laugh when we're together any more? You always used to make me laugh, but now it's always this analysing, all this weird stuff. Jesus, Rez, I'm starting to feel lonelier when I'm with you than when I'm on me own. I –'

'I know, Julie. I said I'll snap out of it, I'm just –'

'But when are ye goin to snap out of it, Rez? It's ever since ye started gettin all those books from yer cousin. I know ye look up to him and ye think he's cool. And there's nothin wrong with that, but –'

'I don't "look up to him",' he said gruffly, pulling away. 'Jesus. Just cos I like talkin to someone about books and films and stuff, ye have to make me out to be some kind of child. For fuck's sake, Julie.'

'But it's not only that, Rez.'

He sighed and shook his head. 'Here we go again.'

'I know ye hate me sayin it. But I mean it, Rez, ye smoke too much. It's messin yer head up. Some people can handle it and some people can't, and you just can't. It's makin ye … it's makin ye into a different person than ye were before. And I don't like bein with ye as much.'

'Don't say that, Julie. I don't smoke that much. Just a joint or two in the evenin, that's all. What else am I supposed to do? I just like it. Dope is my thing, it's not some big deal. It's just for listenin to music and helpin me think about things.'

Her voice was low and she looked dead ahead, across the sea. 'Listen Rez, do whatever ye want. I'm sick of havin the same argument over and over.'

They fell silent. Most of the daylight had drained away. Rez felt Julie shivering at his side. He leaned into her again and buried his face in her hair, breathing her in. 'I don't feel anything any more,' he whispered into the pulse of her neck, a dry sob caught in his throat.

'Shhh,' she replied, stroking his head, looking out to sea.

10 | Matthew

I groaned and pulled the covers over my head. It was Tuesday morning and I was still fucked from the long weekend. My ma was banging on my bedroom door. Dull light filled the room and I could hear the muffled tune of an ice-cream van out on the road. Eventually I willed myself into getting up.

I drank tea and watched telly for a while, though I couldn't concentrate and my ma kept at me to go and look for a job. Then she had to go out. Although I'd had a full night's sleep, I was still affected by the pills: little things irritated me more than usual, but I kept having these surges of euphoria and intense emotion, triggered by random memories or whatever happened to be on telly – even a car ad or the benign smile of a celebrity chef. I watched a few music videos, hoping Christina Aguilera would come on, or just some decent band. In one of the videos, from a rubbish American indie band, four tousle-haired guys were walking down a lane in slow motion as an apocalyptic sunset blazed behind them. There was an old woman standing nearby, with a trolley full of what looked like chicken heads and voodoo paraphernalia. A deranged grin crept over her cracked face. She started to giggle, then it looked like she was choking. An expression of horror came over her, as if she'd peered into the depths of hell. Then one of the band members put his hand on another's shoulder and looked intensely into his eyes. He smiled. His face turned into a frog. At that moment, I had a vision of Kearney smashing the junkie's face. I heard the crack, felt the surge of pain as if it were my own bones being broken. I scrambled to change the channel, calming down only when the screen glowed with a soothing Pringles ad.

My ma had come back. 'I'm not tellin ye again, Matthew,' she said harshly. 'Get on out there with them CVs and find something. There's no shortage of jobs, you'll have something by the end of the day if you want.'

What I wanted by the end of the day was to be drunk and stoned. To this end, I called Cocker.

'Listen,' I said when Cocker picked up, 'I need to get away from the gaff for a while. Me ma's houndin me to join the workforce. The only force I want to join is, like, Delta Force.'

'Or Air Force One,' said Cocker dreamily. 'That'd be alright. What *is* Air Force One? Is it the plane, or all the planes?'

We arranged to meet in town and head to the beach. Cocker rang Rez and I rang Jen. No one rang Kearney.

We took the DART to Portmarnock, already two cans in apiece by the time we got off at the station and walked across the bridge, then out on to the beach. It had turned into a sunny day, a brief opening in the grey cloud-wall that had hidden the sky for months. There were a lot of people making the most of it before the sky-blue was swallowed up again. Pasty parents laid out mats and kept an anxious eye on their children, who waded into the sea like a generation of suicides. Every father, no matter how young, seemed to have a beer belly, and all the mothers had flabby, cellulite-lined legs. The men stripped off their GAA or English football jerseys. The women wore bathing suits of pink or idiot-yellow. In the hazy sunlit drunkenness I felt deflated by the scene.

'All the happy families,' said Cocker as we spread out a blanket and sat down.

'Don't ye think ye'd ever like children?' asked Jen with a playful grin.

'What, with you? You're off yer head.'

'No, not with me!' she protested, taking the bait. 'In general, I mean. I wouldn't let you put your seed into me, Cocker. In your dreams.'

I looked at her. 'In your dreams' – did that mean Cocker and Jen hadn't actually had sex the other night? The dejection brought on by the sight of the milky sunbathers disappeared and I perked up.

'No, I don't think I'd ever want to have kids. But who knows, ye know? What do ye reckon, Matthew, do ye see yerself as a da some day?'

'No way.'

I meant it. Shrugging, I cracked open a can. 'The thought depresses me. I don't see myself livin that kind of life. It just doesn't appeal to me. Once ye have kids, that's everything fucked. Ye may as well give up on yerself at that point. And as far as I can see, that's just what people do. They give up on themselves. They get these flabby bellies and start listenin to fuckin FM104 and they start to think that a visit to Atlantic Homecare on a Saturday is a great day out. Goin on about motor tax and fuckin wheelie bins. No way.'

Jen laughed. 'Well, ye never know.'

'I do know. I know very well. But what about you, Rez?'

Rez was staring at the sea, sipping his can. He turned to me, gazed for a few moments and said, 'What?' He was scarcely with us at all. His face looked grey, sagged with worry. A surge of vicious feeling – hatred for Rez, the desire to see him suffer – flared up in me, and then was washed away by the blur of drunkenness. 'Children?' he said eventually. 'Jesus. The thoughts of it. I don't even know if I want to be in a relationship any more, let alone have kids.'

'Well don't go tellin Julie that,' said Jen with a smile.

We sat there and drank until our heads felt fogged and heavy in the high afternoon sun, and all was hilarity. The fact that everyone else was sober made us feel drunker, and we sneered and denounced the beach, the humans, the whole wide world. Cocker announced that he'd 'gotten the goo' on him and insisted we start doing shots of vodka, not that we needed any insisting.

When we had just downed our third shots, an inflatable ball plonked down into our midst, throwing a coating of sand over the fringe of our blanket. A little blonde girl trotted over, naked except for a vest. I looked at her, my head starting to spin. She reminded me of my sister Fiona when she was little, when I used to tell her stories in bed and feel big and strong, protecting her. I picked up the ball and smiled at the girl when she was beside us. She held out her hands with an impatient look, frustrated at every second spent away from her playmates. I held the ball out to her. She grabbed it and ran, shrieking with delight. It all made me feel sad.

'I'm a bit fucked,' I said. 'I think I'll take a swim.'

The water wasn't too cold, or rather it probably was cold, but the drunkenness acted as a kind of wetsuit. I crashed into the foam, exhilarated by the sudden sensation, opening my eyes underwater to a silty murk.

I flapped around for a few minutes, lying on my back and floating as low waves washed over my face, dissolving on my eyes to leave the vacant blue sky and the bare sun high above me.

When I came out of the water, Jen was sitting alone on the blanket. Rez and Cocker had gone off somewhere. Jen watched me approach, shivering as I grabbed a towel to wrap around me.

'Have fun?' she said.

'Yeah. You should get in. Fuckin hell, that's sobered me up a bit. I need a drink.'

I sat down beside her, still shivering and pulling my towel tight around me. I wanted badly to lean against her, draw in her warmth. To my embarrassment, I noticed I was getting an erection. I tried to move my left leg in such a way as to hide it, but I thought she had noticed.

After a while she said, 'So have ye worked out what ye want to do if ye don't get the points to go to college?'

'Not really,' I said. 'Get a job, I suppose. Which is actually what I'm supposed to be doin now, but, ye know … just something to keep me goin. I don't want a career or any of that crap. There's nothing here that I want to do. All I want to do is get drunk and hang around with me friends.'

'Nothin *here* that ye want to do,' she said. 'That's just how I feel. That's exactly why I want to go away. There's a lot going on out there, in the world. I mean, like, there has to be.'

'Are ye really plannin to go away?'

'Yep.'

'But have ye worked out where ye want to go yet?'

She was gazing out at the sea. There seemed to be fewer people on the beach now. Clouds had stolen in from nowhere to swoop across the sun.

'I don't really care where I go. Just somewhere far away, somewhere different. There has to be more in the world than, than *this*.' Leaning back on her elbows, she lifted her chin to indicate the beach, the Dubliners, the city.

'I don't know if there is, though. I mean, I get the feelin it's the same everywhere. It's all America now. Everywhere ye go you'll probably still be in America. Ye can't really get away from it. Know what I mean? Fuckin shopping centres and parades, all that stuff. Cars and houses to buy, big furniture superstores. God, when I even think of it I just want to swim out to sea and drown. But then again, there's always Mexico. Where those weird pyramids are …'

I turned to see if she was listening, and found that she was looking right at me, smiling faintly. Her eyes sparkled as the sun broke out from behind a bank of cloud.

'You're nice, Matthew,' she said simply.

'I'm not "nice",' I protested. 'What do you mean, I'm "nice"? Niceness is just fuckin blandness, just fuckin … just fuckin Dublin.' I was working myself up, using the outburst to hide my nervousness.

But she cut over me: 'I'm only sayin you're nice, Matthew. It's true, ye are. You're angry and fucked up and a nervous wreck, but I think there's something a bit more to ye.'

I didn't know what to do, how to act. But as I was hesitating, she put her hand on mine and I blurted out, humiliatingly, 'Can I kiss ye?'

She burst into laughter at the question. 'My God. Why not send a formal written request next time, like applying for college or something. But yeah, go on, you can.'

We kissed for the first time in the weakening late-afternoon sun. I had wanted to do this for a long time, but now I found that the moment was in danger of being ruined – the drink was making my head swim. I felt her tongue on mine, tasted the vodka on her breath and saliva, felt my vodka mix with hers, an airlock of alcohol forming between our wet mouths. I had to open my eyes because the spinning was getting worse.

'Uv to gsick,' I mumbled, pulling away.

I clambered to my feet and looked around for a discreet place to vomit, but there was nowhere because we were in the middle of a beach. In desperation I ran towards the sea. I was almost there when I threw up, dropping to my knees and spewing over the wet sand. For a few moments I was oblivious of everything but the sensation of vomiting, the gagging and nausea, the heaving and stench and the vile taste. Then I became aware of the people around me, the families and couples who were still on the beach. I looked to my side and saw the little girl with the ball, standing there, still wearing only a vest. She watched me quizzically, her little sister waddling towards her to take her hand. Then the girls' father hurried over to take them away, saying, 'Come on, come on over here, let's go.' I started to laugh and let myself fall forward on the sand, my head thudding into the ground beside where my vomit lay in multi-coloured splatters.

I lay like that for some time. Then I got up and plunged into the water, washed all the vomit off my face and felt better.

Sobered up with the vomiting and the cold water, I felt more embarrassed at what I'd done and kept my head down as I paddled about in the bobbing waves, watching the people onshore with a shaded gaze. But I laughed inwardly, looking forward to telling Cocker and Rez about it. I could see Jen lying on the blanket, still resting on her elbows, looking out at me. I waved. After a few minutes I emerged from the water and sat back down beside her.

'That was so romantic,' she said, putting her hand on my leg. 'I'm glad ye enjoyed kissing me so much.'

I smiled and put my hand on her thigh. She put her hand over mine, stroking my fingers. 'Where are the lads?' I said.

'They said they were goin to walk down and find a shop to get some skins. All Cocker's were ruined. A can burst open in his bag.'

We watched the dwindling crowds depart. It started to get cold and we put on our shirts and tops. I kissed her neck. She put her hand on the inside of my leg, her fingertips near my balls. When I scanned around and saw no one was looking, I slid my hand up her thigh, letting it rest between her legs. She was wet and warm.

A few moments later, I drew away from her.

'What is it?' she said.

'Nothin.'

'No, what is it?'

'No, nothin. Never mind.'

I gazed at the sea. She watched me for a while. Then she said, 'Matthew, are you annoyed because you think I was with Cocker the other night? Is that it?'

I didn't respond.

'Well, I wasn't. Just so you know. Nothing happened, Matthew, I promise. Yeah okay, I was with him once before, but that was ages ago. The other night he slept in my brother's room.'

I turned to look at her. She met my gaze. 'Seriously?' I said.

'Yeah, seriously. I've been hoping something would happen with you and me for a while, Matthew. But ye never seem to do anything. Ye just, like, go into yerself, ye sit there scowling and smoking, ye never make a move. I was always just waiting around.'

I was silent, wrestling with the question of whether I could believe her. Eventually I smiled. I put my head into her neck, kissing her hair.

Some time later, Rez and Cocker appeared on the horizon, silhouetted against the rocks where seagulls squawked. Me and Jen were lying together, hand in hand. I waited to see if she'd take her hand away from mine when the lads got close enough to notice. She didn't.

'Jesus Christ, what are you two up to? Can't leave yis alone for half an hour,' said Rez with a look of mock disapproval when they reached us. He seemed cheerier than he had been earlier on. We smiled. Cocker didn't seem at all bothered.

'Let's have a smoke, will we?' said Jen. 'Half past eight and we've only had a couple of joints. What's goin on?'

It was getting chilly and soon we decided to leave.

When we got up and walked off the beach, there were still a few people remaining: a lone child building sandcastles, an elderly couple on deckchairs. They wore sunglasses even though the sun was waning, giving no more warmth.

———————

It was nearly dark by the time we got back to town. Jen stayed on the train for Blackrock. 'Let's meet up again in a couple of days, will we?' she said as I was getting off.

I tried to persuade the others to stay out with me for a pint, but they said they had to go home. I thought about having one on my own, but suddenly the idea only depressed me, even more than the thought of going home to bed depressed me. I had been euphoric about getting with Jen but now the feeling had vanished. I kept thinking of the junkie's broken face and feeling that *I* was to blame. I wandered around town for a while as the rain started falling on the twilight streets. I had enough hash left for a couple more joints, so I went into the jacks in McDonald's on Grafton Street to roll one – a McSpliff, as Cocker had dubbed such efforts. Then I walked home along the canal, smoking on the way.

The streets were unusually quiet and there was no one else on the canal-bank walkway. Loneliness and melancholy swirled inside me, thickening the more I started feeling stoned again. I paused near a bridge to watch a swan gliding over the oily-black surface of the water. The swan was quite small; probably it was very young, and everything about it gave off a sense of fragility. I looked up and down the canal but could see no other swans, no brothers or parents for the little thing.

Deeply stoned now, I found myself captivated by the creature. Its long, slender neck seemed so delicate. I had a vivid, awed sense of all the ultra-fine nerve endings, bones, muscles and other parts that must have been in there, functioning in complex ways beneath its smooth white exterior. It seemed a miracle that the swan had survived this long without being mangled or smashed to death.

Enchanted, I followed the swan as it floated downstream, its black eyes tilted towards the water. It was drifting closer to the dark mouth of the tunnel formed by the bridge's arch.

Suddenly I was overwhelmed by anxiety: I became convinced that something awful was going to happen to the swan. In an instant every muscle in me had tensed up, my heart started speeding and my palms sweating. I was breathing too quickly, staring through blurring eyes at the little white shell of life floating through the dark water. I wanted somehow to protect the bird from whatever horrible thing it was that was going to happen, but I felt I would never be able to. The swan was tiny and weak and the world it drifted through was brutal and pitiless like some awful machine. The crazy thought occurred to me that maybe I should bash the swan's head in, just to get it over with as quickly as possible.

I watched the swan drift towards the tunnel's mouth. Just as it was about to be swallowed up in darkness I averted my gaze. I hurried away, badly disturbed and struggling with an anxiety that verged on outright panic. I crossed the road, getting away from the lonely canal, and forced myself not to look back, not even to think about it any more.

11 | Kearney

Late on Tuesday evening Kearney took the house phone up to his attic bedroom and called his girlfriend, Rachel. (Kearney thought of Rachel as his girlfriend, but she didn't see it that way and neither did anyone else. What she thought was that Kearney had shagged her one night – or tried to shag her, but shot his load before he'd even got it fully into her – and she'd avoided talking to him ever since.) He vaguely realized that he hadn't spoken to Rachel in months, but that wasn't important: he was eager to share an idea he'd had while off his face on ecstasy, for a follow-up to *Sleeper Cell*, provisionally titled *Sleeper Cell Command: Call of the Prophet*. He knew she would be keen to hear.

'Ye play this mad fuckin preacher over in London,' he said when she picked up. 'Ye have to recruit these young Islam lads with propaganda and all, but without gettin caught by the filth or MI5 or whatever. Then –'

'Joseph,' Rachel said.

But Kearney was absorbed in his account and kept going, '– ye plan the attacks and send the suicide bombers out on the right buses and Tube trains to earn Max Kills and Max Carnage, and –'

'Joseph.'

'– and ye eventually move on to bigger things: WMDs; spectacular attacks, like 9/11 but even better; assassinations; cyber-crime. Maybe ye can, like, gravitate the moon towards New York or something. And ye can join up with different groups, the Palestinians or Pablo Escobar or whoever. Maybe even the IRA.'

'Joseph!'

He had been speaking with increasing fervour but now he stopped, confused.

'Wha?'

'Why are ye tellin me all this?'

He shrugged into the phone. 'I dunno. I just thought ye'd be interested. I –'

'Well I'm not. What do I care about yer bleedin sick ideas? Games are for children.'

'No, they're not. Not any more.'

'They are, even if the children are seventeen or twenty or thirty-four. They're for children. Why did you even ca–'

Kearney cut her off by calling her a fucking minger, then hung up.

He played a therapeutic game of *Grand Theft Auto*, laying waste to a massive swathe of urban geography, being particularly brutal to a brunette slut with big tits he named Rachel, finally pounding her face in with his bat. Then he took out his notebooks and worked on some of the finer details of *Call of the Prophet*. He could feel it: if only he knew how to get these ideas out there, they would be hits. Rachel couldn't be expected to understand – Rachel was a silly cunt.

He put away his notes and lay on the bed. Time for a wank. First he thought of Miss Nolan, then of Christina Aguilera, and finally of Rachel getting her face kicked in by a metal boot as Kearney rode her out of it from behind. Wank concluded, he lay there looking at the ceiling for around fifteen minutes. Then he thought he'd have another wank because the first one had been crap. He got to it, only to give up almost immediately because, in fact, he had no desire at all – for anything. The problem with Rachel, he reflected, was that she was a ridiculous fucking cunt. The other problem was that she thought *he* was stupid. So did all the others – particularly Rez, the pretentious arsehole. Rez seemed to think that walking around with a book in his hand meant he wasn't a fuckhead, which is precisely what he was. Books, mused Kearney – what was the use of them?

He turned his head to regard the lone volume lying amid the CDs, magazines and Rizla packets cluttering the room. There it was: The Novel, which Kearney had been forced to study in sixth year. For all that he detested it, Kearney had had to concede that The Novel was a formidable creation. On the day Mr Foley stood before them and read aloud its opening line (something about marriage, manners and money – the typical shit of literature), Kearney's eyes widened in a sudden, powerful realization of the colossal boredom they were about to be put through. And indeed the boredom had been both severe and relentless. The Novel was so radically, suffocatingly boring that it became, paradoxically, an object of fascination for Kearney. He hated *reading* it, but the very fact of its existence was astonishing to him. The fact was that The Novel was not only regarded as a classic, it was popular as well – people actually *liked* this shit. Whenever Kearney tried to read even a paragraph, his brain would short-circuit, feelings of rage and inadequacy would consume him, and he would have an unnervingly vivid sense of how utterly different he was from the rest of the species, from *official* humanity.

It wasn't that he didn't like reading. He regularly devoured not only *Gamer, Gamezone, Extreme-Gaming, Nintendo Hardcore* and *Ultragame*, but also a fair portion of the more sophisticated and specialist literature: *Strategy Gaming, The RPG Magazine* and the wonderful *Shoot-'Em-Up Heritage.*

Reading these magazines gave Kearney the sense that when he closed the hatchway to his attic bedroom and sat down in front of the screen he was aligning himself with a proud tradition, an illustrious video-gaming heritage. Playing games was not just exciting and absorbing but something grander, almost a spiritual activity. One Saturday afternoon he had found himself instinctually rising to his feet and pushing his chest out with pride, having finally completed *Call of Duty*. He never would have admitted it to anyone, but a lone tear even wetted his cheek as he heard the swelling victory music, saw the flag of freedom fluttering over a blackened Europe, and watched the end-of-game credits scroll away to the very end. It was a landmark moment in Kearney's young life.

But just try telling Rachel about such grandeur, he concluded, still fondling his now-flaccid prick. The problem with Rachel was that she just didn't get it – Rachel was a moron. Rachel had no fucking *soul*.

Kearney banished her from his thoughts. Soon he fell asleep in sweet anticipation of the havoc to be wreaked tomorrow night at the school: scene of the trauma, focus of his purest loathing, nemesis to all that he was.

12 | Matthew

The graduation ceremony was about to take place in the church on the school grounds, inside the railings and next to the main building. We had converged outside the front gates at a quarter to eight. Kearney brought the bottle of vodka. None of us had seen or spoken to him since Monday morning, but tonight we were too excited to hold anything against him.

The church loomed in front of where we stood drinking and smoking, guarded by the high iron gate, like a castle under siege. We were a barbarian army. A phrase came into my head from the news: the Clash of Civilizations. By now, carfuls of family were rolling in, all dressed in their finery. We howled and jeered at them from a distance, sequestered – we were undesirables, the rogue element.

Then everyone was inside, the ceremony getting underway without us. We threw shapes and sneered and drank our filthy vodka. We had no plan of action, but inspiration would surely flare up before long.

'Lads, do yis reckon Miss Nolan is in there?' said Kearney.

'I'd say so, yeah,' I said. 'I wonder if she's wearin those boots.'

'Primed for the fist,' said Kearney. 'Simply ready for the ride.'

Rubbing his hands together, Cocker said, 'Lads, listen to me now. I would really enjoy havin sexual intercourse with her. Will I tell yis what I'd do? First I'd stimulate the vaginal region. I'd manipulate the nipples and breasts with me mouth and me hands so as to get Nolan primed for the sex act. By this stage it's fair to say me own sex organ would be more or less engorged. But I'd keep stimulatin the nipples and the clitoris and the other erogenous zones until her vaginal passage was well and truly lubricated. I mean glistenin. Then I'd insert me erect member in there –'

'You'd blow yer load!' shouted Kearney.

'I'd lash it in and out in a repetitive fashion until there was enough friction to trigger an orgasm. I'm talkin about me own orgasm, but it's possible that she'd be stimulated enough by this point to have an orgasm as well. Who knows. But I wouldn't be doin any of this for the purposes of procreation, now. No way, lads. I'd be doin it purely for the pleasure of it. Too fuckin right I would.'

After a few minutes the bottle was two-thirds gone. Cocker, lightweight as ever, was already wobbling. Cackling, he shuffled over to the gate, pulled down his zip and started pissing through the bars. 'There yis go,' he shouted. 'Christian Brother paedo brigade. That's what I think of all yer mercy and all yer bleedin …' His voice trailed off in boozy mutterings, his head slumping against the bars. 'Loada me hole,' he added.

'Put that thing away, Cocker, you're killin the planet,' called Rez.

'Yeah well, I have to kill it before it kills me,' Cocker slurred back, trying to spit and dribbling it across his chin.

'That's true. I'll give ye that.'

Kearney pointed through the bars of the gate at the chapel.

'God is in his church!' he declared.

We looked at him.

'God is in his church!' he repeated, giggling like a perv.

Rez swilled on the vodka, gasped at the harsh taste, and passed it my way. I drank and then looked through the gates at the chapel.

'Do you believe in God, Rez?' I asked, for no real reason.

He grinned, looking at the church and then back at me. 'Are ye serious?'

I thought about this. 'No,' I said. 'I don't think I am.' For some reason this seemed hilarious and we both cracked up.

When the giggles had subsided Rez said, 'Nobody believes in God any more. Everyone knows it's bollocks. These kiddie-fiddlers in their black fuckin gowns are the only ones who don't realize it.'

'That's why we drink so much, because we don't believe in God,' I said. The thought had only occurred to me as I was saying it. It struck me that my most penetrating insights happened when I was off my face.

'Do ye reckon?' said Rez, considering this, smiling faintly at Cocker who had turned and was wagging a finger at us, eyes half shut and face puffy red. 'Yeah, actually I reckon you're right. It's like, if ye believe in God and that yer goin to go to heaven and all that, ye don't really need to have a mad one down here on earth. But if ye know that it's all just dreams and that we're just down here on our own and there's nothing better goin to come of it, then ye may as well take a load of pills and get fucked all the time and try to have a bit of fun.'

'It's kind of sad,' I said unsurely.

'No it's not. Why? Past people used God stories to get them through life and make it all seem okay, and we use other things. Why shouldn't we? There's nothing sad about it.'

'Yeah, I suppose so,' I said. I was warily watching Kearney who had circled back towards us, still grinning at fuck knew what. He seemed different to me now, after I'd seen him loafing the junkie.

Kearney held his two fists up, wrists facing me, doing a weird little dance. Again he said, 'God is in his church!' This triggered a laughing fit so severe he had to bend over until it passed.

' "If God does not exist, then I am God." Do you know who said that?' asked Rez.

'Robbie Keane,' said Cocker.

'Pat Kenny,' I said.

'Bertie fuckin Ahern!' roared Kearney.

Cocker gulped on the vodka. 'Do yis wanna hear a joke, lads?' he said.

We nodded eagerly.

'Why do women fake orgasms?'

We didn't know.

Cocker shrugged. 'Who cares?'

A moment later he held up the vodka and said, 'Here lads, the bottle's just about empty. I dare someone to fuck it at the school.'

No sooner had he said it than Rez stepped forward and grabbed the bottle from Cocker's hand. He drained the vodka, reached back and then hurled the bottle over the gate. We watched it lope through the air and explode against the red-brick wall of the school, narrowly missing a classroom window. We cheered, excited by the eruption of violence, of destruction for its own sake.

A moment later Mr Landerton appeared. He came running out of the school – apparently he had been up to something in there before heading into the church – and bounded down the driveway towards us. His face was pink with rage. We stood our ground, brave with drink, and sneering as he bore down on us. Then he began to slow, and the fury in his face changed to doubt, caution. He was realizing that, as of last week, things had changed between him and us.

He came to a halt with ten yards and the high iron gate still separating him from our group. We laughed and waved.

'You haven't got any power over us any more, Landerton,' said Rez calmly. No one had ever called Landerton anything but 'sir' to his face before; it sounded weird.

'Get out of here, yee cretins,' he barked. 'I'll call the police if yis don't.'

'Ye faggot,' said Kearney with a sneer.

'Come out and have a drink with us, Landerton,' I called.

'You, Matthew, I'd have expected more from you. And from you as well, Richard.'

'And not from me?' called Cocker. 'Ah sir, me feelins are hurt.'

'I'm goin to call all your parents!'

Cocker shook his head and said, 'Landerton, we really couldn't give a fuck.'

Landerton was about to say something else but then his eyes widened and his body visibly tensed up. During the exchange, Kearney had slunk in behind us and now he reappeared holding a rock. He gripped a bar on the gate with one hand and then hurled the rock through two other bars. All of us flinched; only Landerton didn't move a muscle as the rock flew from Kearney's hand. We watched in amazement as it shot right for his head. But it missed him by inches, whizzing overhead with momentum enough to carry it right through the stained-glass window above the church door. The entire pane shattered, and shards of purple and indigo rained down into the doorway.

'Leg it, lads!'

We scurried away into the night, exhilarated. Laughing as I ran with the pack, I looked back once at Landerton before we ducked into a side road, out of sight of the school. He wasn't shouting after us; he didn't even look angry any more, or disgusted – only sad. Mystified and sad. I snuffed out the flicker of pity I felt for him, and I whooped as we vaulted a wall into the darkness of the neighbouring industrial estate, and kept on running.

13 | Kearney

**Snapshot Number 5: Kearney contemplates his
Leaving Cert prospects**

You have been FUCKED!

> Subjects passed: 2 of 7
> Honours achieved: 0 of 7
> Likelihood of getting into college: 1.5%
> Life prospects in the Big, Bad World: 9%
> Appraisal: Slacker/Fuck-up/Degenerate

Fallen Henry the Titan says: *Don't sweat it kid. You still mah nigga. You and me both know that there ain't nuthin to be gained through all that shit, the real meat be elsewhere, baby. Shit. Soul on ice, mother-fucker, soul on ice. I still got your back, lil nigga, remember that. Fallen Henry ain't gonna desert your ass just cos you didn't get no grades to please these pussy-whipped motherfuckers. Hell no. You be cool, Kearney, hear? You be REAL cool. Shit.*

14 | Rez

The evening after the graduation, Rez avoided eye contact with his ma as he fixed himself a mountain of toasted sandwiches in the kitchen and a giant mug of sugary tea to wash it down. He went into the sitting room and sat on the armchair. His da was on the couch, arms sprawled out like he was being crucified, legs parted obscenely. His mouth hung open and his unquestioning eyes rested on the glow of telly. They exchanged grunts.

Everything was coming at Rez too intensely. He wished he wasn't stoned, though he knew he'd do it again if he had the chance. He peered into the flux of telly, first at ads and then the war. It seemed to him he couldn't tell the difference between telly and non-telly, as if the TV-reality was leaking out of the screen, submerging the sitting room. Or perhaps the telly was a black hole, slowly sucking in all of *real* reality, annihilating any difference between itself and the world it glowed out at.

Rez's da shifted on the couch and bellowed to the house in general, 'C'mon, it'll be startin any second now.'

His ma hurried in from the kitchen, then Michael came bounding in and fell on the couch beside their da. Rez's ma opened a huge packet of crisps and they all dug their hands in and began to munch.

On-screen, various young people were sitting in a house, doing nothing. Now and then, two or three of them would fall into conversation: about the people outside looking in; about how it felt to be watched all the time; about having conversations about being watched all the time *while* you were being watched. Occasionally someone would scratch themselves, or cook some pasta, or politely leave a room. There were scenes from inside the bedrooms: people were sleeping, serene under night-vision green – it reminded Rez of the Iraq invasion. There were indicators of the passing of time, then more meandering conversations that petered out into the background hum of steady, amiable senselessness.

He had seen *Big Brother* before – it had been going for two and a half years now. But it was tonight, stoned out of his head and alive to every glimmer of meaning, that he first recognized the sinister brilliance of the programme. With a dark thrill, he saw that the *Big Brother* house was really the world, and the people inside it were none other than Rez himself and his family who sat with him in awed fascination before the screen. And not only them: everyone else on the planet was in the *Big Brother* house too, watching themselves being watched, admiring themselves admiring. In the house, nothing of significance was spoken about; there was no purpose whatsoever to anything that went on. Unlike the on-screen version, however, in the *real Big Brother* house there was no outside, nowhere normal you could get back to.

Rez stayed rooted to the armchair, mesmerized by the shuffling, sighing, prattling humans on-screen, by the purity of their self-consciousness: how the slightest move they made, everything they said or did was performed, simultaneously sculpted and scrutinized by a hundred million pairs of eyes. He wondered if some rebel instinct in one of the contestants ever drove them to attempt an unself-conscious act. If so, it would have been futile. In this, Rez knew he was no different from the on-screen humans – his condition was to be forever outside himself, looking on, appraising and comparing. The innocent gesture had been annihilated. Even when there was no one around, it was impossible not to act as if you were being watched. This was the infernal genius of *Big Brother*: it was a decoy, an alibi, a playfully sustained illusion that *it* was the show, but which in the end pointed you back to yourself – the *real* show. Even now, sitting in the armchair, Rez watched himself from outside: a bright but troubled youth, an alienated outsider, drowning in suburban banality and hi-tech senselessness, adrift from family, law, meaning and morality. He saw himself sitting there, eyes closed, his insane family guffawing all around him. Despite everything, part of him relished the image.

He needed to get away. He left them there, his da happily rubbing his beer belly, and hurried upstairs to his room.

Usually Rez's bedroom was a refuge, a place he could go to block out the weird signals that came to him through telly. But tonight he felt oppressed even in here. Harsh, frightening thoughts swarmed in on him. He tried to remember the last time he'd felt genuinely happy, but this only made him feel worse, because all the happy memories that occurred to him seemed false, like there'd been no substance to how he'd felt, only a grinning desperation. He fumbled to put on some music, trying to distract himself. Menacing, tribalistic drums throbbed and then Ian Curtis started singing, his voice deranged.

After lying in the dark for some time, listening to the music, Rez gasped for breath, grabbed the phone and called Julie.

'Julie …' he said when she came on the other end.

'Rez? What is it? It's late. I was just goin to bed.' She sounded annoyed.

'Sorry, it's nothing, I'm just relieved to hear ye. I just wanted to hear yer voice.'

She groaned. 'Are ye alright, Rez? Ye sound like something's wrong. What's happened?'

'No, I'm alright, I think. It's just … fuck, I don't know, it's just what ye were sayin out at Howth. You're right. I should probably just cut down on the dope, ye know? Me head's gettin a bit weird. It's … I don't know.'

Julie was yawning. 'Yeah Rez, I've been sayin that for ages. But all that stuff ye worry about, it isn't real, ye shouldn't think about it. You'll drive yerself round the bend.'

'I know, Julie, I know. Don't worry, I just wanted to hear your voice. I feel a lot better now. Listen, I'm really sorry for wakin ye up. Go on back to sleep, I'll see ye tomorrow. I love ye, Julie.'

Julie said she loved him and hung up. He did feel better; Julie was good for him, she kept him grounded. Saying 'I love you', though – that was the worst. He meant it when he said it – at least he thought he did – but actually saying the words was excruciating. It was impossible to say the phrase without feeling embarrassed – not because you were expressing your feelings, but because you were saying something that you'd heard a million times, in the dodgiest of places, like romantic comedies and shit pop songs – everywhere that was wrong.

Some time later, he heard his parents locking up downstairs and going to bed. Then the house fell quiet, and soon he was asleep.

15 | Kearney

– Dwayne Kearney
To: Joseph Kearney
Email received at 6:23
18/06/2003

wats up faggit?

how r things back in gay ireland? im off me fucking trolly right now so sorry if i talk a load of shite except im not sorry at all u little queer. haha im only messing with u joseph dont be so touchy u faggit. listen joe drop wat yr doin an GET DE FUCK OVER HERE – amerika is unFUCKING beleievable. trust me. im only hear a cuple of days but allredy i never want to go back to shitty ireland again. seeiriously. im working like a nigger but fuck it we slEEp on the job and take coke every day and there is a session EVREY NITE!!! book yr tickets right now nigga!! or wud u prefer to stay in dublin smoking shite dublin hash all summer!!! cos hears de ting. over here i can alreddy get watever de fuck i want. wen i want. theres dis guy called Stu and hes been sorting me out with whatever de fuck i want wink wink nod nod. seerieously yu hav to meet him hes a cool moterfucker. and forget them dry cunted irish mingers as well joe. when u come over hear ill have some real wimen ready for ya. cute little bitches man i meen it u wont beLEAVE it. u have to pay of course but u no what dey say – theres no free lunch joe!! except a fuckin dog or sumting. dont take my wurd 4 it come over and sea 4 yrself.

get on dat plane joe!!!

later homes!

yr loving brother Dwayne INsane

PS seeriesly i am off my fuckeng tits here i swere to fucking god. me mate egon says hello. seeriously egon dats his fuckeing name like the bleedin gostbusters. i am off mi fuckenng hed and heres the thing i dont even no the name of wat we took but fuck me joe its fucking great GET OVER HERE!!!!

PS haha jus like Mortel Kombat tho u wudnt no cos yr 2 young u fagget

16 | Rez

Rez woke early and hung about the house for a few hours, trying to read, not knowing what else to do with himself. Around noon he went into town to meet Julie. It was another drizzly, overcast day; it felt like the summer would never begin. When he saw her standing with her hands in her army-jacket pockets on the cobblestones outside Eamonn Doran's, Rez shrugged off the heavy mesh of obsessive reflections he'd been entangled in, enough to offer her a smile. But instantly as he did so, he realized by the look on her face that something was wrong.

He took her hand and they started walking. But after a few steps, as they passed under the archway leading out to the Ha'penny Bridge, she slid her arm out of his and put her hand back into her pocket, muttering that it was chilly.

They wandered aimlessly for a while, saying little. Rez was tense, his mind crowded with grim and painful thoughts. He wished he hadn't smoked that joint on the way to the bus stop before coming in to meet her.

Their wandering led them up O'Connell Street, across the junction and into the Garden of Remembrance, where only the odd tourist stood admiring the mythical-swan statue or throwing a coin or two into the long, low fountain. Inside the walls of the garden it was both peaceful and strangely desolate.

They sat down on a bench. Still they said nothing. Rez was growing sullen, irritated by her distance and moodiness. Julie looked away, watching a young couple who had just walked in, pushing a buggy and laughing together, both absorbed in a funny anecdote the woman was telling.

Then she turned to Rez and said, 'Listen, I don't know how I'm supposed to say this, but I've been thinking a lot and I don't ... I don't think we should be together any more.'

He looked at her in silence, stunned even though he'd been half expecting it.

'What do ye mean? What are ye talkin about? But ... I'm in love with ye, Julie.'

She shook her head. 'It hasn't been the same for ages. Yer changing. I don't know, I just don't feel good around ye any more. Ye always seem so distant, like yer half in another world, staring off into space all the time.'

'Look, I know what ye mean, I have been a bit off, but it's just temporary, I've just been worried about a couple of things, there were just some things on me mind. But I'm grand, I'm fine. I promise ye I'll be back like the way I used to be. I promise ye.' A whining, pathetic quality had come into his voice but Rez didn't care; he didn't want to lose her.

But his pleading only had the effect of strengthening Julie's resolve, which had begun for a moment to flicker, as if about to give in to comfort, pity and the lure of the familiar.

'No,' she said firmly. 'I'm sorry, Rez. I've made up me mind. I do love ye, but it's just better to be on me own at the moment. It's not you, it's me.'

She winced, as if embarrassed at having uttered such a cliché.

Rez was close to tears. 'For fuck's sake, Julie,' he pleaded. 'What am I goin to do? Ye can't just do it like that. Ye can't. The summer's only after startin, I was just under a lot of pressure with the Leavin Cert and everything. Can ye not just give it another chance?'

Julie looked downcast but she remained resolute. The more he pleaded, the more she hardened against him.

She sighed. 'Look, Rez, I've decided I'm goin InterRailing with Gráinne and Anne. I know I said I wasn't goin to but I've changed me mind. So it's better I say all this now, okay? I'm sorry, Rez.'

'I can't believe this,' he said, hands on his knees, looking at the ground. The couple with the buggy walked past, having circled the fountain; they noticed the scene and lapsed into an embarrassed silence.

A while later Julie stood and walked back up the steps and out of the Garden of Remembrance, leaving him sitting there, alone and dejected, as a cold drizzle began to mist up the dull Dublin sky.

17 | Matthew

I got a job on the forecourt of the Shell garage down the road. It was easy work. On my first shift a dazed Ukrainian showed me what I had to do: fill up cars, occasionally go over them with the hose from the washer, and 'keep an eye on things', whatever that meant. By the second half of the day I was confident enough to get stoned off my face, smoking furtively over by the wall. I imagined a spark from my lighter sending the whole place up, a mushroom cloud expanding across the southside, like one of the videos Kearney was always watching. The wet and dreary weather had returned, which suited me fine. I stood against the wall and listened to the rain lashing down on the plastic Shell logo and the concrete, and when the car headlights came on they left lovely, blurring trails across the grey.

I was to meet Jen on Friday. On Saturday she was going away to Spain on holiday with her da – a present for all the study she'd done.

I hung around the house that afternoon, waiting for her to call. When my phone finally rang, I let it ring three times to show how cool I was. Then I picked up.

'How's a goin,' I said.

'Hi.'

'So listen, where do ye want to meet? We can go see a film, or just hang around, or whatever. What do you want to do?'

She gave an awkward laugh then said, 'I'm really sorry, Matthew, but that's what I was calling for. I wanted to tell ye I can't meet up today after all. I want to, but it turns out that this is the last chance I have to see Siobhan before she leaves on her trip. I thought I'd get to see her tomorrow morning but –'

'What about later on, then? Can't we meet in the evening?'

'No, I can't, Matthew. My dad's taking me and Padraig out for dinner. Part of his big "Thanks for working hard for the Leaving Cert" effort.'

'Oh,' I said.

In a perkier voice she added, 'But we can meet up as soon as I get back. I do want to see you, it's just … I'll only be gone a little over a week.'

'Yeah,' I said.

Jen said goodbye. Now the empty day loomed ahead: all those hours, a grimy crater into which depression and boredom always poured. There was only one thing for it: to get fucked.

I called Rez. His voice was heavy and slow, like he was drugged.

'I think I'm stayin in,' he said. 'I start the new job tomorrow anyway. I just want to hang around here today. Sorry.'

For fuck's sake. Maybe he'd been fighting with Julie or something. I hid my irritation, hung up and called Cocker.

'I'm in town now gettin stoned with Kearney,' he said when he picked up. 'He's after bookin a cheap last-minute flight to Boston. He leaves tomorrow. He says his ma paid for most of the ticket, just to get rid of him. Can't blame her. I told him I'd pay for a euthanasia job for him if he's up for it. Stall it in, we're headin out to that big hill up on Killiney. I've got a lovely eighth here. Hopefully it won't piss it down, though, with these skies.'

My intention had been to avoid Kearney until he left for the States but I wasn't going to sit in today and do nothing. One more session before he went away was neither here nor there.

'I'll be there in half an hour,' I said. I could hear Kearney singing operatically in the background. We hung up.

———

I sat next to Cocker on the DART. 'What do ye think is up with Rez?' I asked him as we came out of the city.

'What do ye mean?'

'Well, I don't know, it's just that half the time these days he seems miserable, ye can't even talk to him. When I gave him a ring this mornin he sounded like he could hardly speak, ye know? Like he was fuckin miserable. Sometimes he seems normal and then he's great craic but a lot of the time now he's that way, all gloomy-like.'

'But it's just cos of Julie,' said Cocker. 'They haven't been gettin on at all.'

'No, even before that. He's always frownin and goin off on his own. He just seems dead edgy, or cagey, or whatever the word is.'

'Yeah,' said Cocker. I thought he was going to elaborate, but he just muttered, 'Nicholas Cagey.' Then he turned to look out the window at the passing coastline.

Kearney was sitting in front of us. I could hear relentless techno played at full volume on his headphones, but he must have been listening with only one ear because he turned around to face us.

'Maybe he is depressed,' he said.

'Why would he be depressed?' I asked.

Kearney grinned. 'I don't really know. Possibly cos he's a willy master. As gay as a pink doorbell.'

'Give it a rest, Kearney.'

'I'm only messin with ye, Matthew. I'm only messin with ye. I'm only messin with ye. I'm only fuckin messin with ye. Rez is a fuckin quality fella. A-One, boss. I reckon he's a saint or the second comin of Jesus Christ. I'm goin to name me first three sons after him. The fourth one will be named after Gay Byrne.'

'What about yer daughters?' said Cocker.

'Riverdance,' said Kearney. 'And Slán Leat. If I have a third, I won't give her a name. I'll lock her in the attic and throw her slabs of meat.'

'God help any kids you'd ever have,' said Cocker.

Kearney grinned again, taking it as a compliment. He was known to be anti-life, pro-compulsory-abortion. He turned back around in his seat.

'Do you reckon Rez is depressed?' I said to Cocker.

'I don't know. He was in great form the night of the gig, when we were flyin on them pills. Well yeah, he got a bit quiet-like, and then goin on about weird stuff. There's always this stuff about reality or whatever. It's like he's obsessed or something. But ... ah, I don't know. Fuck it. He'll be grand.'

The train bombed along and a few minutes later we reached Killiney Station.

––––––––––

We got off the DART and walked along a spiralling road that petered out into a muddy track that took us to the top of the hill. We drank whiskey and watched the dark clouds swarm in on the city from the sea. From up here Dublin looked like one enormous suburb, a dreary sprawl of semi-detached houses, electricity pylons and new roads leading to new suburbs, to roundabouts and Atlantic Homecare superstores. I wondered if every other place in the world seemed so dismal to the people who lived there.

'So how's this new job goin?' Cocker asked.

'Grand. I mean, I've only done one day, but already it's the easiest job I've ever had. Total lack of responsibility. It gives me time to, like, ponder things.'

He laughed and said, 'You'll end up like Rez.'

'He's startin a job as well, tomorrow.'

'Yeah I know. Doin night security work at some office block out in Citywest.'

'No way.' I'd assumed he'd be working in a supermarket or a garage. I pictured Rez sitting alone all night in an empty building in some deserted business park. 'It sounds like something from *Fight Club*,' I said. 'I'd say that's the last thing he needs, though. He seems to be gettin weirder the more time he spends on his own like that.'

Cocker shrugged. 'Well, he says he's lookin forward to it. He has a big stack of books he's goin to read up there. He says it'll give him time to think and write.'

I snorted. 'What's he goin to write?' Really I was envious: I should have thought of being a writer first. Maybe I could be a musician instead. Or an artist.

'Mostly just more of that stuff he's always scribblin, I suppose,' said Cocker. 'His philosophy. All these essays he does write – he has tonnes of them by now. But apparently he's writin some kind of book as well. All about our lives. Something like that.'

Kearney sniggered. 'The world is really holdin its breath for that one.' He handed me the shot he'd just poured. 'Here then, let's drink to Rez's new job as nightwatchman, and to my departure for the pussy farm that is Boston. Total fanny holocaust it'll be.'

We lit cigarettes and felt the kick of smoke in our throats, laughing and looking down on the city. It didn't feel like it was our city, or our country, or our people. I scrolled my blurring eyes over the sprawl and felt a loathing for all of them, the fuckers who lived down there and raised their families, worked their jobs, asked no questions and listened to Joe Duffy or Gerry Ryan or whoever-the-fuck-else.

As the whiskey pulsed into my brain, the hatred kept gushing out of me, laying waste to the city in a crescendo of contempt. Ecstatic, I wanted to drink myself into the ground, into total oblivion, and let all those cunts do what they wanted.

'What are ye up to this weekend?' I asked Cocker some time later. Kearney was off throwing stones towards the town. 'Do ye want to meet up tomorrow?'

'I'm workin tomorrow,' he said.

'Yeah, but after that?'

'Eh, actually I'm goin out …'

I waited.

'I'm headin out to meet another couple of friends. I mean, like, ye wouldn't really know them.'

'What, is it a party or something?'

'Sort of. Not really a party, just a little thing. It'll probably be crap.' He laughed weakly and looked at the ground. He said nothing more.

Now Kearney was standing a bit down the hill, pissing and waving it from side to side, giggling to himself. It looked like he was pissing all over Dublin. 'God is in his church!' he roared. 'God is in his church! How does yer garden grow?'

Turning to me, Cocker pointed at Kearney with his thumb and said, 'Here, this boy is really off his nut, do ye know that?'

'Of course I know that.'

'No seriously,' he said, grinning, eyes wide. 'He's even worse than I thought. Listen to this. I was around at his gaff this mornin, before we went into town. We were havin a spliff up in his room, and then he had to go downstairs for a while. So I started havin a look at his computer, and I found all these videos he's been makin. He's been recordin himself – just him sittin there talkin into the webcam. Just fuckin rantin away, like, makin all these mad voices like some actor. But it's real weird stuff, what he's sayin. All these fantasies of him killin people. Like, he's even talkin about his own ma and all, and weird stuff about homeless people. It's fuckin mental. And there's one of the videos that's different, where he's just sittin there dead still, not sayin a word, just starin into the camera, starin right at ye. I skipped forward and that video is the same all the way through, and it lasts, like, fifty-six minutes. What the fuck? I was goin to rip the piss out of him when he came back up to the room, but when he climbed the ladder and saw that I'd found the videos he started screechin his head off and havin a total fuckin mickey-fit, like pullin his hair out and screamin at me and everything. What a fuckin nutjob.'

'Jesus Christ,' I said, laughing. Cocker was laughing too, so much he couldn't talk any more. Kearney was coming up the hill, watching us.

'What's so funny, Cocker?' Kearney asked.

Cocker pointed at him. 'You are!' he replied, still shrieking with laughter. 'You and yer home videos. What the fuck is all that about, Kearney?'

Kearney stood looking at him, saying nothing. He stayed like that for a long time, while we laughed till our stomachs hurt. Eventually, Kearney sat back down beside us. I poured a shot and passed it to him. 'We're only havin a laugh, Kearney,' I said.

We stayed up there for a good while. We drank the whole bottle of whiskey and then, all of us pissed, we wanted more.

In the town, me and Cocker feared we wouldn't get served because none of us had remembered to bring our fake IDs. But Kearney strolled into the first offo we saw and emerged moments later with another bottle of whiskey in his hands. 'Yis owe me four quid each,' he said.

We walked on through the genteel coastal town, vaguely in the direction of the DART station.

Cocker said, 'I've to go for a piss, lads. I'm burstin. I'm leggin it back to that pub down there. Go on and I'll catch up with yis in a few minutes.'

'Alright,' I said as Cocker trotted back the way we'd come.

Kearney started singing, though it was more like roaring. Up ahead a woman was walking along with her two little girls, who both had curly blonde hair. The woman looked harassed, weary, the way parents always looked – people were crazy to want to have kids, I reckoned, or, more likely, they just didn't think about it, they simply did it. She was telling one daughter to hurry up, stop lagging behind, while trying to restrain the other from running too far ahead. The girls were cheerful and oblivious.

Kearney kept up the singing and I joined in. The mother trotted on a few paces, calling in an annoyed way at the taller of the two girls, the one who kept running ahead. As she did so, the younger girl behind her stepped on to the road.

There was a squeal of brakes and the scream of a horn, and then it had already happened.

I saw it clearly, we both did: the car bounced over the little girl with a crunching double-thud, one for each set of wheels. It skidded to a halt a few metres ahead of where the girl now lay. Tracks of gore ran through her smashed head, branded into her golden crown and the tar.

Then the mother was screaming, everyone was screaming, running about with hands to mouths, crying, not knowing what to do, or knowing there was nothing to do but not accepting it.

We had frozen in the road. I felt myself going cold all over. I was transfixed by the sight, the horror of it. I couldn't look away, though seeing it made me want to crawl off into some pit, renounce life as something brutal and wrong. The dead girl was still, her wine-coloured life force pulping out of her, one eye open in what looked like wonder, the rest of her face flattened and smashed into a horrible mess.

Then I had to look away. When I did, my eyes passed slowly over the calamity of the scene, on to Kearney's face.

Kearney was smiling. Despite my shock I saw this clearly. It wasn't a showy smile but one that looked instinctive and natural, almost innocent in some terrible way. He looked like he was in a state of ecstasy. Then he became aware of me and his eyes locked on mine. His face was radiant – I had never seen him looking so alive. I couldn't turn away.

The spell broke. Kearney looked back at the dead girl, no longer smiling. The trance-mask vanished from his face, as if it had never been there.

An ambulance had arrived. The mother was howling and shrieking like some animal being ripped apart by predators. Other people on the street were doing the same; it was like a scene from the Bible.

I felt my legs taking me off the road. I bumped into Kearney and heard myself say 'Excuse me' in a hysterical voice. My legs were weak and I dropped to a crouch. Then my guts heaved and I threw up all over the concrete.

———————

Later, we had to give a police statement. The guards spoke to us in gentle, weary voices and sent us home, telling us we'd be contacted if they needed us.

'Do ye think yee'll be okay?' said the sergeant, a ruddy, friendly man from the country somewhere.

I nodded and so did Cocker, who had accompanied us even though he hadn't seen the accident itself, only the broken, bloodied body that remained. He'd hardly said a word since, and was as pale as I imagined I was.

'And you, Joseph,' said the sergeant. 'How are ye feeling about all this? Nobody should have to see such a thing. I hope to God yee'll get over it somehow, lads.'

Kearney answered: 'It was terrible, I don't know how I'm ever goin to sleep again without seein her face, like, the way her head burst open like that, the blood everywhere and all.'

The sergeant shook his head in anguish and sympathy, closing his eyes and breathing slowly – and the very moment he closed them, Kearney turned and stared at me. His stare seemed to demand something, an acknowledgment or admission.

And, to my disgust, I realized that I was smirking at him, too cowardly to remain stony-faced or glower at him like I wanted to.

Before the sergeant led us out of the station with soft pats on the back and murmurs of compassion, I had to go to the toilets and throw up again.

18 | Kearney

Snapshot Number 6: A History of Violence

Kearney had always loved the slaughter, always loved to watch. The news was great for that: there was no shortage of carnage broadcast for Kearney's delectation. Already he had lived through the twilight years of the Troubles – kneecappings, bombings and reprisal shootings – various wars set against various backdrops, atrocities here and there, the occasional terror attack that sent little joy-twinges through his cock and balls. There were hijackings and high-school slaughters, genocide and outrage, nerve gas and the nuclear threat. When there was a dearth of these things in the news Kearney felt empty, deprived, like a football fan in the summer months with no matches to watch.

But what he'd got back then was never enough. Riveted to the screen, gorging on bloodshed, Kearney had always willed the body count to rise higher, to multiply, to *soar*. He had craved nothing less than the apocalypse, an atrocity that would end history itself. Kearney, in his way, had yearned for the Absolute, with all the earnestness of a desert-hard mystic.

He had waited, knowing something big was coming. And sure enough, when he was fifteen, there came the day when his patience was rewarded: 11 September 2001. Like everyone else, Kearney would always remember where he was when the planes hit the towers and *official* reality became so suddenly, blindingly interesting.

He remembered where he was: he was at home, playing *Grand Theft Auto*.

'Joseph!' came his mother's cry from downstairs.

Kearney's initial assumption was that she wanted to berate him over something he'd done that she had taken exception to, like forgetting to flush the toilet after taking a shit. That was why she usually roared his name. After three more cries of 'Joseph!', Kearney slid down the ladder from his bedroom, cursing under his breath. He bounded down the stairs and into the living room – and found the camera eyes of the planet fixed in awe on the blackly billowing New York skyline.

He dropped instantly to the floor, legs folding automatically beneath him like some meditating *sadhu*, and his eyes didn't stray from the screen for many hours. When the second plane hit, he became very quiet, very still. A great peace came over him. All his restlessness melted away in the radiance of tranquillity that infused him, brighter by the second, brighter as each flailing stick-man fell from the sky-high roofs, as the Gemini spires combusted and crumpled, and clouds of cinema-smoke tumbled through the filmic canyons of Manhattan.

Kearney couldn't look away. He couldn't eat, couldn't sleep; he didn't think of sex or games or anything, for days. The news channels played the clips again and again, from every possible angle: the planes whacking into the buildings; the huge, liquid-flame explosions bursting from their sides. It was worthy of any movie, undisappointing even to senses jaded from a lifetime of sleek, carnage-dense blockbusters. Kearney felt dwarfed, humbled by this mighty event. This awesome twenty-first-century breed of atrocity offered Kearney his first glimpse of what others called the sacred, the numinous, the unsayable.

Everyone else, he noticed, was as fascinated as he was. Day after day, week after week, the telly pulsed with decimation. It was planetary death-porn, the greatest show on earth.

Then the global focus had shifted to Afghanistan where Kearney gorged on the carpet-bomb ejaculations, the rapacious ground offensives, and all the delicacies heaped on for mass consumption, for Kearney consumption. The way some people are fanatical about Man United or Liverpool, Kearney became fanatical about Al-Qaeda and the Taliban. He read everything he could find about what the papers called the 'Islamic death cult', Al-Qaeda. Soon his attic bedroom became transformed into a shrine to 9/11. Posters and photos of the exploding buildings, of New York and Washington staggering under attack, gradually filled every available inch of wall, creating a cocoon of holy violence to block out any seepage from the mundane world, from dull, squalid reality. Never a day passed that he didn't look, with undimming awe, at footage of the World Trade Center attacks. They had even begun to feature in his dreams: erotic dreams of curvaceous boom-clouds, bulging red-black orbs like bums, like body-curves; dreams of belly-dance carnage; of screams of indistinguishable terror and ecstasy – an orgasm of hate.

19 | Matthew

My alarm clock was going off. I pulled the covers over my head and whimpered, wanting to stay there forever. I only got up when my ma's calls from downstairs got too angry to ignore.

Five minutes later I was staring into my bowl of cornflakes, watching them float on the surface, turning soggy. I heard the house phone ringing, then my ma stuck her head into the kitchen. 'It's Joseph on the phone for ye,' she said. 'Come on out and take it.'

I cursed under my breath, stood up wearily, and went into the hallway.

'Alright,' I muttered into the phone.

There was silence on the other end. I listened to the electric hiss, waiting. In my black humour it was easy to resist the pressure to speak.

Eventually, in a quiet voice Kearney said, 'Matthew, ye can't pretend that wasn't unbelievable.'

'The girl fuckin died, Kearney. She fuckin died. That was real. That was her mother there, screamin cryin. And she'll be cryin for a long time.'

'I know all that, Matthew,' Kearney said softly, placating me. 'I know all that. I do. I'm not sayin it was a good thing that she died – no way. It's terrible, you're right. But the fact is, we didn't do it. It wasn't our fault. We just happened to be there to see it. It would've happened anyway. How we feel about it doesn't affect anything. People die all the time. Right now it's happenin, all over the world. I'm just sayin, actually *seein* it with me own eyes – it was … I've never felt like that before. Do ye know what I mean?'

'No.'

Kearney sighed. 'I'm just sayin, it was *powerful.* That's all I meant to say. Yeah, it's sad that she died or whatever. Yeah. But Jesus, it was just … I haven't slept a wink. I've never felt so awake. Me mind feels really fuckin clear. Seriously. I've just been sittin here in me room, in the quiet, for hours and hours. It's hard to explain.'

'Kearney, what are ye on about?'

Silence again. Finally, he exhaled. 'Nothin, Matthew. Never mind. And never mind that ye smiled at me in the cop shop yesterday. I just thought that you felt it as well. But okay, I made a mistake. Ye did smile at me, though. I remember it dead clear. All me memories are clear. Soon I'll be on a plane. I'll be thinkin of ye on the way over. I'll email ye.'

We hung up. I walked slowly up the stairs, back to my room. 'Is everything all right?' my ma called after me. I ignored her and locked the door from the inside. I lay down on my bed and stared at the ceiling.

———

Later that day Kearney left for America. Rez started his new job as a nightwatchman. Jen was off in Madrid with her da, and Cocker seemed to be drifting towards a new crowd. I sat in my room that night and listened to music, afraid to smoke a joint for fear of the thoughts and visions it might trigger. I felt utterly alone.

That was how our summer began.

PART TWO

DIVERSION ENDS

Disciple: Oh enlightened Master, most illustrious and illuminous Sage, oh Teller of wise and profound Truths, oh superior Mind that splits Diamonds and splits Hairs, oh Prophet, oh Seer, oh Saviour, is it really true, as the Thought has come to me in my Hours of Anguish, Despair and Gloom, when my Soul has craved, in its Urgency, some Glimmer of Solace – is it true, that, behind the apparent Veil of Multiplicity, Strife and Separation, we are all, ultimately, One?

Master: Probably not.

—Killian Turner, *Visions of Cosmic Squalor/The Upheaval*

20 | Rez

Why I am Not Real and Happiness is Impossible in the Modern Age. To be read after my demise – by Richard Tooley

Section 23: Why Thinking is a Disease

Part A

I remember one day I was kissing Julie. Usually kissing is considered to be normal and uncomplicated but this is not always the case. If you think too much about what you are doing, it will be <u>unspeakably ruined</u> for you. You will be <u>genuinely paralysed</u>. Julie and I had just eaten dinner at Rick's fast-food place after we had been to the cinema to see Irreversible. *We were waiting at Julie's bus stop and we started kissing. Suddenly I couldn't stop thinking that a few minutes ago Julie had put into this mouth that I was kissing the body of a dead animal. (She had eaten a cheeseburger and chips.) It was one body inside another. Not only that, but the animal she had put into her mouth had been processed, cut up, cooked and mangled.*

Maybe it wasn't even just one animal, but <u>the merged flesh of several</u> <u>animals</u>, compressed in a factory into a single burger.

I tried to just kiss her and feel pleasure, but I couldn't put it out of my head. Now I could smell it, the dead animal which she had put into her mouth. And it struck me that 'mouth' was just a name for a hole in her face.

She kept kissing me 'passionately', but I was going weak with disgust. I tried harder to just enjoy the kiss. I closed my eyes. But it was ruined. It was too bizarre and disturbing for me to pretend it wasn't happening: inside her, at the end of the dark tunnel in the hole in her face, <u>the dead</u> <u>animal whose chewed-up flesh I could smell was being squirted with acids,</u> <u>the purpose of which was to decompose the dead animal and merge its</u> <u>flesh with Julie's human-flesh</u>. Like some horror film. I pulled away from her, unable to continue kissing the hole in her face. It was like there was a dungeon of freaks beneath the surface of Julie.

That happened a month before we broke up. For the last month that we were together, whenever we kissed I had the same thoughts. Sometimes it wasn't quite as bad but it was always there. Kissing was ruined for me forever. I had thought about it too much.

Part B

I envy animals. They are part of nature. I am part of nature too but it's ruined for me, because <u>my mind is a virus</u> and it attacks me every minute of the day. I'm out of sync with everything, all screwed up.

The reason I envy animals is that they are programmed by nature – just like we are – to live in the normal way (eating, sleeping, having sex, tearing each other to pieces). Unlike us, however, the animals cannot deviate from nature's programme – they haven't got a sabotage-mind that sticks itself into the gears and sends everything haywire, all sparks and hissing smoke.

Animals do not think, which means they do not doubt. They are pure instinct. They never trip up over themselves: they just do it. All I am is doubt. I am tangled up so badly that <u>I know</u> I'll never be normal again. This is the root of my <u>abject misery</u>.

'Just do it' – like the Nike ads. That is how animals are. And not only animals: also the majority of humans, such as jocks, meatheads, footballers etc. They never trip up because they never think, they just do it. They are animals. That's why they like wearing Nike and all that crap. In spite of my <u>abject misery</u> I am proud that I am not one of them. It is better to think than not think, even though thinking is a disease and it kills everything, so that soon you can't relax and just fucking enjoy life like a normal human being.

21 | Matthew

For a week I didn't see any of the others. I was working in the garage most days. That was okay because I didn't want to be at home on my own. It was a relief to be distracted from thoughts about Becky, the little girl who had been run over. But at times nothing could distract me: I would see her crumbled, bloodied face superimposed in sudden flashes over the face of my boss, or a customer, or another employee.

I didn't hear from Jen all week. I emailed her once, but after that I resisted the urge to try again. In the email, I told her what me and Kearney had seen out in Killiney. I didn't tell her how I'd smirked at Kearney in the police station, or how much I'd hated myself ever since. I didn't say that to anyone.

Becky had been on the news and in the papers. I'd kept all the stories about her, and all the pictures. I'd put them in a little wooden box that my granda used to own, and hid it in my bedroom. I told no one.

Jen was due back on the Tuesday. On the Monday two things arrived: an email from her and a postcard from Kearney.

In the email Jen said she was sorry she hadn't replied earlier, but she had deliberately stayed away from phones and computers. I skimmed over lines about art galleries and beaches and her father, until I found the parts about me: she looked forward to seeing me again, and could we meet up in town on Wednesday?

So she hadn't changed her mind about me. There it was, the proof on-screen.

'Matthew, there's a postcard here for ye from Joseph.'

I didn't know if my ma's voice from downstairs actually sounded ominous, or if I only heard it that way because of what she'd said.

I went down and picked up the postcard. The photo was of the World Trade Center, before the plane attacks. Thick letters coloured in like the American flag said:

USA STILL STANDING TALL – HEROES LIVE FOREVER

In black marker Kearney had drawn the planes swooping in, a big explosion ripping out of one of the buildings, and the little stick-men falling from the sky. I turned the card over and read:

greetings from Great Satan

ive come strate down to New York with Dwayne for a cupple of days. its AWESOME! U can stil see the ruins and rubbel at Ground Zero, its the best thing ever. we set off an antrax scare on the Subway this morning 4 a laff, It was gas!! hoho no pun intendid nigga Seeriusly though America is deadly – in spite of all the infidels. theirs a lot of FUN STUFF here – u know what I mean.

keep it real black man. Allah Akhbar!!!

The K

For fuck's sake, I thought. Now I'd probably be put on some CIA blacklist. They'd take me in the night and waterboard me or something. Not to mention what my ma would think. I took the postcard back up to my room. I tore it in half and shoved it in the bin. I lay down but I could still see the glossy cardboard jutting out of the bin. I took the two pieces back out and ripped them up into many smaller parts, then shoved them all into the bin and put a sheet of paper on top so you couldn't see them. I lay down on the bed and closed my eyes. I could see Kearney's grinning face on the red spots and darkness of my eyelids.

A few minutes later I got up, had my breakfast and walked down the road for my morning shift at the garage.

———————

I met Jen that Wednesday. We went to see *The Matrix Reloaded*, which was sort of a let-down but actually alright once you took it for what it was. From then on, me and Jen started seeing a lot of each other. We had always seen a lot of each other, but now it was different: we saw each other alone.

Nearly every day I would meet her in town and we would get stoned together and go to films, or hang around Stephen's Green or Temple Bar or Merrion Square. She wasn't working for the summer but she always had more money than me. One afternoon we sat up on a hill in the Phoenix Park under puffy clouds and watched the summer waste away. I had some hash with me and kept thinking about making a spliff, and in the back of my mind was the idea of getting some drink, but I kept putting both intentions off because we were having a good laugh as it was, and in the end we did neither. We just joked around and had mess fights and kissed on the grass. Jen put on songs by The Cure and Radiohead and we listened with one earphone each and it felt like the love scene in some film.

Jen rolled over to look up at the blue sky. She was smiling. 'It's funny how it all works out, isn't it?' she said.

'How do ye mean?'

'Nothin. Just, ye know, you and me gettin together like this. You know, like you have the idea or the image of it in your head, and then it really happens, and it feels funny, that's all.'

I had a vision of ten million other young lovers across the globe, having the same conversation, each of them feeling beautiful and unique but really just acting out some script, given to them by nature or maybe television. Rez's theories played out in my head, threatening to spoil the afternoon. But I looked at Jen's face, the way her eyelashes moved as she watched a plane trailing high up in the sky, and all those doubts seemed frothy, needless. Rez was wound up way too tight – maybe he just needed to relax and look carefully at things, or feel the sun on his face, or lie down beside a girl on the grass in the Phoenix Park.

Later we walked into the city centre. It was still sunny so we wandered into Stephen's Green and sat on the grass. People had their shirts off and Frisbees flew through the air, everyone laughing and smiling. While we were sitting there my phone beeped in my pocket. It was a message from Rez: '*alright matthew listen r u around? i really need 2 meet up with u, i can come over r wherever u r.*'

I was puzzled by the text. He didn't say what he wanted: whether it was to get stoned, or drink, or go to a gig, or what. It was the first I'd heard from him since he'd started his security night job. Jen said, 'Who's that?'

'Just Rez. He sounds a bit … I don't know. He says he wants to meet up.'

Jen watched me and said nothing. I texted Rez back: '*Hey Rez cant meet up now. Might be around this evening. U around later? Want 2 get stoned r whats up?*'

When I'd pressed 'Send' Jen said, 'There's something going on with him, Matthew.'

'Yeah, there probably is. He'll snap out of it. He'll be grand.'

'Well, are you sure?' she said.

'What do ye mean?'

'Just that I wonder about him. I emailed him back when I was in Spain, and the reply he sent me, it seemed … I don't know, it was frantic, it was hard to make sense of. It was kind of disturbing, actually. I mean, you hear so much talk these days about depression. And suicide. Young men especially. I read this article in *The Irish Times* and, like, more men between eighteen and twenty-five kill themselves in Ireland than in any other country *in the world* – apart from Norway.'

'That makes sense. Ireland would do that to ye,' I said. But my instinctive cynicism was boring even to me. I thought for a moment then said, 'Maybe they see through things, though. Maybe they do it because they're aware of the reality of what we're living in.'

I enjoyed hearing myself pontificating so I continued: 'I mean, like, maybe the ones from this generation who kill themselves are the ones who would have been, like, priests in earlier times, or, like, shamans in other parts of the world. Ye know? Like maybe they're kind of, like, diviners for, like, the emptiness all around us, and they kill themselves because while everyone else just rushes out to buy things and smile at the computer and all that, these suicide fellas know that it's all bollocks, there's nothing out there. Ye know what I mean? Like, have ye ever seen that film, *Logan's Run*? Me and Rez watched it a while ago. It's mental. There's this underground society hundreds of years in the future, and every year there's this ceremony where some of them try to escape to the earth's surface to find this place called "Sanctuary" – but they always get killed before they reach it by this big laser thing. But then this fella Logan actually manages to escape to the surface but all he finds is, like, desolation. Just total wilderness. So he goes back down and he starts screamin, "There is no Sanctuary! There is no Sanctuary!" But the rest of them have such a need to believe in it that they just hate him. And, like, I think they kill him or something. I can't remember, we were fairly stoned by that stage. Ye know what I mean, though? Maybe there is no Sanctuary.'

'Yeah, maybe,' she said. But her mind wasn't on my speech or on *Logan's Run* – it was still on Rez. 'You should go and meet him,' she said in a low voice. 'In the article in the paper it said that the big reason most of these guys kill themselves is that they feel isolated, they can't talk to anybody about what's goin on in their inner lives. Maybe that's how Rez feels.'

'But Rez does talk to us. He tells us all his ideas, all this stuff about why the world is so used up and he can't connect or whatever.'

Jen didn't reply. She watched a little girl playing on the grassy slope with a rubber dog. The girl reminded me of Becky.

My phone beeped again.

'never mind its fine just thought maybe u were around c u later.'

I showed Jen and shrugged. 'He must be alright.'

She made a vague noise, looking into the distance, thoughtful.

A while later she said, 'I wonder what it was like to live hundreds of years ago.'

'Why are you thinkin about that?'

'I don't know, it just came into my head.'

I pondered for a moment. 'It wouldn't have been very good, probably. I mean, ye wouldn't have been allowed to do anything, just get married and work and be poor.'

'Yeah, but do ye think they were happier than we are?'

'I don't know. It's possible. I remember talkin about this with Rez once. He reckoned that people were happier in the past, anyone who lived before these times, basically. He reckons it's impossible to be happy in the modern world, because we're not human any more. We're just, like, abortions of technology or something.'

'Do you agree with him?'

I shrugged. 'I don't know. I don't really get what he's talkin about. Or only sometimes I do. Rez can be kind of pretentious. I mean …' I hesitated, feeling bashful. 'I mean, I feel kind of happy at the moment. Like, here with you.'

'Awww!' She laughed and jabbed her finger into my side. I grabbed her leg and tipped her over on the grass. She squealed in pleasure as she fell, pulling me down on top of her.

As we lay there I had an urge to tell her what had happened out at Killiney, how I had grinned for Kearney after the horror. But I couldn't do it. I leaned down and kissed her.

We lay quietly in the grass and put our sunglasses on. An expanse of cloud glided across the sun and in a few minutes we felt chilly. We got up and walked out of the park. We wandered around to George's Street Arcade and browsed the CDs. Jen bought me a Mercury Rev album that she had heard at a friend's place.

'This will get you out of that punk-rock ghetto you've been living in,' she said. She kissed me and added, 'There's more to life than only hate and rage, you know.'

When I got home that evening I put on the Mercury Rev CD, and lay down to listen to it. Life was better when Kearney wasn't around, I decided. Being with Jen was helping me see that. Kearney was a deadener, a nullifier. He talked things into nothingness and you got sucked in by his cynicism, drawn into a void where everything was at the same zero level, pointless and contemptible. Rez had said before that Kearney was a nihilist. I'd replied that we were all nihilists, that was why we were into punk and sabotage and all that stuff. Rez had said yeah, but Kearney was different: he loved death and hated everything else. I hadn't really seen it at the time, but now I felt stupid for having been so blind.

The music played on, strange and mysterious, as if floating in from some other, more magical realm. Soon I drifted off to sleep, into weird and enchanted dreams.

22 | Rez

The instant before Rez opened the email, a shiver of dread ran through him. What if it was a premonition? Maybe he should just turn it off and never log on here again. But then he clicked the message and it was too late.

Before he even fully read it, the blood had drained from his face and his insides seemed to melt. He stood up, but his legs were weak and he had to sit back down – and then he saw them again, her words on the screen like atrocity footage. He clicked the browser closed but he knew it was too late: this would be with him for the rest of his life.

He grabbed some money and ran out of the house. The 151 took him to Parnell Street. He got off, went straight into an offo and bought a naggin of Jameson. The man at the register was about to ask for ID, but when he looked in Rez's eyes he just muttered the price and handed him the bottle. Then Rez was outside, swigging greedily.

He paced on to Parnell Square, outside the walls of the Garden of Remembrance – the very place where she'd dumped him. He swigged again on the whiskey. Why hadn't she changed her Hotmail password? She knew he knew it. Had she known he was going to look at the emails she sent to her friends? Did she get some kind of buzz out of it? A diving instructor, on a fucking Greek island! Rez could see him, this Marley, in his mind's eye: a hulking shadow-man, handsome, ruthless and predatory. He could see him boasting about it afterwards – how willing Julie had been, how eager, how *orgasmic*. It was all there in the few lines he'd read. Nothing could have made him feel more inadequate. He swigged long and deep but the words sliced into his most vulnerable parts: '*It's like I didn't even know what sex was before him. Last night he made me come twice before he even, you know, put it inside of me – after that I lost count! Rez NEVER used to make me come.*'

Outside the Hugh Lane Gallery he brought his hands to his face, clawing at the skin. He felt he was about to vomit. An old woman stopped to stare but Rez ignored her.

'*Rez NEVER used to make me come.*'

The worst part was how she had capitalized the word 'never'. He paced around Parnell Square to the front of the Ambassador. He crossed Parnell Street and headed down O'Connell Street. Outside Dr Quirkey's Good Time Emporium a teenager in a hoodie broke away from his gang to stand in Rez's way. He sneered and opened out his arms in challenge. Rez knocked him aside with his shoulder and didn't turn around when the teenager's mates jeered and called out threats. 'He's a mad fuckin thing, did ye see the head on him?' the teenager screeched behind him, trying to save face.

'*Rez NEVER used to make me come.*'

His feet took him back along the Liffey Boardwalk, over the Ha'penny Bridge, through the alley, under the archway and into Temple Bar. Already the pisshead crowds were out, singing and swinging from lamp posts with their crewcuts and football jerseys. On the cobblestones of Crown Alley he had to wade through an English hen party, drunk and leery, wearing devil-horns and policewoman uniforms. The women grinned at Rez and gave wolf whistles. 'Ooh. Do you think I'd go to jail if I went home with him?' said one in a pink wig.

'Maybe, but he'd be worth it,' replied her friend. They all laughed but Rez tore away from their trailing hands. 'Ooh, feisty! I fink you need to relax, love. But we can help you with that, innit.'

There was another uproar of laughter as he turned the corner beside Purple Haze. He stomped up the few steps that led from the back of the Central Bank to the plaza. In the sheltered walkway was a young-looking homeless woman, sitting with her legs straight out and covered by a blanket. She shook her Styrofoam cup at Rez. Without thinking he shot her a look of bare derision, his mind crackling with sudden cruelty. But then he remembered Kearney smashing the junkie's face and was overcome with shame. He fumbled in his pocket for all the coins he could find, and dropped them into the woman's cup. He couldn't meet her eye.

On Central Bank Plaza he scanned the clutter of grungers, skaters, Goths and rockers who fringed the severe black railings that had been erected to obstruct their loitering. He wasn't conscious of who he was looking for until he saw him, sitting on a slab of stone in his full-length leather jacket: Aido the Death Metaller. Rez approached him. A couple of skater lads were trying, without much success, to perform jumps and tricks on the steps and along the steel railings. Aido looked on, either frazzled with contempt for the inept skaters, or just wasted. Rez stood by the stone slab and said, 'Alright Aido.'

Aido looked up. He stared at Rez for many seconds, his face utterly blank. Then, in a deep-bass drawl: 'Richard.'

'How's things man.'

'Pretty good, pretty good,' said Aido in an elongated American accent. Rez and Aido had been in the same year at school but already this was among the longest exchanges they'd ever had.

'Listen,' said Rez, 'I know this is sort of out of nowhere. But I heard you might be able to get speed. I'm tryin to get some. Today I mean. Like, right now if possible. Do ye think ye can help me out?'

Aido didn't respond at first. Then an expression of anguish came over him. He turned his face to the ground and shook his head violently. Finally he looked back up at Rez and said, 'Yeah man. Do ye want to go and get it now?'

An hour later and Rez was feeling no pain. He paced the streets of town, filling up fast at the onset of Saturday night. His earphones were in, distortion raging in his skull.

He left Temple Bar and stepped on to Dame Street, inciting a barrage of car horns from taxi drivers who veered to either side of him. What would it matter, in the long view, if he went under their wheels? What did anything matter? He walked across College Green, towards the arched entrance to Trinity. From there he turned around and surveyed the traffic-filled expanse of the so-called Green at the end of Dame Street. They used to hang people here – he recalled learning this fact during some childhood jaunt with his da. The speed was running high, coursing through him in dark visionary waves: he imagined an alternative Dublin, one where public executions still took place. Looking over at the taxi ranks and the V where Dame Street forked either side of Trinity, Rez imagined huge black gallows rising up from the traffic island; he heard the screams of the victims, their agony drowned out by the clamour of consumer zeal, the shopping and the drinking; he saw necks breaking and bodies gasping towards death, and no one caring, barely even aware; he saw Stephen Horrigan being led to the gallows, a belt placed over his head like a garland, solemn children pointing at him from the cradles of their laughing fathers' arms.

The vision passed. Rez spun on his heel and marched away, through the grounds of the college. He lit a cigarette. Now he was outside himself again, looking on, relishing the glamour of his alienation. Tonight he didn't care how hollow he was, how non-human and insubstantial: in fact he revelled in his flimsy condition. Nothing could touch him; not the unreality of his world, not the void of space and time, not even Julie. He called up her image and, sure enough, he was unmoved by it. She couldn't hurt him where he was now. This was splendid isolation. Rez was the king of infinite fucking space.

'*Rez NEVER –*'

The words were incinerated before they reached his heart, fortified now like the Death Star. He reached into his back pocket and took out another of the bulges of speed wrapped in a cigarette paper. He swallowed it. Shoot speed kill light, he chanted in his head. Shoot speed kill light, shoot speed kill light. He came to the Long Stone pub across from the walls of Trinity and went in. The music blared as he pulled out his earphones and scanned the crowds: girls in clusters with shiny dresses and too much makeup, laughing too hard and watching to see if they were being watched; young men watching them, swaggering, broad-shouldered and nakedly aggressive. Shoot speed kill light. He ordered a whiskey and drank it down, basking in *film noir* glamour. Shoot speed kill light. He ordered another one and drank that. Then a third. The whiskey and drugs mingled inside him, like mercury fingers kneading his guts. That last speed-bomb was coming on strong. Tremblingly lucid, he walked downstairs with deliberate slowness and entered the Gents. He stood before the mirror above the sink and looked at his own face. Minutes passed. People came in to use the toilets and wash and dry their hands, but to Rez they didn't exist. 'Yeah bud yer gorgeous. Now go on back out there and don't be so bleedin vain,' said a drunk man, slapping Rez's shoulder and looking into the mirror with him. But Rez gave no response and the guy left him there, muttering that Rez was some kind of weirdo. Still Rez stared: there was only him. There was nothing else.

He left the pub and paced the streets again. He came to a bridge and put his hands on the side rail. It was dark now and the Liffey shimmered with dollops of light from the quays above.

He closed his eyes. His lower lip trembled as the speed pulsed out waves of rapture and awareness. Dublin was a den, a cauldron, a brothel, but he was beyond it all. He began to imagine the vastness of the universe, the silent darkness that stretched out forever, a limitless void. All that back there – the city, the lights and noise, the shopping and drinking, the music and roaring – it was a conspiracy, a cover-up in which everyone colluded and whose purpose was to deny it, the nothingness that Rez could feel now, crushing in from afar, burying the planet and all the creatures that scuttled across its surface. He revelled in the insignificance of human things, of sentiment, of self.

He opened his eyes and peered into the quick black swirls of the river beneath. Up ahead were the docklands and then the open sea. From here he could discern the ships and rigs and cranes of the port. It occurred to him that although he had lived his whole life in this city he had never followed the Liffey up there, to where it merged with the sea. He set off, pacing past hotels and pubs, and empty office blocks with lights still glowing inside their glass shells, until the noise of the city centre was behind him. Soon he was at the end of the river. The pathway was blocked by an iron fence, but Rez clambered out over the water and managed to swing himself around. Nearly slipping, he leapt on to the other side: a thin strip of rubble-strewn, overgrown wasteland, then the river's mouth. Shards of rusted steel curled up from the darkness ahead. A rat scurried through the weeds at his feet. He walked across the strip of wasteland to the edge of the quay and looked down: a ten-metre drop, then the black rush of the river. The speed throbbed in his brain and body and he closed his eyes again. Then he thought: why not? Why not just step off, right now, and disappear in the black water? No one would see, no one would hear. He would simply vanish. He realized that his intent was serious, that he was indifferent to whether he lived or died.

He stood there, intensely aware of everything: of the carousing city behind him; of the rushing water below; of the starless night sky and, beyond it, the *real* darkness, the true night that lasted forever and knew nothing of Rez.

Rez lifted his right leg forward, over the water. He let the weight of it pull him out, slowly but inexorably until, silent and unseen, he fell forward and plunged into the dark river.

23 | Kearney

– Joseph Kearney
To: Matthew Connelly
Email received at 6:23
05/07/2003

alrite connelly! u nob jockey

watz up horse

jesus krist i just dont no were to start. im havin de best time of me life over hear and i just wanted to rub yr face in it hahaha. tell de others 2. any1 who stays in dublin must be a rent-boy r some kind of demon queer. dats all im sayin. u benders havent got a clue

evry single day and night ive been off me fucking face. im off me fuckin facr right now in fact!! me and dwayne an his mate egon hav just hoovered up a gram of coke in 15 minnets excpet now ders some debate as to weather it was actually coke at all. apparently not. maybe amphetamine or benzadrine r some other brain fucking powder … who knows. de question is purely akademic im fucked off me face and dats all dat truly matters lol;/winkwinkwank when i got to de airport last week dwayne was der waitin for me. he was wearin dis poncey hat like pork pie hat or wotever. and he lifts it up and ders dis ROW of joints on the in side and dat waas only de start of the fun haha. straight to NYC for days of may hem and den back to d apartment in boston were hesstaying with 12 other mad irish cunts … all dat weekend we didnt sleep der was dis dj in the gaff playin hard house and ders no fuckin furniture just bare floorboards hahaa. smokin CRISTAL METH n everything. and boston is HOT!!! i mean HOT!!! as in: scald yer bollox off

last nite we went to a gig. techno is de best but ill go to hardcore rock gigs with dwayne de metaller. as long as its hard and RELENTless and i can get totally monged who really gives a fuck!! de band was called DRUG ORGY and neither of us had heard of dem but it was obvious dey were goin to be gud with a neme like dat or so we taught!!! so we drop a cuple of yokes and drink a bottle of sambucha wiht de lads up on the rooftop n den we head in on de trolly (dats de tramline nigga) and get into de gig fucking REVVIN for it. as soon as we get past de bouncers dwayne goes to me "stick me finger in yr mouth!!" and i goes "wot yr off yer head u insestuous kweerboy!!" but he goes "shut de fuck up and suck me fuckin finger nigga" so i do and d taste is pure mank like dis metal taste pure chemcial taste and i goes what de fuck is dat!!! and he goes "MDMA!!!!" its a fuckin WUNDERDRUG!!! yeah boyeee

den the band cums on and weere fuckin totally off our heads just like screamin at de hevens and dwayne has dis drool comin out of him his eyes are rolled back in his head totally mad out of it fuckin zombie holocaust. n den de band comes on and weer ready for total metal holocaust but suddenly we see its dis nerdy bunch of little cunts with trousers n glasses n der was even 1 girl in de band. a girl with pony tail and glasses!! n me n dwanye look at each other in like pure horrer goin Is dis DRUGg ORgy r u fuckin seerious? and dey start playin dis warbly fag music with banjos and flutes and all dis shite and d song i swear to fuck i looked it up online afterwords cos i was so distorubed. de song was called HOMEMADE PESTO AND CHILEAN WINE WON'T SAVE US FROM THE ABYSS!!! it was about trees and organic bred n such bollix. adn den anoter song was called OH CLIVE, THERE IS MORE TO LIFE THAN POE AND FAULKNER. total faggits!!!

me and dwayne wer redy to get de fuck out uf their. but wile dwayne is at the bar gettin one mroe shot each for the road dis hot little indie bird beside me starts lookin at me. lovely tits on her like ye just want to stick yer face in and go nuts and fuckin bite dem off hahaha. and i start gettin big rushes of blood to me mickey cos im fucked off me head and i smile at her tinkin id luv 2 put d willy inside hur but suddenly its not just her its her friends too. male friends all of dem starin at me and no one is smilin like. and i think wat de fuck is rong now? and i start wonderin if dey are anti irish or somethin. and dis big lanky cunt shakes his hed adn goes "dis ain't cool man" and sticks his finger in me chest and goes "de fuck is dis huh?" and i goes nothin cos i dont know wat de fuck its all about and now the little indy bitch goes "do u tink its like cool or sometin. is it all a joke to u. or do u really think its cool to like masscacre 3000 people" and i goes "i didnt massacre anyone!!!" and im totlally lost thinkin "Do dey think im an A-rab or sometin??!"

an den de penny drops n i look down at me t shirt n i remember dat its de one, u know d black one i had made back in dublin with JIHAD!!! printed across de frunt. id fuckin forgotten i was fuckin wearin it an be now everyones shoutin at me n slappin me hed and im panickin goin wheres dwayne but hes over by de bar laffin his hed off n the bouncer comes flyin over n goes "de fuck outta here!!!" he goes "n dont come back or i break yr neck asshole!!" he goes

so dat was dat dey fucked me out and i put on my hoodie wit like quiet dignity den dwayne comes out and we went off into de nite to get fucked off our merry little heds. fuckin deadly

i taught id tell u that little story for a laff hhahaha fuck dem infidels. bush. fuck dat de only bush i care about is yer fuckin mas bush!!! hoho!!! did u get me postcards oh niggz. i hope so n gess wat. dis fella Stu is comin up next week from LA or sumwer n dwayne goes "now weell get sum real drugs" n apparantly he has sumething else but he wont say wat it is … not drugs but sumeting real interestin. dwayne says stu is a total mental cunt so lets wate n see.

been on dis fuckin computer 4 ages. its only cos i love ye n i want to ride de hole off ye ye fuckin ride ye

B COOL BiTCH

ALLAH FORGIVE U!

THE K

SHAME ON DA NIGGA!!!!! I FUCK YO ASS UP!!!!

PS wats dis?? ' *

anser: a 1-eyed chink blowin u a kiss hahaha

perhaps u put yr DICK tru his eye???

haha lightin up im only jokin

off me fuckin chops i am

jesis kirrst

24 | Matthew

I deleted Kearney's email and didn't bother replying. Then I turned off the computer and took a bus into town to meet Jen for her birthday.

It was the fifth of July, a Saturday, and another warm, beautiful evening. We walked around randomly, chatting and happy. I'd bought her a book about some girl who had travelled around Asia looking for magic beads or enlightenment.

When we were in George's Street Arcade looking at old vinyl records, my phone beeped with a text. It was from Rez.

'jesus matthew i did something v stupid last night it could have been disastrous. im all fcked up i think i need help dont say it to anyone … jesus.'

'What the fuck?' I said, staring at the screen.

Jen frowned. 'What's wrong?' I showed it to her. 'Oh my God. What's he done? Is he okay? Call him, Matthew.'

I called but it rang out. I tried again with the same result. 'He's not answerin.'

'This is really bad,' she said. My phone beeped again.

'haha just kidding, nothing wrong. was only having a laugh. will call u later about tonight R.'

I locked the phone and put it in my pocket. 'He says he was only kidding. What a sap: he had me thinking he had gone and tried to do a Stephen Horrigan or something.'

Jen said nothing, eyes narrowed, reflecting. 'I'm worried, Matthew. There's something wrong. We should do something.'

But there was nothing to do. Rez would be seeing us that night anyway, we reasoned, so we could put it out of our minds and enjoy ourselves. We went for pizza in a fancy place behind George's Street. The waiter put a candle on our table.

'I'm excited,' said Jen, wiping her lip with a napkin. 'I can feel it, it's going to be a great night.'

I smiled and leaned across the table to kiss her. All of this – having a girlfriend, eating pizza in town, planning to meet your friends later for a night out – it all seemed right – kind of normal, but not in a bad way.

'Happy birthday,' I said.

I paid for the pizza. That meant I was fairly broke, but Jen's da had given her a wad of notes 'to have fun with'. After we'd eaten we walked through the grounds of Trinity for a while, watching the people out and about on a fine sunny evening, drinking coffee or orange juice, everyone relaxed and cheery. Then we went to an arcade near the Screen cinema and had a two-player game of *Time Crisis II*.

'You look deadly holding that gun,' said Jen after we'd completed the second level.

'So do you.'

She laughed and pointed the gun at my head and fired.

At half seven we walked to the Foggy Dew to meet Rez and Cocker. To our surprise, Rez was in a good mood from the moment we met him. 'Ah I'm sorry about that stuff earlier, I was only havin a laugh, it probably seemed a bit weird,' he said. I watched to see if he was faking it but he seemed cheerful, up for a wild night.

'All set for the Noosehound tonight?' said Cocker as we squeezed through the bustle and sat down around a table with cocktails that Jen had paid for, even though it was her birthday.

'Yes I am,' I said. The plan was to get a bit of a buzz on us here before moving on to the Noosehound, our favourite indie and punk night, just around the corner in Temple Bar.

'Let's make this one to remember, lads,' said Cocker, feeding on the collective eagerness. 'In the sense that we won't remember it at all. To be totally honest with yis, I had a brief moment this mornin when I thought I might not be able to make it. Fuckin destroyed I was from last night. Seriously, I don't think most people recognize the effort ye have to put into this drinkin business. These hangovers. That's real blood, sweat and tears, lads. You'd never do it if ye didn't feel ye were part of something important.'

Jen smiled and shook her head. 'Gary Cocker, you seem hell-bent on poisoning your body and mind. All of you do. Imagine the remorse you're all goin to feel when you're old and your insides have stopped workin, because of all the toxins you've poured into them down the years.'

'Hah!' said Cocker with a cheery grin. 'The future me. Ol' Dirty Bastard himself. Me only aim is to fuck him up as badly as I can, while I can.'

'The idea is to plant time bombs against our future selves,' I said, explaining to Jen the half-arsed philosophy that Rez, Cocker and I had cooked up over a night of vicious drinking, back before the Leaving Cert. 'Ye have to sabotage yer own future. That way, when yer future does come and yer nerve fails ye and ye want to sell out, it won't matter because certain, like, avenues won't be open to ye any more.'

'The avenues of cowardice,' added Rez, who had first come up with most of this stuff – me and Cocker went along mainly because it sounded cool. He continued, 'There's no use pretendin that when it comes to it, yer really goin to have the courage of your convictions, and ye'll be faithful to the facts ye saw so fuckin clearly when ye were eigh-teen. That's the same mistake that everyone makes. They get older and no matter how idealistic and how, like, clear-sighted they were when they were younger, they start to *collaborate*. And they tell themselves that it had to be that way, that passion and intensity are bound to give way to a more, like, mature version of the world. But it's still the same evil, degraded, capitalist world. Only they've smelled the honey and become collaborators. So fuck it, poison yer mind and body now, and decimate the future enemy. Annihilate the collaborator.'

Jen raised an eyebrow and smiled, unsure if we were deadly serious or only having a laugh.

'So have ye heard any more from Julie?' Jen asked Rez a few minutes later. 'Sally MacLennane' came on the speakers and me and Cocker cheered.

Rez looked at her for a moment, as if weighing up whether to say something. Then he told us the story about the diving instructor, the island, how he'd read Julie's email.

'Oh, Rez,' said Jen when he was finished, instinctively reaching forward to put a hand to his face. I liked the way she did that. 'That's really awful. I can't believe Julie would be so hurtful.'

'She didn't know I'd read it,' muttered Rez, looking a bit sheepish now that he'd told us of Julie's betrayal.

'Fuck that,' I said. 'Don't mind her Rez, she'll come beggin to be with you again when she gets back.'

'Marleygate,' said Cocker.

'Sex, Dives and Videotapes,' I added.

'Expert muff diver,' said Cocker, then regretted it and looked down at the table. But Rez didn't seem to have heard.

Jen shook her head sympathetically.

'Fuckin Julie,' Rez muttered. The topic was clearly threatening to darken his evening. 'Anyway, let's get wrecked. Surely that's the mature and intelligent way to resolve all the complex problems that, like, vex me.' He raised his glass.

'To Marley and his aqualung of love,' said Cocker. 'May he get the bends because he's actually a bender.' We clinked our glasses and drained the cocktails. 'Rez, this'll cheer ye up. What do a woman and a KFC meal have in common?'

'Tell me.'

'If ye take away the legs and the breasts, there's nothin left but a greasy box to throw yer bone into.'

Rez smiled and shook his head.

Jen sighed.

Just after ten we went to the Noosehound. As usual, the bouncers pretended to be convinced by our crap-looking fake IDs, and in we went. Usually when we came here we smuggled in our own vodka or cans of Dutch Gold, but tonight Jen insisted we let her take care of the drinks. 'Relax, don't forget it's all on daddy's bill,' she said when we made a faint, insincere protest. 'I know he'd want us to have a good time.'

'In that case I'll have rum and Coca-Cola,' I said in a Jarvis Cocker voice as we pushed into the clamour of sweat and electro-clash. 'Actually, no, I'll have a double vodka and Red Bull.'

'Same for me,' said Cocker.

'Me too, please,' said Rez.

Me and Cocker clambered up to the DJ box and requested punk songs, and Cocker screamed that if the DJ didn't play 'Accelerator' by Primal Scream he would sneak into his house at night and eat his children, or his mother if he didn't have children, or his bollocks if he didn't have a mother. The DJ didn't hear him properly and merely gave a pompous nod in recognition that we existed at all.

'Cheers, you fuckin spanner!' yelled Cocker, smiling and giving the DJ the thumbs up. 'The fucker can't hear anything.'

Jen decided that what we needed to make the night perfect was some pills; she'd been dead curious to try them since we'd all raved to her about how amazing it had been the first time.

They weren't hard to find. Jen paid again, though we made some show of cobbling together a few coins to help out. We bought eight pills and took one each, washing it down with vodka and Red Bull. Then we rushed on to the dance floor because 'I Wanna Be Sedated' had come on. As we danced I kept thinking that looks were passing between Cocker and Jen. I considered putting my fist through a mirror. But moments later the pill came up on me and all the rage and jealousy fell away.

'I FUCKING LOVE YIS!' I roared to the three of them on the dance floor.

Cocker threw his arms in the air and screamed in euphoria. I decided he was my greatest friend of all time.

'So it's working then, guys? You're coming up?' Jen called out.

'OF FUCKIN COURSE I AM! I'M HAVIN THE TIME OF MY FUCKIN LIFE!' I roared back, already too fucked to catch her irony. As I roared the words, it seemed like I was proclaiming a manifesto, the sum total of all there was that was worth saying. Jen was rocking with laughter.

A few minutes later, she was coming up as well. She had been dancing a few bodies away from me and now she approached, eyes huge and clear. She took my face in her hands and said, 'My God, these are incredible.' I nodded and grinned as 'Debaser' came on. She pulled me in again and said, 'Matthew listen, I just want to tell ye, I think yer amazin, I'm *so* glad we got together. I've always liked ye. Did ye know that? I never told anyone and I never did anything about it, but I've always liked ye, I always thought there was something different about ye, something more interesting.'

I took her face in my hands and kissed her; we pressed our foreheads together and gazed into each other's eyes.

Then we prised apart, and suddenly I was babbling at her, the words pouring out of me, uncontrollable, one leading to the next.

'Jen there's things ye don't know about me, like I'm not who ye think I am, or there's somethin wrong with me, I don't know how to explain it, like I'm not a normal human bein or, or I don't know, but when me and Kearney saw the girl gettin killed, I mean it was horrible, Jen. But Kearney was really into it and I smiled at him and it's like, now when I see them bombin Iraqis on the news and the children dyin and all that stuff it's like I can't even feel angry any more, like I'm no better than they are, I'm just a Yank up in a gunship, like shootin into schools and chewin gum or …'

I stopped talking and closed my eyes. I was sure I'd said too much and now she would leave me and go off with Cocker, or someone else who had integrity and substance.

I opened my eyes and Jen was still smiling a wide, lovey smile. She didn't look shocked or disgusted. Still dancing, she put her hands behind my head and kissed me on the lips. She purred in my ear, 'You're amazing, Matthew.' I realized that she hadn't heard a thing I'd said. But still I felt better, like I'd been to confession and spilled out my sins to God, only there was no God, the sky was empty and there was only Jen and me and Rez and Cocker, and the music and the drinks and the ecstasy that surged up through me now and everything was radiant and epic and there would never be another moment like this one in the entire span of the universe. I beamed at Jen, euphoric, suddenly forgiving myself for all the terrible things I'd felt I'd done for years and years, without even knowing what they were. Then I thought of Kearney over in America and sort of wished him well but understood very clearly that I had to move on from him, that a lot was at stake here, there was more to life than hate and rage and it was crucial that you liked yourself and a good girl could help you do that, and so could friends like Cocker and Rez and –

My thoughts got scrambled because at that moment the song that had been playing fell away and the first scorched beats and squeals of 'Accelerator' tore through the speakers. I planted my feet shoulder-width apart, clenched my fists, threw my head back and howled: 'UUUHHEEEAAAGGGHHH!'

The next thing I knew a bouncer was shoving me towards the side of the dance floor with his shoulder, pushing me against the wall, saying, 'Don't be a fuckin cock-merchant, alright? Give it the fuck over or ye can gerrou.' I looked in his eyes; he was pure brawn, skin-headed, and scarred under the right eye. But in his face I saw wound-edness, strangled compassion and the capacity for immense love.

'It's okay man, don't worry about it. Yer a great guy, I know ye are. Here, have a cigarette' – I pulled the pack from my back pocket and held it up to him. A joint protruded from the top; I ignored it, putting the pack away again. 'It's great, I know yer only doin yer job, I know I'm actin the bollocks a bit. It can't be easy, like, on a Saturday night and all that, but fair play to ye. I mean like, yer not bad at all. I respect ye, ye know what I mean? I really fuckin do, I respect ye. All I'm sayin is I think yer great, man, seriously.'

'GET THE *FUCK* OUT, YE CHEEKY LITTLE CUNT!' he bellowed, grabbing me by the scruff and dragging me to the front door, then shoving me on to the street. For a moment I thought he was going to hit me. 'Ye can forget about ever comin back here again.'

'What's wrong?' I pleaded, genuinely bewildered.

But he repeated that I was a cheeky little cunt and walked back into the club, rolling his shoulders and making sure he looked mean and cool. I held out my opened hands in a futile gesture to no one, an orphan before howling cosmic winds. Moments later, Cocker and Jen came hurrying out. Jen was laughing. Cocker's face was a glaze of indiscriminate bliss.

'I'm barred!' I announced. The words sounded momentous, prophetic, and once again I started to come up, mad with euphoria.

'The important thing is this,' Jen said, pulling a cocktail glass from underneath her jacket. 'I smuggled out your drink.'

Some time later we were in the Iveagh Gardens, sitting on a bench, surrounded by the darkened windows of office buildings and the faintly rustling treetops of the city-centre green space. We were passing around one of the bottles of red wine we had bought from a secret, late-night counter. With all the drugs inside me the wine felt strange, like a trickle of cool, sweet blood running down to my guts. I had the vivid sense that as long as there was wine and cigarettes, everything would be okay. I looked up into the sky and felt a magnificent, heightened peacefulness. You never know, I thought, maybe there *was* something out there; not like a God, but something vast and beyond our understanding, some immense mystery that gave everything a kind of dignity and even a meaning. I thought of Becky and how she died but still I felt serene – maybe even that horror had a significance as part of some great cosmic blueprint. It seemed that everything was basically alright, that even tragedy and violence were not proof of how vile the world was, but only elements of it I couldn't yet understand.

Each reflection triggered many more, my mind cascading with wonder and insight. Then I wanted to be with the others. 'Try Rez again,' I said to Jen, gurning my jaw, lighting perhaps my thirtieth cigarette of the night. 'Rez is a great guy, pure fucking quality.'

There were purrs of agreement, then Jen phoned him.

'We're in the Iveagh Gardens, come on around, we're all waitin for you,' she called into the phone. I could hear the crackle of speech on the other end. Jen laughed and put the phone in her pocket.

When Rez arrived a few minutes later, we greeted him like he'd been away for years. There were hugs and cheers, roars of random approval and aggressive bliss.

'The last I saw of you, Rez, you were chatting up some gorgeous girl at the bar,' said Jen.

'I saw her as well,' said Cocker. 'Fuckin cracker. That was just before Matthew got slammed by the bouncer. What happened to her, Rez?'

'Ah, I don't know,' said Rez, looking a little sheepish. 'I think I scared her away. It was a bit of a rant.'

'What did ye say to her?' I asked.

'Ah, some stuff, I don't know. I told her about how the music at the club, it wasn't any good, most of it was ten or fifteen years old. I mean, the music *was* good, but it's not of the here and now, it's not our music. Ye know what I mean? All this is music that came out years ago. It's like the epiphanies of other generations, in Manchester or wherever. Like, it's great music, but I wish we could hear real music from now, instead of what people were amazed by fifteen years ago. It all feels second-hand. The music that they do play from now doesn't count, cos it just sounds like the stuff they put out back then, regurgitated.'

'No, I don't agree with you,' said Jen. 'It's not all like that. There's some amazin stuff we listen to that's just come out.' She named some good bands from the here and now, a few electronica acts, some techno stuff.

'I know, yeah, you're right. But that's only a little part. Mostly we're listenin to The Clash or The Stone Roses or MC5 cos they came from times when things still meant something, or when it felt like there could be something new, or … ah, I don't know. I mean, I'm only sayin.'

'What about Joy Division? You're obsessed with them,' I said.

'Even Joy Division. Even The Smiths. It's amazin stuff but it's not my music, it's a different era.'

'I don't know,' said Jen, looking at Rez in a thoughtful way. 'It seems almost like your brain is made like that, that you can only see what ye don't have, or like you're determined to believe that everything is corrupt.'

'So this girl didn't like what you were sayin?' I said.

'Well, no. But it wasn't only about the music, I was really fucked and I started tellin her how everyone in the club, every person I saw as I looked around, was made up of bits of television and films. It was true – it was really fuckin incredible, I saw it all so clearly, with completely new eyes. We're just not real people any more, we're all just types, it's like our personalities are these costumes we wear, and we choose them and mix and match from a fuckin pre-designed range of possibilities.'

'I don't really get you,' Jen said. I saw that she was listening keenly, though; Rez had that power. He had started to cut through the air with tense, slicing hand gestures, and I imagined I could see veins bulging at the side of his head, but it might have been an hallucination. He drew people in, Rez; he could unnerve you. Talking to him was exhausting; you couldn't do it for too long or you'd start to feel as lost as he was. But that was what made him so interesting. His mind was a vast, sinister labyrinth – I saw all this clearly, in a moment of deep chemical insight – and Rez was down there somewhere, running through it, looking for a way out but only losing himself more hopelessly. Maybe he wasn't trying to run towards the exit, though, maybe he knew he was running away from it, deeper and deeper. Maybe he didn't want to escape.

Rez kept speaking: 'What I mean is, everyone is a type. It's like the replicants from *Blade Runner*. You're an artificial personality construct who thinks it's human. We're not human any more, we don't have any real feelings, we don't have any depth. We're just types, just fuckin reflections, echoes. Like, ye can be the cynical outsider, the slacker guy, kind of doomed and romantic, but it's only an image, something that the fuckers let ye have to keep ye off the streets. Or ye can be, I don't know, the family man, or the quiet, intellectual type in a white shirt, or whatever. Or the artist or the punk or the nihilist. They're all images, outfits; they're not real. Nobody is real any more.'

I was becoming entranced by Rez's monologue, which accelerated and intensified as he got into it. It was almost too much – there was the feeling of hurtling towards the edge of an abyss, with Rez screaming and leading the way with mad eyes and raised fist, dead set on hurling himself into the void.

Cocker was the one who put the brakes on it: 'Lads, I am off my fucking head!' he declared.

Rez seemed to snap out of it too: 'Yeah, fuck, those pills are amazin. But have we still got the one left each? Please God tell me we do. It brought me down when I scared that girl away. I thought I was in there. I reckon if I can get with some other girl it will take the sting out of what Julie did.'

A loved-up Jen groaned sympathetically and gave Rez a hug. 'Aw, don't worry Rez, there are plenty of gorgeous girls out there who'll be crazy for you.'

I said, 'You're right, Rez, we should take the last pills now. Where are they again?'

'Here,' said Jen, taking them out of her purse. 'Who's goin to be the priest this time?'

'You do it, Jen,' Rez said. 'It's about time we had female priests in this fuckhole of a country. Though I still wouldn't go to Mass, obviously.'

Jen took the first pill between thumb and forefinger and raised it in the air. 'Body of Christ, Rez.'

'Amen.'

She put it on his tongue and he swallowed. I could see his face tensing in the thrill of anticipation, the forerunner to the actual effects of the drug.

'Body of Christ, Cocker.'

'Body of Christ.'

'You're supposed to say "Amen", not "Body of Christ".'

'Amen.'

Cocker swallowed his pill and washed it down with a bottle of water we'd bought in a 24-hour Spar, along with more cigarettes, chewing gum for our gurning jaws and a needless surplus of skins.

When Jen said 'Body of Christ' to me, she put the pill on her tongue. I took it from her with mine, swallowed it, and then kissed her, though in an asexual kind of way.

'You may go in peace to love and serve the Lord,' said Jen.

'Thanks be to God,' said Rez.

'Thanks be to fuck,' said Cocker.

We all sat down on the bench and drank some wine, and there was silence for a moment; a full, vibrant silence. Drugs, I thought, are fucking wonderful. *Contrary to popular opinion.* I thought of writing the phrase down, then decided it was better not to write anything down, nor even try to remember it.

'Lads and ladies,' said Cocker, standing up and taking a theatrical swig on the wine bottle. 'Here we are tonight, us four. Here we are for evermore.' He threw his arms out as if to embrace the sky. 'Oh holy fucking Jesus Christ almighty, I swear to God this is UN-FUCKING-BELIEVABLE!'

We lay down on the grass in a circle looking up at the sky. The world was starting, very faintly, to brighten, a galactic purple radiance seeping into the sky above the rooftops.

We lay there, speaking occasionally, quietly, as the sky slowly became infused with dawn light, pale at first but galloping towards brilliance.

'Lads,' I said. 'Lads and ladies, or one lady I should say, but listen, this is the best night of my life. I mean that. I couldn't imagine a better night, and better people to be here with than youse.' Usually this kind of talk would have been instantly ridiculed, but tonight there was no question of that. We all felt it: the ecstasy, the city at dawn, the cool grass beneath our bodies. We lay there and watched, listened, breathed. A gust passed through the gardens, cool, making my skin tingle.

A few moments later, Rez spoke. There was pain in his voice as it floated free of him, out into the universe.

'This is all we have left,' he said.

I was going to say, what do you mean? I was going to contest him, not in an argumentative way, but only to try and show him that there *was* more, that things may have been bad but they weren't *that* bad – even when he was high he thought that way. I was going to tell him that yeah, the world was fucked up beyond belief, that the times we were living in were atrocious, and maybe, as he put it, nothing was real any more, reality was a thing of the past. Maybe all of that was true, but that only meant there was nothing to hold us back, nothing left to lose, only sheer giddy freedom to do whatever the fuck we liked, to hell with everyone else.

But I didn't say anything. I watched what looked like a satellite tracing a lonely arc across the brightening city sky, but maybe I was hallucinating. It was hard to tell.

25 | **Rez**

Why I am Not Real and Happiness is Impossible in the Modern Age. To be read after my demise – by Richard Tooley

Section 146: Forgetting Considered as
Metaphysical Annihilation

Consider the infinitely and profoundly troubling nature of our <u>fundamental existential plight.</u> No matter how intense, unique, beautiful or interesting your experience, it will be wiped away so fully that there will be no evidence it ever existed at all. This is a <u>fundamental truth.</u> I never forget it for a moment. It's like when you go to a party and say something funny and clever. You feel good – but as the night wears on and people get stoned and wasted, your clever remark gets lost, sort of muddied out. People forget who said it, or what exactly was said. By the following morning, no one can remember it, except maybe one or two, but even their memories are already fading; and anyway you can't even be sure they

remembered at all, unless you call them up and ask. But that would be too
embarrassing – you would be considered a weirdo.

   All humans are <u>profoundly shocked</u> to realize that everything vanishes:
their loves, hates, passions, thoughts. Also how good they looked, and how
unique their personalities were (or seemed to be – that in itself is a <u>major</u>
<u>question</u>). Imagine if The Clash had played all that music but there was
no way to record it. People would whisper about how amazing it had been
but no one else would really get it and the ones who'd heard it would even
begin to doubt their own memories – was it really as great as it seemed?
Until all memories are washed away, <u>like sandcastles in the tide</u>.

   Yes, such is our <u>human condition.</u>

26 | Matthew

When the wine was almost finished we left the Iveagh Gardens and walked through the early-morning streets. It wasn't cold, but there was a freshness in the air, a coolness that made us feel purer than we would have done, coated as we were in mingled smoke and sweat, reeking of drink.

All was quiet as we passed Stephen's Green Shopping Centre. We walked down Grafton Street where only a drunken tramp stirred outside HMV, lying on the paving stones. I wondered if it were possible for me to ever end up like that. I had to look away or the sight of him would have brought me down.

Jen suggested we go into Bewley's for cups of sugary tea. It seemed a good idea but then Cocker said, 'Why don't we go to an early house?' and it was settled.

The pub was on the quays. The four of us stepped from the bright morning into the wilful gloom of surly old-Dublin workers and resolute alcoholics. We felt self-conscious. There were maybe six people drinking there, all of them male, all greyed and dusty with life. We ordered pints of Guinness and sat down quietly in a corner, our movements jittery and our faces bright with ecstasy-wonder.

We drank our pints, smoking cigarettes and talking in low voices; disjointed, keen conversations that bubbled over now and then into affectionate laughter. The feeling of being there together was so good it was almost painful – I wanted things to stay exactly that way, that one moment forever, but everything was always slipping away, nothing was fixed. I beamed at my friends, love and affection for them pulsing out of me. I wanted to express it and tried a few times, but settled for simply smiling, laughing, watching them.

The old men and other drinkers didn't bother us, bar the odd funny look. Mostly they played darts and left us alone, and when one white-haired old man was passing our table on the way back from the toilets, he leaned in and made a friendly joke in a gruff, heavily accented voice. We laughed and nodded to him.

On the third pint the plunge came; the sudden, shattering emotional drop following the high that was so perfect you sometimes forgot you were high at all. It was like being pushed into icy water on a bitter-cold day, a horrible shock, all the grief and betrayals of a lifetime condensed into one instant – a feeling of sheer, desolating loneliness. It was as if the visible world vanished and you found yourself stranded on some cold dead moon, lashed by winds and darkness.

Anguish breaking out on my face, my hand reached over for Jen's. She turned to me slowly, gazing at me from across a gulf, locked into her own incommunicable grief. I smiled weakly at her and she tried to do the same; hers was a frail and frightened smile. I saw that we were both utterly alone and could never be otherwise. Rez had gone quiet, retreating from the front of his face into some sunless, barren place deep within himself. I realized it was beyond me to imagine how bad things got for him, but now I had some sense of it, the depth of his loneliness.

It lasted maybe a minute or two – this exile on a faraway moon – and then it passed. The feeling level readjusted; I was no longer ecstatic, and no longer buried in anguish. I was somewhere in-between.

We drank another pint and went outside. It was well after midday. We were drunk, and none of us wanted to go home or to be alone. Its primary effects worn off, the ecstasy continued to work on us, providing a moderate but constant bassline of enthusiasm and pleasure.

'I wish we had more pills, just one more each,' said Cocker. But I thought it was better that we didn't; to take more now would be only to fuck ourselves up and it would mean that the crash, when it came, would be unbearable. Better to slow-drink our way through the day, listening to music if we could, and gradually come down together all the way, easing ourselves back to something like normality.

Jen had told us that her house would be free for the afternoon. Her da was going away for a couple of days and her brothers would be at their girlfriends' houses, or out on the lash.

'What about drink?' asked Rez.

'We can get some at the offo near my house,' she said.

We took a bus along the coast. It was a lucid-dream kind of day; the people we saw on the streets, or walking along the strand, seemed hardly to be there at all, like pencil sketches. The sea out past Lansdowne Road was a thick blue, without lustre, drinkable-looking. We sat upstairs on the bus, wary of making eye contact with two crewcut lads in tracksuits in the last row, rolling joints and broadcasting their scorn in abrasive whines. The whiff of their hash filled our nostrils, queasy-making.

We bought sixteen cans of Dutch Gold and drank them throughout the rest of the day, smoking joints from Jen's ounce of hash, listening to Mogwai and Leonard Cohen and Radiohead. We were quiet whenever Padraig, Jen's older brother, was in the room, and he ignored us but for a few surly grunts as he made sorties into the kitchen. When he left to go to his girlfriend's we felt more relaxed.

The light faded outside, sped-up like in a film, until eventually we turned on the lamp in the corner of the sitting room. Our conversations got more jangled and fragmentary, our outbursts of laughter more frayed and weird-sounding. Strange voices gabbled in my mind in the quiet between songs, and my eyes darted randomly, all fucked up and playing tricks on me. I remembered how I'd felt last night, all the grand thoughts I'd had about the universe, about how everything was ultimately alright, redeemed by some immense mystery. Now, frazzled in the gloom, it was hard to connect with those ideas and emotions. A dead girl was just a dead girl, there was no grand solace to be found. My mind was clogging up with dark, confused thoughts and I started to nod off. Just as I was about to sleep I gasped: from the corner of my eye I saw that Kearney was in the room, dressed in black and silently watching me from the couch. I jolted upright, but now I could see that it was only the shape of Cocker's jacket that had confused me.

Sad, reflective music filled the room. Our talk gradually petered out, then Cocker stretched out on the couch and fell asleep. Rez was sitting up on an armchair, head resting in his hand, an image of desolation.

'You alright, man?' I asked.

'Yeah,' he rasped, in a way that made it painfully clear he wasn't. I didn't know what to say.

'Ye sure?'

'Yeah. I'm grand. Just a bit … down.'

He was making a massive understatement and he knew I knew it, and he wanted me to know it.

'Okay. Well, em, it was a great day.'

'Yeah.'

'I'm glad you were, ye know, here.'

'Was I?' he said, then laughed scornfully at his own pretentiousness. At least he was laughing.

Rez sighed and turned away, back to his bleak thoughts, the labyrinth he was lost in.

Jen was sitting beside me on the smaller couch, and she put her toe into my side and wiggled it. I turned to her.

'Will we go to bed?' she asked with a smile.

'Okay.'

We walked slowly up the stairs holding hands, then into her room, which I had been in a few times before but never as what we were now: more than friends. Lamplight glowed low and soothing; there was varnished wood and soft curves to everything. It was uncluttered but cosy; the kind of room you wanted to be in.

We sat on the bed and kissed slowly. Her hands came up, pulling me towards her. She inhaled sharply, like she was trying to breathe me in. We both smelled of alcohol and drugs. She guided me on to the bed and I held her head in my hand, resting on the pillow. She began to undress me. My heart was thumping, my muscles tensing, partly in anxiety and partly in excitement. I slid my hands up her thin blue cotton top, cupping her breasts in my palms. They felt warm. I drew my right hand down and rested it on her flat stomach. I kissed the pale skin of her neck.

She unbuttoned my jeans, then guided me free with her hand, between the buttons of my boxer shorts. She held it, squeezing slightly, looking in my eyes. We kissed again and I put my lips on her nipples, and rubbed between her legs with my hand. She had started to moan softly, making sounds that seemed to form gasping, melodious little sentences I couldn't understand. She reached over to the wooden bedside drawer and took out a pack of condoms, then helped me put one on.

We started kissing again. She was moaning more, her eyes closed, almost grimacing as if she was in pain.

She put her mouth to my ear and whispered, 'Come into me.'

I pressed myself towards her, trying to slide into her without using my hand.

Nothing happened. She opened her eyes and looked into mine. I reached and then looked down. My dick had gone soft. The condom hung loosely on it, curving in the middle. In fast-rising panic I tried to shake and coax it back to action.

She did a little laugh but I was aghast, terrified. 'What the fuck is happening?' I pleaded.

'Relax …' she began.

'But what's going on? Why isn't it hard?'

I was freaking out, close to despair. She tried to calm me down but I felt humiliated. Visions of lifelong impotence bombarded me, smothering me in horror.

'Just relax,' she said. 'Here, lie back.' She took it in her mouth and kissed it, licked the tip, flicked her tongue over it. I watched in extreme anxiety.

'It's no good,' I moaned. 'Why is it happening?'

Eventually, through Jen's licking and coaxing I achieved what felt like a very precarious half-erection. 'Now, put it in me,' she whispered. I obeyed: as soon it was inside her I could feel myself coming. I tried to stop it but it was too late. I closed my eyes, devastated. Something in me seemed to expire, with a final, humiliated groan.

I lay on top of her and buried my face in her shoulder. She was trying to comfort me, saying sshhh and stroking my hair, while I stared in shock and agony at the wall. 'Don't worry, it's fine, it happens to lots of men. It's all the drugs you've taken. That's what happens, it's normal.'

But I didn't believe her: it wasn't the drugs, it was something badly wrong with me, an affliction I had now for life. I was ruined; there was nothing left for me but to kill myself, or live like a hermit on some mountain, reading books and shunning society. I was ruined.

I pushed her away from me and lay on the bed, shivering with the comedown, helplessly viewing an inner montage of disgrace, humiliation and shame. She put her hand on me but I shoved it away. After that she didn't try any more. She turned away on to her side of the bed and we lay there in silence, no longer communicating, no longer together. It took me a long time to fall asleep.

27 | Kearney

He awoke to find a black T-train driver shaking him roughly by the shoulder. 'Okay son, gotta get off now, this the last stop.' Kearney gazed up at the man, bewildered – and was blitzkrieged all at once by the fork-stabs in his brain, his heaving, sloshing gut, his parched mouth. As he stumbled off the train, squinting at a sign to try and work out where the fuck he was, it all came back to him – the party, the club, the fighting, the after-party, the wanking into a cake for a laugh, and finally everyone pouring on to the morning train to get home from the other side of the city. Then he must have passed out and the cunts had just left him there. Thinking of it, he started to giggle, despite the stabbing in his head and his ravaged condition.

He boarded a T-train going in the opposite direction, hoping it would get him back home. Whenever the train hit open air, rain slammed against the window, blurring up a near-black sky; Boston had been enduring a three-day torrent of rainfall, as if the blazing summer had imploded under its own extreme pressure. It showed no signs of letting up. Kearney tried to distract himself from his headache by listening to the Spanish conversation of the Latino man and woman who shared his carriage. They spoke quickly but he made out the words for food – *hermano* – and for party – *mañana*. Not bad, he thought, considering he had hated Spanish in school and surely failed it in the Leaving Cert.

An hour later, racked and raped by his hangover, Kearney finally found his way through the city's polluted deluge to the apartment. (One of the lads had previously told him, 'If you ever get lost, just follow the sirens and the screams of dying crack babies.') The apartment was empty: despite the interminable downpour all the lads were up on the rooftop terrace, shirts off, roaring and stomping in pools of water, drinking cans of Budweiser. A Pogues album was playing on a tiny CD player kept under shelter, Shane McGowan's feral howl an incitement to lunatic drinking. It was eleven o'clock.

A big cheer met Kearney when he stepped on to the rooftop. The lads grinned and congratulated him: 'So you made it back. Good man, Joe, you've passed the test. Give the man a can of wife-beater!'

'We were about to start takin bets on whether ye were raped and then murdered, or murdered and then raped. But it seems they didn't bother to kill ye after the rapin. Fair play to ye though, ye made it.'

'You're a fuckin mad thing, Joe. Takin after your brother so ye are.'

Kearney grinned. His T-shirt was soaked and water streamed down his cheeks. He didn't mind that they'd abandoned him on the train after he'd passed out – all that was part of it. He loved having the chance to hang around with these older lads.

Now Dwayne approached and gave Kearney a brotherly punch in the shoulder. 'Good man Joe. That was a rite of passage. Gettin abandoned on the train in a foreign city when you're too hammered to even stand up. Fair play though, ye made it back in one piece. You're becomin a man.' He slapped Kearney's back. 'So how's the head?'

'Not too bad now. I bought some Aspirin in a 7-Eleven on the way back.'

'Good man. Get a few drinks into ye and ye'll be grand. We've all had a bit of speed as well, let me know when ye want some. Last night was good craic but that's only the start of it. This whole weekend is gonna be fuckin mental. And listen, Stu is comin tomorrow. I'm dyin for ye to meet him. He's a sound cunt. He keeps tellin me about this special surprise he has. Fuck knows what it is. But c'mere, I have somethin for you as well, a little present for me kid brother. C'mon and I'll show ye.'

Kearney followed him down the stairs, into the sepulchral filth of the apartment. They stepped over bare mattresses and strewn clothing, dripping everywhere. The stench of beer, cigarettes and a million farts was repulsive even to Kearney. Dwayne found his own mattress in the corner and rooted out his money belt. From it he retrieved a little plastic pharmacist's jar. He opened it and spilled the contents into his palm. Kearney leaned in to see as Dwayne held something up between his finger and thumb: a green plastic capsule.

Kearney started feeling excited. 'What is it?'

His brother paused dramatically, then said, 'Date rape, Joe. Rohypnol. Pour this into the drink of some young one and she'll do whatever ye want. She'll be as horny as fuck and then ye can do her whatever way ye fuckin like, and in the mornin she'll just think she was drunk and mad up for it.'

'Have ye tried it?' said Kearney, fascinated by this drug he'd heard a lot about but never seen for himself.

Dwayne laughed. 'What ye should be askin me is, how many times have I tried it. Trust me Joe, when ye have this stuff on yer side ye can punch *well* above your weight. Not that a brother of mine needs any help in that department. But still, why have cotton when ye can have silk, know wharray mean? But here, I'm only givin ye the one; I don't have many of these. Save it for the right moment, when the romance is high.' He handed Kearney the capsule.

'Nice one, Dwayne.' Kearney beheld the capsule rolling innocently in his palm. This truly is the land of opportunity, he thought – date-rape opportunity!

'That's what family is all about, Joe. Just never let it be said, d'ye hear me, never let it be said. Now c'mon upstairs and we'll show this gang of mickey-swingers how to drink, wha?'

Kearney put the pill in his wallet and climbed the creaky wooden ladder, behind his brother, and together they re-emerged into the relentless rain, and the sky the colour of war machines.

28 | Matthew

On Monday my work shift passed like a sinister dream. The other staff kept looking furtively at me and turning away when I caught them. Customers made bizarre remarks and jokes I didn't get. It all felt unreal. My body ached and I had no energy. I smoked a spliff around the corner but it just made the paranoia worse.

The next day I still felt dreadful. I wasn't working so I stayed in my room with the door locked. Rez rang me in the afternoon.

'Do ye want to come over for a while?' he said when I answered. 'I've something to show ye. We could have a smoke.'

'Are your parents not there?'

'No, they're in work. Stall it over.'

'Right, see ye in a little bit,' I said, relieved at the chance of company.

Half an hour later we sat in Rez's living room, skinning up and talking.

'How was the comedown, man?' Rez asked.

'Not very good at all. I still feel down.'

'Yeah man, suicide Tuesday. Do ye know about that?'

'No. What is it?'

'It's like, after people started usin ecstasy in the eighties, Tuesday was the day when everyone started toppin themselves on. Ye go out droppin yokes on a Friday and a Saturday, and it takes a couple of days for the full lag to kick in, so ye feel shit on a Tuesday. Then ye go and hang yourself or drive your car off a pier or whatever.'

Music videos were playing on the telly. Christina Aguilera was simulating various sexual manoeuvres, wearing a skimpy denim miniskirt and thrusting her ass at the camera. I watched it and felt nothing. I thought of Jen and then reflected, for the thousandth time in two days, that I would never be able to satisfy a woman sexually. I pushed the thought out of my mind.

'So what was it ye were going to show me?' I said.

'Me album,' he replied. Rez had been talking about making an album for some time, but I hadn't realized he had actually been working on it.

'Ye mean it's all done, you've finished it?'

'Yeah, more or less. It's not really an album, though, more one long track.'

'What about the songs ye wrote, aren't they on it?'

'No. I can't even look at them any more. They were totally fuckin delusional. What I've made now is more ...' He searched for an expression, licking the backs of the skins in the meantime. 'More honest,' he said eventually.

'Well let's hear it, then. I'm dead curious.'

He went up to his room and returned with a CD.

'Let's have a smoke first,' he said.

We lit up and then he put in the CD and turned up the volume. Straight away, the peace of the room was violated by searing sheets of noise, screams of feedback and harsh metallic clanging. There was no rhythm or melody, and it was hard to even tell what instruments, if any, were being used. The noise constantly mutated but didn't go anywhere; it sounded like a black, amorphous worry-cloud. Random shrieks flared up and then died. Drills and hisses rose in volume till they smothered everything, then dropped away again into more clanging and hammering. It was the most discordant, abrasive din I'd ever heard.

Then, emerging from the squall of noise, human voices could be heard, arising for a while before being swallowed back up by the black cacophony. I heard what sounded like a child weeping. Then there was a cold, deep male voice with an English accent. I strained to make out some of the words: '... took him out to the factory where we had the cameras and the equipment. It was three hours before he finally died ...'

The voice fused into a steam-hiss of static noise and vanished, then there were more sobs, and screams of fear and pain, like the sound of people being tortured. There was a ranting voice in a foreign tongue, maybe Asian, furious like Hitler. Then it was Hitler himself, and more crying and wailing in the background. The screeching, metallic din kept warping, disfiguring itself further, slowing down and speeding up without any kind of pattern.

Now a racist thug was gloating about how he and his friends had beaten a Pakistani man to death in a public toilet in some deserted park. An American woman described how she had microwaved her baby. After several minutes, many voices, sobs and screams converged together, merging into a featureless panic of sound that rose in pitch until it was a single, shrill tone. The tone played out for a few seconds. Then, abruptly, everything stopped.

There was silence but for the whirr of the CD as it came to rest.

Rez exhaled smoke, looking ahead of him at the CD player. I studied the side of his face. Neither of us said anything for a few moments.

Then, stubbing out his joint in an ashtray on the arm of his chair, Rez said, 'So, what do ye think?'

'Well ...' I didn't know what I thought. 'It's fairly fuckin powerful.

I've never really heard anything like it. Do ye have a name for it?'

'*King of Pop*,' said Rez.

My stoned imagination was hurling out all kinds of speculations about the black sprawl of noise he had played me. I had a vivid, thrilling insight into just how fucked up Rez was getting, how lost he was. It occurred to me that this recording, this *King of Pop*, was Rez's cry for help, the aural equivalent of a half-hearted suicide bid.

A few minutes later I awkwardly tried to respond to the appeal. 'Listen, Rez, are ye alright these days? It's just, ye seem different, you've changed a lot. Ye never seem happy any more.'

'Of course I'm not fuckin happy,' he snapped.

Stung, I proceeded more gingerly. 'Right, relax, I'm only talkin to ye. It's just, I mean, yeah. Ye need to relax man, you're too wound up. Look, I know that the way things are in the world is horrible, and that life is meaningless, and all this stuff we've talked about. But … but there's more than that.'

'There's nothing more to it than that.'

'There is. Or maybe there isn't, I don't fuckin know. But what I mean is, ye seem in a really bad way and, and I'm worried. So is Jen and so is Cocker. I think you're only seein the world the way you're seein it because you're depressed or something. Maybe ye need some kind of help. Ye know? I'm worried that you're going to, ye know, do something to yerself.'

Rez scowled. 'Do something to meself. Jesus Christ, don't give me that.' He looked right at me with an intensity, an anger that unnerved me. I was feeling more and more uncomfortable, wishing I was elsewhere, wishing I wasn't stoned.

'Don't kid yourself,' he said. 'Part of you, the *honest* part of you, would love nothin more than if I went and topped meself. That'd be excitin, that would be a good story to tell people, it would make ye more interestin. Something to tell girls to make them fall for ye: "Oh, it's rough, me friend hanged himself." You'd love it if I went and killed meself.'

I looked away.

'Just as I would love it if you went and did yourself in,' he added.

'Fuck off, Rez,' I said. 'I was only tryin to talk to ye. I won't bother any more.'

'Yeah, well don't fuckin bother,' he sneered. 'All I asked was what ye thought of the music.'

'It's not music, it's just noise. Anyone can make a racket like that, and then just stick on the worst quotes ye can find. It's just fuckin lazy.'

'It's not lazy. It's just honest. That's the only way to get through to people any more and make them feel something. Everything else is just some fuckin false memory that ye get from a car ad or somethin. Do ye know what I mean?'

'No.'

'I mean, like, ye can't trust anything else, emotional songs or melodies or anything like that, anything with feelin in it, cos it's all part of the system, it's all been fed to ye by these fuckers who only want ye to keep consumin things and not cause a fuss and …'

He frowned, angry at not being able to articulate himself better. I glowered at him, hurt and furious, relishing his confusion.

I said, 'It sounds to me like you hardly know what you're talkin about, Rez. You're inventin some political statement or whatever just as an excuse to make something dead vicious. It's just cruel, that's all it is. You're just wallowin in all this misery and hidin behind some concept. That music is more like something Kearney would make. Maybe you're not that different from him. At least Kearney is honest about what he's into.'

The comparison incensed him. 'Well fuck you then, why don't you fuck off and make something decent, since it's so easy for you to criticize?'

'Fuck off yourself.'

I remained in my seat, tense and shocked. We had never fought like this before.

'I'll go then,' I said.

'Yeah, off ye go,' he replied.

'Thanks for the smoke,' I said, ridiculously.

I was out the door and thirty metres down the road when I heard him racing after me. He caught up with me, panting.

'Listen, I'm sorry Matthew. I'm sorry man. I didn't mean it, I just felt a bit, I don't know, insulted or something, or trapped.'

Now there was something pathetic to him. I had the sense that he really didn't want me to go, and that if I did, it would be disastrous.

I sighed. 'Look, forget about it. Ye can't be talkin to me like that, though. I was only askin ye if you were alright.'

His face darkened like he was going to snap again. 'I am alright,' he said, but then he made a visible effort to smile and soften his tone. 'Look, come on back to the gaff, we'll have another spliff. I'll nick some of me da's vodka and we can have a drink. I'm sorry man, I was just bein fuckin ridiculous.'

We walked back to his house together. Rez actually seemed to lighten up a bit after that. He even made a few jokes and did impressions of some of the teachers, like in the old days. He flailed his gangly limbs about while telling an anecdote from the couch, and after a while he had me cracking up, like there wasn't a thing in the world wrong with him, and our nasty argument of earlier seemed to be forgotten about completely.

We listened to Nine Inch Nails and Orbital and played a game of *Zero: Retribution* (Rez had borrowed the game from Kearney while he was in the States). An hour before his ma came back we opened the windows to air out the room and get rid of the hash smell. He poured some tap water into the vodka bottle, refilling it to where it was before we'd started lashing into it. Then I said goodbye and walked home, stoned and drunk, thoughtful and confused at once.

29 | Matthew

I didn't call Jen after what had happened in her bedroom. The thoughts of it filled me with such shame, I couldn't bear to face her again. Besides, I had no doubt that she was secretly hoping I'd leave her alone – who would want to stay with a guy who couldn't please a woman?

On Thursday evening I was sitting in my room, looking out the window, worrying myself into depression over my penile affliction. My mobile started ringing. I looked at the screen: it was her. I placed the phone back down on the desk beside my bed and let it ring. Eventually it stopped, only to start again a few seconds later. After it had rung out for the second time, it didn't ring any more.

The next day I phoned Scag. I wasn't sure if he had meant it when he'd said to give him a shout sometime, but today I couldn't sit at home and wallow. I needed to be out, getting annihilated and forgetting all this crap. It was too miserable.

'Story, Matthew,' said Scag when he picked up. 'Good to hear from ye, bud. Are ye lookin for a few yokes, is it? I'm afraid there's a bit of a drought on at the moment, sunshine. What about a bit of speed?'

'Em, the thing is, I wasn't actually lookin for any pills. I was just, ye know, givin ye a shout, seein if ye wanted to, like, meet up or something.'

There was a pause, then Scag said, 'Sure thing bud. We should meet up for a bit of a chinwag, have an oul smoke, see if we can get to the bottom of this thing once and for all, know wharray mean?' He laughed like Dustin the Turkey: 'Hua hua hua.' There was something mad about him, but basically Scag seemed alright.

'So what's the craic with ye these days, then?' he said. 'Are ye still refusin to work?'

'Actually I got a job. Just doin a few hours a week down in the garage around the corner from me. It's dead handy. The best thing about it is that I don't actually have to do any work. Or at least, I don't do any work.'

'Fair enough, man, fair enough. Like I told ye, just don't get into bed for less than ye got out of it for. So c'mere, are ye doin a line these days?'

I was puzzled. 'What, ye mean cocaine?'

'No, no. Not cocaine, I mean, are ye seein a bird. Doin a line.'

'Oh. Well, em, I was yeah, until recently. But it's, ah, I don't think it's goin anywhere.'

'Ah well mate. Fishes in the sea and all that. Know wharray mean? But c'mere, I'm just here in town havin a smoke and a can with a few old pals.' I presumed he meant junkies or winos. 'I'm in Dublin Castle. Stall it in and we'll have an oul chat.' He paused. Then, 'Have ye got a few quid on ye for a can or two? I'm a little bit skint to be honest with ye.'

'Yeah. Well, I mean, I can get a bit of drink … I'll jump on the bus now and see ye in there in half an hour.'

'Grand, yeah. I'm wearin me gold suit and a top hat, so ye can't miss me.'

'Yeah?'

'Yeah.' He cackled and I heard the old friends in the background guffaw along. Even their laughter sounded slurred. 'C'mere Matthew,' he said, 'I reckon we've been havin a bit of an Iraqi summer here in Dublin: it's a little bit Sunni, but mostly it's Shi'ite!' The chorus of laughter flared up again. It was cheering me up to talk to Scag.

I went upstairs to my bedroom and stuffed whatever money I could find into my pocket. Then I thought I could do with a little more – you never know where we might end up – and had a quick rummage in Fiona's room to see what I could borrow, but she never had any money because she was only fifteen and hadn't worked a day in her life. I gobbled a big bowl of Frosties to keep me going, then wrote a note to my parents saying I was going out and would more than likely stay with a friend. I put on a jumper and went to leave.

On the floor under the letterbox there was another postcard from Kearney. Fuck this, I thought, picking it up. The picture was of a little smiling girl with blonde hair, looking into the camera, full of trust and warmth, on the grass of some city park, next to monuments and a duck pond. I turned it over.

greetings infidel,

dry youre eyes Matt – ill be home very soon. Roll out the red carpet mofo. lissen man Ive' seen sumthing over here your not going to beLEAVE!!! trust me blood u aint never seen shit like this before. Ill tell u when i get back but put it this way it makes that stuff we seen with the little girl look like CHILDS PLAY!!!!

Dont trust Whitey

The Kronic

I shoved the postcard into the pocket of my jeans, and left.

Scag was in the public gardens of Dublin Castle, by the big grassy circle outside the Chester Beatty Library that was designed to look like a Celtic symbol or something. As I approached I saw him standing beside a bench, engrossed in telling an anecdote to, as I had guessed, a pair of shabby alcos who sat on the bench and watched him. It was a warmish summer's day but Scag still wore the black, fingerless glove on his left hand he'd had last time, and the black leather jacket.

'Ah Matthew, me oul flower,' he called when he saw me. 'Nice to see ye again, man. I thought you'd left me behind in the world. Me more tender feelins were bein hurt.'

'Yeah, I'm sure they were,' I said, laughing.

'These are me mates, Patser and Alfred.'

I shook their hands, and Alfred, a grizzled, badly dishevelled wreck probably in his fifties, said in an almost genteel English accent, 'Here ye go, lad. Get some of that into ya.' He passed me a flagon of cider and I drank some, worried about what kind of diseases swarmed on his cracked lips and gums, but not wanting to seem snobby. You probably had to allow for these things, hanging around with Scag.

Patser, the other alco, shook his head, coughed like there was a swamp in his throat and said through his beard, 'So you've found another one to take under your wing, Scag. Some lost soul lookin for a father figure, is he? Ye never never learn. Pray God he doesn't end up like the last one.'

Scag looked at him, amused and about to say something. But just then, two tall, obviously foreign girls walked by, in their twenties and both beautiful. The two alcos and I just watched longingly as they passed. But Scag called to them: 'How are yis doin, ladies?'

They looked back at him, unsure, not stopping but slowing down a little.

'Are yis havin a nice time?'

They nodded. One of them was frowning, but in a curious way, with a faint smirk on her face. The other one was trying to keep walking, but Scag saw his chance and consolidated the advantage.

'Come on over, we don't bite, like. Where are yis from, girls? We were just havin a little smoke, sure come on and talk to us for a bit.'

Forced by common manners to reply to his question, the girls finally stopped walking.

'Norway,' they said together.

'Ah, Norway – the land of Mr Hans Christian Anderson, if I'm not mistaken. Would yis believe I used to live in Oslo?'

'No,' said the more mistrusting of the two. She had a pale, smooth-skinned face and wavy blonde hair. She wore a white pullover and torn jeans. She was very stylish, I thought. Both of them were. Though not in the boring, fashion-victim way.

Grinning more openly her friend said, 'Actually, Hans Christian Anderson was from Denmark.'

'Oh yeah, of course!' said Scag, only fractionally discouraged. 'I must have been thinkin of Knut Hamsun – now he's definitely Norwegian. Do yis know him? He wrote *Hunger*. It's a book about my life story; this lad comes to a foreign city and does fuck all, and he has no money and goes round the bend a bit. It's a great book.'

The thing about Scag was, he really seemed fairly well read, despite all the junkie stuff and the criminality.

'I've heard of it,' said the girl with the grin. She was tall and slender with long limbs and dyed red hair, and even prettier than her friend.

'Yeah well, yis should read it,' Scag said. 'It's a Norwegian classic, ladies.'

I looked on, impressed, as were Alfred and Patser who, unlike Scag, seemed to shrink and fixed their eyes on the ground when the girls finally decided to come over and give us – or give Scag – the time of day.

I was wondering if Scag really had lived in Norway when the dyed-redhead asked him the same question.

'Yeah, I did. Lived in a squat there for a few months in around eighty-nine. Denmark as well. There's a lot goin on in Denmark.'

'Yeah, I have a few friends who squat in Copenhagen,' she said.

They talked about that for a few moments. Then Scag turned to his two alco friends and said, 'Right lads, I'll love yis and leave yis, I have to be gettin on. I shall be seein yis soon.'

And with that we found – the two girls and I – that we were following Scag, being led out of Dublin Castle and down Dame Street, and across into Temple Bar. He kept up a steady flow of verbiage to ensure neither girl had time to question what they were doing and slip from his grasp.

'It's a lovely afternoon, girls,' he said as he weaved us among the cobblestoned alleys of Temple Bar. 'It would be a sin not to make the most of it by sittin out and havin a pint in a nice oul beer garden. Am I right or am I right?'

We let him lead us through the laneways until, a few minutes later, we found ourselves in a pub. Scag slapped his hands on the bar and said, 'So, ladies and gents, what'll it be?' It was as if we had arrived there magically, having had no say in the matter ourselves.

The girls said they'd have pints of Guinness, and I said the same. I guessed what was coming next. The barman started pouring the pints and then said, 'Fourteen euro forty, please.'

'Fuck!' said Scag, making a show of pulling his wallet open and peering into it. Lo and behold, it was empty. 'I've only got fifty pence. I thought I had another twenty bills on me.'

He started off on what was sure to be a longwinded, regret-heavy explanation, but the blonde girl – we had by now learned that her name was Nicky, and her redhead friend's, Lorna – said, 'Oh no, don't worry. I'll get this one.'

'Are ye sure?' he said, as if it was a completely unforeseen, even bizarre idea.

'Oh yes, of course, no problem.'

I had barely said a word since the girls appeared. The truth was, I found them intimidating. They were a few years older than me, and surely far more interesting. No doubt they were hugely sexually experienced. As we sat down at a thick wooden table and sipped our pints, I remained silent but for a few nervy grunts, and imagined them screaming and sweating in the throes of mind-blowing orgasms administered by calm Jürgens, cool Tibors, handsome Tags.

We quickly finished our pints and then Lorna got another round in. Both of them had now settled into the idea of spending the afternoon with a Dublin junkie and his witless, wordless friend, and they loosened up, laughing and joking, telling us about themselves. They had just finished college, studying architecture (Nicky) and fine art (Lorna). Now they were 'backpacking around Europe, staying with friends here and there, seeing what happens'.

'How long have yis been in Dublin?' I asked.

'Only two days. You're the first Irish people we've met since coming here, in fact.'

'We're the only Irish people here,' said Scag. 'I imagine your dormitory is crowded, is it? The summer and everything.'

'Oh, we are not staying in a dormitory, we have a double room,' said Lorna.

'I see. Well, how about another pint, girls? Like I say, next time it's all on me.'

'Of course,' said Nicky with a grin.

We stayed in the pub all afternoon, getting progressively more wrecked. Every hour or so either Scag or I would roll a joint – at first in the toilets, but after a few pints, under the table – and go outside to smoke it.

The girls were drunker than we were, though they kept up the pace surprisingly well. Scag hardly seemed affected at all. I supposed that, with all the smack and other drugs he must have hurled into his body down the years, alcohol no longer had any effect on him at all, or not very much at any rate.

He was now educating the girls with one of what he called his 'race theories'.

'Ye see, drink pulls ye back into yer body. It anchors ye in yer physical experience, whereas marijuana on the other hand makes ye float further out into the cosmic realms, the non-visible reality.' He vaguely waved a hand in front of his face to suggest enigma and weirdness.

'You mean the spirit world?' said Lorna.

'Precisely. The fuckin spirit world. And that, ladies, is why the Irishman drinks so much: cos he's already far enough out in the other world, due to his inborn Irish nature. He doesn't need something to take him out there to the fairies and the spirits and the bleedin demons. He's already there, so the oul grog helps to keep him grounded, it doesn't let him drift too far out. The drink is better for the Irishman than the weed. That's why I never touch marijuana, girls, not so much as a single toke of the stuff.'

As he finished saying this, he slowly licked along the joint he was making, looking intently at Nicky all the while. He smoothed down the folded papers with his thumb and twisted the end of the joint to finish it. Then he put it behind his ear.

'Very interesting, Irishman,' said Nicky with another playful smirk.

'Mmm. You know, we were supposed to do some of the sightseeing today. So long to that,' laughed Lorna. The place was starting to fill up now, the Friday after-work crowd coming in with ferocious thirsts on them.

'Ah, don't mind that,' replied Scag. 'This is the most authentic bit of Dublin cultural experience yis are likely to get, drinkin all day with two bona fide Irishmen. When in Rome, ladies, do as the Greeks.'

They laughed and raised their glasses to us. Since she had started getting a little drunk, Lorna had begun giving me looks, smiling at me when someone else was talking. I grew tense whenever she did it, looking into the head of my pint and then taking a big, steeling gulp.

Nicky said: 'So we were wondering, do you know anywhere that is good that we can go to, like for going out?'

'Ye mean before or after we go back to yer hotel and have a bit of fun?' said Scag with a grin.

'What!' Nicky protested. 'I'll pretend I didn't hear that.' But she was laughing as she said it.

'What's wrong? I wasn't implyin anything underhand, ladies. I just meant that we could go back there for a few cans and a smoke, like. Save a few sheckles, play some of our own tunes, far from the maddening crowd, know wharray mean? God almighty, ladies, what do yis take me for?'

'Well, we'll see,' said Nicky, playfully. 'But we want to go out in Dublin, what can you recommend?'

'Well girls, the thing is, I thought I had me ATM card with me, but now it seems I've left it back at me gaff. But if yis wouldn't mind buying me another couple of pints, I'd be more than happy to show youse ladies a good night.'

'And you, Matthew? I imagine you've got no ATM card either?'

'No, I'm afraid not,' I said. I had bought one round, but decided to keep quiet about the twenty quid still in my pocket. I was playing it like Scag.

'Well, we don't mind buying you a few more drinks, do we, Nicky?'

———————

We went to a dingy, heaving club off Thomas Street that I'd never seen before. Scag said he knew the DJ and he could get us in for free; surprisingly, this turned out to be true. The bouncer asked me for ID, but Scag and the girls acted outraged and he let it pass. Inside the club, there were four different rooms, each with its own DJ. There was techno of various kinds, and trippy, mellow electro stuff, and in one room, this brutal noise-music, like pneumatic drills and chainsaws, all fucked up. I thought of *King of Pop*, wondering what Rez was doing. There was no point calling him. He rarely came out these days. Besides, every time I met him now I'd come away feeling drained, hollowed out, lethargic. In a different way than Kearney, Rez sucked the life out of you. He was a vampire.

'Girls, listen, I see an old mate of mine over there. If yis like, I can get some yokes off him. They're always amazin from him, and he'll give me them for dead cheap as well cos I'm a pal. What do yis reckon?'

'Yokes?' said Nicky.

'Pills. Ecstasy. Yips. Fuckin disco biscuits.'

'Ah! Okay. Go and ask him, I'll give you the money in a moment.'

The girls danced while I stood at the side of the floor, drinking my pint and feeling awkward. Scag went and talked to his friend, a wiry, paranoid-looking guy in a black Autechre T-shirt. Older guys than me confidently manoeuvred themselves closer to the girls, who laughed and threw back their heads, encircled by admirers, enjoying the attention.

Scag saw them laughing and dancing with the men. He called them away and they came. I followed.

'He doesn't have any yokes, but he does have some charlie. What about it? He says it's amazin stuff, and he wouldn't lie to me.'

The girls looked at each other.

'How much is it costing?' said Nicky.

'Only eighty quid a gramme.'

The girls conferred for a while. Then Lorna shrugged and said, 'Okay, let's get two grammes.'

Scag took their money and returned to talk with his friend. I watched as the friend slipped him something at waist height whilst maintaining eye contact.

'How have you known Scag?' asked Lorna, who had moved up beside me.

I tensed up once more. 'Oh, I sort of met him through a friend, like. He's … I haven't known him very long. He's cool though. He seems to know everyone in the city.'

'I'm impressed.'

'Yeah. He told me he's never worked for more than two months in any job in his whole life. Usually he doesn't work at all, he just gets the dole. He thinks work distracts him. Ye know, from his poetry.'

'Oh yes.'

Scag had wasted little time in telling the girls about *Molesting Your Inner Child*. After meeting him the last time, I'd bought a copy from a dusty, second-hand bookstore on Exchequer Street. Though I liked the poems – short, punchy verses about drugs or violence, or straight-up pornography – I suspected that all serious critics who knew about such things would regard them as shit.

Scag came back with the coke. He slipped the wrap to Lorna.

'Go on in, ladies, and do a line. Then we'll go in when yis are finished. How does that sound?'

'Okay, cool.'

'And yis might get another round of drinks on yer way back, if ye don't mind. Like I say, next time it's all on me.'

The girls merged into the crowd and Scag grabbed me by the shoulder.

'Fuck me, did you see the arse on that Nicky? Jesus God, I can hardly keep me eyes away from it. I swear to good fuck, if we don't end up with these girls tonight, I'm going to rip me own bollocks off.'

Moments later he was grinning and saying, 'How do you make a hormone, Matthew?'

I grinned too, knowing something lewd was coming and enjoying it already. 'I don't know, how?'

'Kick her in the gee!' He roared with laughter at his own joke, and I giggled along.

'Here they come,' he said, alert again, anticipating drugs.

We got the cocaine and went into the bathroom together. There was a black guy wearing a white waistcoat in there, standing by the sink with a silver tray full of lollypops and aftershave, and a container of donated coins. We stepped past him and into a cubicle. I closed the door behind us and Scag started scooping coke on to a glossy flyer placed on the cistern. He chopped out two enormous lines. They were almost novelty-sized, I reflected.

He bent down and snorted the bigger of the pair through a €20 note that he'd had all along. 'Get that into ye,' he said, sniffing and handing me the note. I bent and sniffed. 'Grand. Now I'll just take a bit of commission for after.' He expertly fashioned another wrap out of a piece of cardboard from a club flyer he'd had in his pocket. Then he put a heap of cocaine on the end of the key and hooshed it in. 'There we go. Buyer's cut. Patriarchy, Matthew – it might be on its knees but there's life yet in the old whore.'

I thought I should put up at least a half-arsed defence of ethical decency and said, 'Ah, I don't know, they're nice girls. We've been bummin off them all day. Maybe we shouldn't take some of it. They're bein generous with it, anyway, so there's no real need.'

Scag laughed when I said that: a cheery, pleasant kind of laugh – he'd found what I'd said genuinely funny. Nor did he feel fit to respond, other than saying once more, as his laughter subsided: 'The fuckin arse on that Nicky one, I swear to God.'

When we came back out of the toilets we couldn't see the girls. We pushed upstairs. The music was harder here, more frenetic. Green lasers cut through a fog of black ice. The smell of sweating bodies was thick and lusty. The girls were dancing near the DJ's table, flailing their limbs, smiles streaked across their faces as they pulsed in the hectic lighting.

We joined them. Then we all raised our drinks and clinked. '*Sláinte!*' we roared over the din of music. I saw Lorna smile at me in a white flash of strobe lighting; she looked feral, her smile a blood-thirsty curl. But I was more confident on the coke and I danced beside her, leaning in now and then to shout something into her ear.

I realized that she was slightly taller than me. Then Scag was kissing Nicky. I didn't see any build-up to it – one moment they weren't, and then they were kissing.

Emboldened by Scag's success and by the coke that continued to course through me, I danced closer to Lorna, and soon, unbelievably to me, we were kissing too.

———————

The girls' room was on the third floor of a hostel on the south side of the quays, with tall windows looking out on the Liffey. Scag pulled open the curtains as soon as we all fell laughing through the door. The dark river glistened below with slivers of reflected neon. The walls in the room were blue, and the girls' backpacks were on the floor, beside the double bed. There were a few notebooks on the floor, along with clothes including, I noted with a strange, heady emotion, more than one pair of knickers.

'Crack on the tunes, ladies,' said Scag, nodding towards the set of portable white speakers and the iPod beside the bed. Nicky put on something that was like punk and electro mixed together. I was about to ask what it was, but Scag said, 'So are yis writers or wha?' He was gesturing towards the notebooks on the ground.

Lorna started dancing while we opened up the cans we'd bought with the girls' money, behind the bar at inflated, post-offo prices. Nicky said, 'Ah, yes. Yes and no. Mostly no. I write what I feel and think. It's … I do it for myself. Poems, but not really poems. Feelings and impressions mainly, I guess.'

'And you, Lorna?' I said.

'Me too. The same, I suppose. Feelings, memories. I try to write everything down so I can keep it with me when it's over. When something is finished, how can you know it ever happened, apart from the memory it leaves you? I don't like to take photos too much, so I write it down.'

'Yis can write about us then, your two gentlemen hosts and guides for the night,' put in Scag. 'Make sure ye portray me as havin a smoulderin Byronic intensity. Use that phrase.'

They laughed. 'Yeah, we will, undoubting. Cheers. *Sláinte*.'

Scag mooched over towards Nicky, who was sitting on the bed, and a moment later the two of them were kissing again, laughing, saying hushed, hurried things to each other. I sat on the chair by the bed. Lorna kept dancing. 'I can't sit still when I'm on the cocaine,' she said. I watched her, horny yet anxious. She laughed a little, then stepped over, leaned down and kissed me. She took my face in her hands and guided me to my feet. We started kissing, more and more heavily, and her hands began sliding over my body. Behind me, from the bed, I heard rising groans from Scag and Nicky. He was hardly going to start shagging her here, in a room with one bed while we were here too, I thought. And then I thought: of course he is.

Lorna was shoving me towards the bed, and then we were spiralling down on it. She ran her hands through my hair, bit my lip, and rubbed her groin against mine. I was hard as wood, but kept swerving between lust and distress. I looked to my side as she started kissing my neck: Scag was lying over Nicky, propped up on one hand, kissing the tops of her breasts whilst rubbing vigorously between her legs with his free hand. She was moaning loudly. As I watched, he undid her jeans and pulled them around her hips, then slid his fingers under her knickers.

Lorna was getting more excited too. She clawed down my body and began to unzip me. Before I knew it my cock was freed, exposed to open air. She took it in her mouth. I closed my eyes and tried to forget there were four of us in the room. But I couldn't overcome my self-consciousness. I pulled her head away from me, which needed some perseverance, and grinned awkwardly at her quizzical look.

'Em, can we do another bit of coke or something?' I said.

She smiled. 'Sure.'

I put my dick back into my trousers and zipped up. She looked like she was trying not to appear frustrated as she fixed her hair a little, then reached out for Nicky's jeans, which were now completely off her and flung across the bed. Scag's trousers were off as well, and now they were plainly screwing, he lashing into her, and she throwing her head back and grabbing the headboard behind her.

We watched for a few moments. Scag and Nicky were oblivious to us. I turned to Lorna. She looked at me. There was a strange, wordless moment, the shagging noises intensifying beside us. Then we both erupted in laughter.

She cut out the coke on a book that wasn't in English.

'What is it you're reading?' I said to dispel my nervousness with some conversation – an absurd intention, with Nicky now yelping in what I presumed to be an oncoming orgasm, right beside us.

'In fact it's Joyce, *Dubliners*,' she said.

I looked again at the book, where I now saw the author's name. 'So it is.'

'Have you read it?' she asked, finishing off trimming two thin, tidy lines.

'No. Is it any good?'

'It's not bad. I always try to read about the places I go to. I was going to try to read *Ulysses* but I thought, maybe I'll leave it until a longer trip.' She laughed at this. I laughed too, though I had no idea what was supposed to be funny about that.

She let me sniff up the first line. When she took the second, the two of us looked again at Scag and Nicky. He had hoisted her legs up behind her head and was banging into her with sweaty ferociousness. His grunts were now discernible as curses: Fuck, Jesus fuckin Christ, Holy Jaysus. Nicky started screaming like she was being raped.

'Anyway,' Lorna said, turning to me with a playful smirk.

'Anyway,' I replied. I didn't know what to say after that. But she saved me.

'How old are you?'

I considered lying.

'But be honest,' she said with an encouraging smile. 'It doesn't matter.'

'Twelve.'

'What!'

I laughed a little. 'No, I'm seventeen.'

She nodded at this.

'And what about you?' I said.

'Twenty-four.'

'Right.'

I knew I should have been feeling proud like a conqueror – I knew that I should also be shagging her, oblivious to all but the task at hand, just like Scag, who still hadn't come. But I was feeling too weird, too nervy and fucked-up. I only wanted to talk to her.

'You seem a little nervous,' she said.

'Yeah, I suppose so.' I gave a nervous little laugh.

'Don't you like me?'

'Of course I do, you're gorgeous.'

'Do you have a girlfriend?'

'No. It's not that, I'm just … this is too weird. With Scag here, I mean.'

'There's nowhere else we can go.'

'I know.'

Her disappointment had vanished, if it had been there at all. She lay back on the bed, dangling her head over the edge.

Finally Scag came. I didn't know where to look; after trying out several options I settled on the bathroom door, draining my can in hefty gulps.

'JAYSUS HOLY FUCKIN SHITE!' roared Scag, bludgeoning out the screams issuing from Nicky, who he had now turned over and was banging from behind. 'HOLY FUCKIN CHRIST ALMIGHTY, FUCK *ME*!'

Lorna was shuddering with laughter at the situation, which must have been strange, even for these worldly Scandinavian girls. I started to laugh as well, and soon I was doubled over and hooting as Scag seemed to drop dead, slumping off the bed and out of Nicky with a final, prolonged moan. He crashed on to the floor out of our sight, as Nicky continued to groan and gradually came to her senses. Through my tears of laughter, she looked like she'd just suffered a harrowing and violent ordeal at the hands of some crazed molester, which I supposed she had.

Me and Lorna laughed until we were spent. Then, from in behind the bed where we couldn't see, came Scag's voice, keen and collected as ever.

'Time for another line, comrades, what do yis say?'

30 | Matthew

We left the girls in their one-bed room the next morning. It must have been about nine o'clock, a reassuringly grey Saturday morning in the city centre, Dublin waking up but not yet overrun by the shopping hordes that would descend upon it by noon. We helped ourselves to a free breakfast on the way out, in a dining area with 'Breakfast is *strictly* for paying guests only' printed on a sign on the wall.

We hadn't slept. Scag had had sex once more with Nicky, but this time Lorna and I had left the room, walking upstairs to the rooftop and looking out at the river and the buildings on the other quay, watching Dublin stumble home to bed, howling at taxis and vomiting on its shoes. We had kissed again, but that was as far as it went. Lorna had told me I reminded her of herself when she was my age. We'd taken a good bit of coke by that stage and I felt sure of myself once more. Then we'd gone back downstairs and the four of us danced, laughed and chatted as the river outside slowly ran a dull grey, then murky blue, and it was dawn. Before leaving, Scag had assured the girls that we'd be seeing them again, and taken their

177

mobile numbers and email addresses.

We stepped out on the street after breakfast, our dilated pupils stabbed by the sudden glare. Scag looked up and down the quiet street. 'Sleep is for paedophiles,' he said softly.

'Where to?' I asked, energized by the cool morning air.

'Fancy another schniffle?' he said, clapping his hands together vigorously, as if he'd just stepped out after a rejuvenating night's sleep.

'I'm okay for now,' I said. 'I'm still high as fuck.' But as soon as I said this, I felt not quite as high as I had been. Coming down, I remembered Jen, the scene in her bed, the humiliation of it. Kissing Lorna had helped, but the pain was still there. 'Actually, now that ye say it, I wouldn't mind another whack.'

'Come on over to the boardwalk.'

We crossed the Ha'penny Bridge and sat on a bench on the wooden river walkway. A junkie staggered along and was about to pester us for smokes or money, but Scag shot him a look and he kept going. Then Scag took out the coke he'd siphoned off the girls' purchase. He produced a key, put a little heap on the end and held it up to his nose to snort.

'*Puntitos*, they call them in South America. That's how they do it in Bolivia,' he said after he'd taken the hit.

He sorted one out for me and I sniffed it up. He looked at me and laughed. 'We are all in the gutter, Matthew, but some of us are smoking crack.'

Watching a pigeon on the handrail a while later he said, 'So tell us about this bird ye were seein.'

'Ah, there's not much to it,' I said. But I told him about Jen, how I'd liked her for years but already it was wrecked.

'Yeah. I used to get like that about women,' he said. 'Not any more. There's no point. Listen, the whole aim of a woman's existence is to be impregnated, when it comes down to it. Seriously. I like them for their bodies, but that's about it. Psychologically I'm pure faggot.'

'I suppose,' I said. 'Some of them can be nice, though.'

'I remember a girlfriend I had once, we were together for a couple of years and she started gettin hysterical for me to inseminate her. She said it was the next logical step in our relationship. Jesus Christ. The next logical step. I had to laugh at that. We were arguin about it one night and she goes to me, "But that's what we're *here* for!" And I says, "Yeah, maybe it is. But if *bacteria* could speak, they'd say the same thing." And that was the end of us.' He chuckled at the memory, untroubled by remorse.

We sat and watched the oily drift of the river for a spell. 'Early house?' he said.

'Okay.'

We got a few pints into us in a dim grime-pit of a pub called The Bald Goat, drinking amidst the usual haggard old bastards, surly alcos and darts players.

Scag had gotten an *Irish Times* from the bar and after four pints or so he said, 'Look Matteo, the Festival of World Cultures is on in Dún Laoghaire this weekend. Will we head out, just for the craic?'

I said I was up for it. I texted Cocker to see if he would come too. The reply came seconds later: he had a day off so he'd meet me there in an hour.

We finished our pints of Guinness. Then Scag rolled a spliff and we headed into the fully awakened city.

Along the coast to Dún Laoghaire, the train was crammed full of young people heading to the festival. Within minutes of boarding the train, Scag had effortlessly commanded the attention and allegiance of the entire carriage. He held court for the whole journey, throwing out observational one-liners about fellow passengers, randomers outside the train windows, and the parts of Dublin we chugged past on our way.

'SCAG!'

The roar came from the back of the carriage. I jerked my head around, expecting confrontation. But it was a friend, one of Scag's punk and junk companions from the eighties – the decade when, as he had told me earlier, 'Everyone was poor as fuck and on the dole, but we all had a great time. The city wasn't stuck up its own arse back then.'

The wrinkled, leathery punk shoved his way from the back of the carriage to step into Scag's court, where some Italian lads with dreadlocks had gathered to skin up and be entertained by his banter.

'Howaya, Dowdall. Jaysus, it's been a while, I thought you were dead.'

'I am dead. I'm dead inside.' Dowdall cackled at his own slurred wit and cracked open a can of Devil's Bit. He had a nose ring and his dirty, grey-blond hair was spiked up with grease. There were metal studs on his leather jacket and Damned, Clash and Paranoid Visions badges sewn in drunken swerves along his arms. He looked ridiculous, a farce of all that punk once was.

'This is me mate Matthew,' said Scag, slapping me on the shoulder.

'Howaya,' grunted Dowdall with a complete lack of interest.

'Dowdall here used to play bass with Mickey and the Master Race,' Scag informed me.

'Oh right yeah,' I said, acting impressed though I'd never heard of them.

'Here now, not to mention three years and two albums with Footnotes to Plato, and a tour of Slovenia with Abject Phallus,' said Dowdall, wagging his finger like a schoolteacher. 'The Footnotes were a serious punk act, not like these gobshite posers ye get nowadays. Am I right, Scag?'

'Yis had yer moments,' said Scag coolly.

'C'mere, Scag. I hear ye think yer a writer now,' said Dowdall.

'Sometimes I catch meself thinkin that, yeah,' replied Scag. 'I put out a buke there a while back.'

'That's what I heard,' said Dowdall. 'Don't go expectin me to read it, now. Scag the poet, wha? Merciful Jaysus. I can imagine what they wrote in the biography yoke at the back. "Scag was awarded a C Plus in English for his Junior Cert. His ma considers him one of the top five writers to have slithered out from between her legs. He divides his time between Dolphin's Barn and the Walkinstown roundabout."'

Scag granted him a wry chuckle. 'That's it, more or less. I don't really think of meself as an author, though. I'm more of a conduit. There's a force deep down inside me. He speaks and I just write it down. I call him The Fat Controller.'

I laughed, though I wasn't sure I was meant to.

'I've got two more bukes almost finished,' said Scag. '*Sincerely L. Cohen* and *Fine Day for a Holocaust Denial*.' He paused to observe a passing arse, then added, 'I'm thinkin of puttin them out under me pseudonym.'

'What's that?'

'Seamus Heaney.'

'Tsss. Good night and good luck. So are yis on yisser way out to the festival?'

'Yeah. Sure we thought we may as well. Young Matthew here has had some lady trouble. His tender young heart is in danger of bein broken so I'm takin him under me wing for a bit of a blowout to cheer him up. Yerself?'

'Yeah, I'm goin out. I couldn't give a fuck about the festival but there's a bird out there I have to see. Little Spanish thing. Mad for me mickey, she is. Blank Frank has some yips for me as well.'

'Oh yeah?' said Scag. 'Haven't seen oul Frankincense in a while. How many are ye gettin?'

'Ten. Do ye want some?'

Scag hissed, all indignant. 'Does a bear shit on the pope? When have you ever known me not to want some fuckin yokes?'

There were thousands thronging the seafront at Dún Laoghaire, sitting on the grass in groups of eight or ten, drinking cans and bottles. There seemed to be little point in being here, other than to drink and talk in proximity to others who were drinking and talking. Maybe that's what a festival was: that and nothing more. There was a huge stage up near the Forty Foot but we felt no desire to push through the hordes to better hear the world music that was blasting from it. ('*World* music,' remarked Dowdall derisively. 'Where else is it supposed to be from?') I called Cocker and we shouted into our phones till we found each other.

'Any relation to Jarvis?' said Scag, when I introduced them to one another.

'Yeah, I'm his da,' replied Cocker.

Scag laughed. 'I thought so. Right then lads, I've to head off now for a bit, but I'll be back. I've another mate who lives out here who I haven't seen in a while. I'm goin to drop in on him. Dowdall, if I don't get around to Frank's before yis leave, get me them yokes and I'll fix ye up later, okay?'

Dowdall looked reluctant, but muttered yeah. Scag ducked into the horde, then me and Cocker walked off with Dowdall, stepping over hands and legs till we were past the thickest crowds.

'Where are we off to?' Cocker said, frowning, as we fell a few steps behind Dowdall. 'I thought we were just goin to hang around the festival and have a few cans. Who the fuck is this piece of work?'

'Relax. It's just a mate of Scag's. We're goin to pick up a few pills. It'll be cool, don't worry.'

'These are some weird-lookin cunts,' he muttered.

We followed Dowdall down a side street, passing big, rich houses where I wouldn't have minded living but knew I never would. Blank Frank was paying a home visit to one of his wealthier customers. Dowdall phoned him when we got to the house. Frank appeared a moment later at the second-storey window, mobile at his ear, gazing down at us. He was huge, bald, bearded and leather-clad; Blank Frank was an old-school biker.

Dowdall hung up. 'We've to go upstairs,' he told us. 'Now don't go makin bollockses of yerselves, do yis hear me? These lads won't see the funny side.' In a quieter voice he added, 'Frank is ... he has his problems. He isn't that bad when ye get to know him, but it's very easy to set him off. And that's not somethin ye want to see.'

We ascended a marble staircase, passing framed posters of Bruce Lee and Eric Cantona, and stepped into the sitting room. Other than Blank Frank (who used to be called Frank the Fuck when he did vocals for Consumers of Atrocity back in the eighties, as Dowdall had informed us on the way), there was a bulky, crewcut guy with suspicious eyes. He wore a white T-shirt with *Prada* printed brazenly across the collar in navy lettering. Though it was clearly this man's house we were in, he had that inner-city look to him; the raw, blemished face, the ugliness. There were two women as well, in their mid-twenties, both of them trashily blonde, faces caked with makeup. One of them was resurfacing from the coke she'd just been hoovering up from the glass table. She regarded us coldly. Blank Frank looked at me and Cocker.

'This is just Matthew,' Dowdall said quickly. 'And that's his mate.'

Blank Frank the Fuck shrugged. 'So how's things, Dowdall? Long time no see.'

Bottles of beer were offered all round by our jerky, shifty host, who had obviously done plenty of coke before we arrived. The girls said little, lighting cigarettes and watching us with hard, cynical faces.

'Cut them all a line, Eileen, will ye?' said the host, whom Blank Frank introduced as Seamus. I guessed he was some kind of gangster or high-end dealer. He was an erratic in a rich suburb like Dún Laoghaire, full of posh old cunts who spoke with near-British accents and looked down on the rest of us.

Dowdall, Seamus and Blank Frank sat down around a low wooden table on one side of the huge room, and started exchanging stories and jokes. Me and Cocker sat on a couch, listening to their loud, aggressive, uneasy laughter.

After some chat, Frank asked Dowdall how many yokes he wanted.

'Ten for me,' said Dowdall.

'We'll take ten of them as well,' said Cocker, fishing out some notes from his jacket pocket.

Frank the Fuck looked up. Cocker fidgeted beside me, putting the money back in his pocket. The girls watched Frank. Suddenly he made a sweeping gesture and said, 'C'mon up here lads, sit down with us for fuck's sake. Yisser lookin all lonesome over there, huggin yisser beers.'

We shuffled over, smiling awkwardly, and sat down with them.

Now Frank was slamming his massive paw on the table and saying, 'Dowdall, did I ever tell ye about the time me and Seamus here got caught with five hundred yokes outside the Point when Orbital were playing?'

'No, what happened? Did yis get arrested?'

'No, hang on and I'll tell ye. We were just outside the entrance about to get in past security – the plan was to sell the yokes inside – and suddenly this plain-clothes cunt comes out of nowhere. I've still no idea how he knew we had the stuff. But he grabs hold of Seamus's shoulder and starts screamin into his walkie-talkie, and he's obviously callin the lads for reinforcements. And while your man has his hand there, Seamus just looks at me for a moment, then he turns around and CRACK, he loafs him right in the face. So your man goes down like a sack of fuckin shite and we leg it, peggin it down along the quays, in through the IFSC. We legged it down this lane and went into a pub and that was that. They didn't catch up with us. We ended up goin on to some fuckin club – where was it, Spirit? – and sellin most of the yokes in there instead. And then all I remember is

Seamus wearin the face off this big fat trendy bird, and next thing I follow them into the jacks and he's ridin her over the fuckin sink!'

Seamus was slapping his thigh and laughing proudly at the anecdote. 'Ye know what they say, lads: when war is ragin, every hole is a trench. Fuck me, that was a good night. I was still pissed off we never got to see Orbital, though.'

'Orbital, now there's a great band,' said Cocker, nodding his head – even though he'd never listened to them in his life. No one paid him any regard.

Seamus said, 'The next morning I bought an Aer Lingus ticket to Amsterdam and I fuckin stayed over there for nearly two months. I was bleedin shittin it that they were goin to hunt me down and lock me up for years. Or do ye remember that time we dropped a fuckload of acid and went to see *Blade* in the big cineplex on Parnell Street, do ye remember that?'

'Fuckin right I do,' said Frank the Fuck. 'Or at least I remember coming to me senses in the cell the next mornin. Fuckin hell.'

Seamus was in tears of laughter. After a couple of false starts, he managed to get a few sentences out to deliver the anecdote.

'We'd taken a whole sheet between the two of us, and we were just gettin into the film – which is total shite, by the way – and Frank was gone dead quiet, just fuckin engrossed in the film, or so I thought. And then, completely all of a sudden-like, he starts screamin his head off, just fuckin screamin like a mad cunt, this mad, high-pitched fuckin noise, like a lamb bein slaughtered. It was like he was on fire or somethin, or some mad fuckin animal. He had his hands to his face and it was like he was tryin to tear the skin off it, and all the time these mad fuckin screams comin out of him. People were leggin it out of the cinema and everythin, thinkin there was some kind of fire or I don't know what the fuck. And I'm just sittin there pissin meself laughin, and next thing Frank is leapin up on the seat, lashin out at everythin. Kicked me in the fuckin jaw. Then he falls over into the next row and gets up, still screamin his fuckin head off and clawin at his face, and he legs it down the aisle and out of the cinema, into the fuckin foyer or whatever ye call it, upstairs where the bar and café is. By the time I managed to get up and leg it out after him …'

He couldn't go on because he was laughing too much. We were all laughing by now. After a while Seamus controlled it enough to continue.

'And so I leg it out after him, and I'm completely off me fuckin tits as well. And every cunt in the cinema is standin there in shock, starin at this mad cunt. He's after leapin in behind the bar and he's just pullin bottles down off the rack – whiskey, vodka, all kinds of shite – and he's fuckin them out of the bar, at the walls, on to the ground. He must've smashed about thirty bottles by the time the big golliwog security guard came burstin in and floored him.'

'Kicked the fuckin shite out of me too, when I was on the ground,' said Blank Frank proudly. 'Or he must have done, cos when I woke up in the cell I was in a right fuckin state. Me head was like the fuckin Elephant Man.'

'He did, he knocked the bollocks out of ye. He fuckin had to, man, ye looked like ye were a total fuckin psychopath. Every fucker there was shittin themselves. I thought ye were goin to kill someone.'

'It's a miracle I didn't, hurlin all them glass bottles across the gaff like that,' said Frank wistfully, eyes wet from laughing.

'What did the police do?' I asked.

'Not a fuckin thing. I was able to convince them that I was off me trolley and therefore me actions were beyond me control. It wasn't that hard to do – only a fuckin genuine nutjob would do somethin like that, that's how they saw it.'

'They weren't fuckin wrong,' declared Dowdall.

Blank Frank was drying his eyes. 'Fuckin hell, I'm goin to piss meself.'

Beside me, Cocker had gone quiet and still. I thought he was freaked out and wanted to leave. But just at that moment, he jolted upright in his chair, slammed his palm on the table and said, 'That's very funny. Frank, you sound like a real demented cunt alright.'

The room fell silent. Surely Cocker hadn't meant it to, but it had come out sounding like a blatant insult. The two girls on the sofa jerked their heads up, scenting brutality. Blank Frank stared at Cocker, who melted into his chair. Seamus inched backwards, eyes locked on Frank.

I expected an explosion but when Frank spoke, his voice was low and even.

'What the fuck did you say, sunshine?'

Cocker stuttered. Unable to work up a sentence, he attempted an ingratiating grin. I heard myself speak: 'He wasn't bein sarcastic, Frank. That's just how he talks.'

Blank Frank turned to me. I could see his lower lip trembling. His breathing was fast and shallow.

'Didn't mean anything,' whimpered Cocker. The two girls were squirming with anticipation.

Frank turned back towards Cocker. Dowdall was looking at the floor, shaking his head and muttering under his breath. The room felt like it was about to implode.

And then:

'GET DOWN HERE AND LET ME IN, YIS NEFARIOUS NAZIS!'

The roar came from outside, beneath the balcony.

Dowdall broke into hysterical laughter. Seamus leapt up and looked down on the street. Leaning over the balcony railing, he called out, 'Scag ye mental cunt, look at the fuckin state of ye!'

Frank turned his head. 'Ah Scag's here, the brazen cunt. I haven't seen oul Scag in ages.'

In the few seconds it took Scag to come upstairs, Frank turned back to Cocker, pointed a finger at him and said, 'You just take it easy, sunshine.' But it was almost good-natured, the menace all dissipated from his tone. Cocker nodded frantically. I began to breathe again.

When Scag entered the room, Blank Frank grinned at him and said, 'Scag, me oul flower! The last time I saw ye, ye were rollin about on the ground down some fuckin lane, with yer jaws round the ankle of some cunt in a suit. Frothin at the mouth ye were. Ye just wouldn't let him go. What in the good fuck was all that about?'

Scag smiled. 'It'd seem very reasonable if I told ye who that person was. Which I'm not goin to do. Ye know me, Frank, I prefer to abide in the mystery.'

Frank roared with laughter and slapped his belly. He was like a gigantic baby. 'Yer a fuckin headcase!' he bellowed.

Scag noticed me. 'I hope yis are bein nice to young Matthew here,' he said. 'This handsome renegade, he's a good skin.'

'A mate of yours, Scag, is a mate of mine,' said Frank.

Everyone was cheerful now, opening beers and cutting out lines. We stayed for half an hour. Then Frank gave us our pills. Me, Scag and Dowdall swallowed one each. We said our goodbyes and wandered back towards Dún Laoghaire.

When we were away from the house Cocker said, in a deflated voice, 'Listen, I'm gonna head home.'

'Ah come on, we only met up an hour ago. The day's just gettin started. What's wrong? It's gonna be deadly.'

He shook his head. 'I don't feel up for it any more. You can hang on to those pills. Just throw us a few quid whenever ye have it.' I tried to persuade him to stay out but he was adamant. 'What were we doin in there, Matthew?' he said quietly, letting the other two walk ahead. 'This isn't our scene at all. These people are horrible. Why don't ye stall it home as well? Or just come for a pint in town.'

But I wasn't ready to go home or even to have a normal night. I left a pale, diminished Cocker at the bus stop, then hurried to catch up with Scag and Dowdall.

'Is there anything decent on at this festival?' Scag was saying as I fell in step beside them. 'What about this bird ye mentioned earlier, where is she? She might have a few mates for me and Matthew here.

Oul Matthew, he's a bit of a fuckin sex-hound, you'd wanna see the fuckin cracker of a Norwegian he scored last night.'

'No, man. The Spanish bird's on her own,' said Dowdall. 'I've to meet her here and then we're goin back to her place, that's the plan. I'm goin to drop a few more yokes and nail her to the wall. That's if I can even get it up. But are ye not throwin it into that big jungle-momma ye were with last time I saw ye?'

'Not any more,' replied Scag. 'It was alright for a while but I started gettin fed up. She had this big fanny on her as wide as the bleedin Congo. Ye couldn't get a bit of friction in there at all. It was like throwin a sausage up O'Connell Street.'

Dowdall chuckled. 'Still and all, fine set of mangoes on her. But right, I'll have to love yis and leave yis, lads. Have a good one, don't stop till ye get enough.'

When Dowdall disappeared into the crowd, heading towards one of the smaller stages, Scag turned to me and said, 'What a wanker. I really doubt there is a little Spanish bird he's goin to see. He's fucked off now and he's goin to be yoked out of it on his own all day, just cos he had to pretend that he was meetin some bird to impress me. What a tosser.'

I could feel the ecstasy coming up on me, bleaching through the tiredness and the jerky, frazzled anxiousness that had crept in across the weird hours.

For a while we smoked spliffs with black lads who were watching a reggae band in a beer garden. Then we gave up on the festival and took the DART back into town, attaching ourselves to a bunch of Poles who sang and guzzled litre bottles of Paulaner and Lech. We swallowed our second pill each as the train was pulling out, and I lost all sense of where the highs and comedowns from the various drugs – ecstasy, cocaine, alcohol, grass – began and ended.

We blathered with the Poles all the way into town, punctuating our rants with peals of madcap laughter and slugs of lager. Scag gave up on the farcical attempt at meaningful dialogue and took to leaping up and down the length of the carriage, swinging from the metal bars between ceiling and floor, screaming 'COME ON YEE BASTARDS!' over and over. People laughed and cheered him on, but everyone looked tense whenever he got close to them. He was all loved-up on the pills, though, and meant no harm.

The Poles invited us to see a Polish DJ. It was in a club on the city-centre fringes of the northside that I'd never been to before called McDargle's.

In the club I felt invincible. Strobe lights pulsed; hard techno tracks broke down in the middle, then built up to prolonged, obliterating climaxes. We swallowed more pills. Scag was kissing a girl, a punky, blonde Pole who was like a boy. Then he was at my side, screaming into my ear that there was a guy who had microdots, did I have a tenner and we'd trip our bollocks off. I passed him my last note and danced some more. There was a different DJ now, or maybe not. Then Scag was dragging me into the hallway leading to the toilets, his face a cackling devil-mask. 'Let's drop this fuckin acid!' he yelled.

'Are ye sure it's a good idea, with all this other stuff we've been takin?'

'Relax, man. It'll be fuckin cool.'

'I'm a bit nervous. I've never done acid before.'

'Don't worry, it's deadly. Remember I'm here – if you're gettin paro or it seems a bit full on, talk to me. I've been takin acid for decades. I was takin it when you were in nappies. I was takin it when *I* was in fuckin nappies. There's nothin about it that can faze me, man.'

'Okay, thanks.'

We put the tabs under our tongues and let them dissolve.

The walls were spilling with the colours of music, and there he was, Matthew, standing in the middle of the dance floor, knowing what was to come, moving without moving, zooming through the cosmos while his body stayed very still, and all the surfaces bled together.

After the club we went back to a house on a dark, narrow street near Christ Church with the Poles, where the party continued. The acid was incredible; it must have been six hours after taking it and I was still tripping hard. The DJ from the club had come back to the house. At one point the techno got more intense and there was this Polish girl dancing in front of me. I could see that there was something wrong with her face. I peered at her through the smoke and noise – and then it was little Becky's face and it caved in on itself, spurting out gore and crushed bones as the one eye peered at me from hell. I screamed and leapt back, falling to my knees and covering my head with my arms. Scag had seen what happened and took me by the shoulder and guided me to my feet. I was shaking and babbling as he pulled me aside, away from staring revellers. 'Relax, Matthew, it's only the acid. Don't fight it, nothin ye see can hurt ye, it's only Samsara, don't fight it.' I smoked a cigarette and tried to calm down. I started to cry. I turned my face to the window so no one could see. Later I wrote Jen a text that scrolled on for three pages, but I deleted it.

The techno thumped all night. Even the Poles dropped out before we did. Some time after dawn most of them had retired to the bedrooms to sleep, or have sex; or come down in more intimate groups, or gone home; or laid out on the floor of the sitting room, front room and kitchen to pass out.

Scag was sitting on an armchair, peaceful-looking, a roll-up dangling easy from his left hand. He was gazing out the window, emanating thoughtfulness even as the veins in his temples bulged to the point of rupture. I sat down on the carpeted floor at his feet – there were no empty seats – and listened to the ambient waves of soothing, vaporous silver that dissolved around us, the DJ's gentle-comedown set. I felt sleepy and my head dropped forward a few times, eventually coming to rest against Scag's leg. I closed my eyes and let darkness flood over me, thinking as I blacked out that dying would not be unpleasant at all.

'I reckon it's time to split, Matthew,' Scag said after a while. I stood up and rubbed my eyes.

We took four cans of lager from the heaps of unconsumed alcohol that lay scattered around the various rooms, and left.

'Fuckin hell,' I said when we were out on the grey, early-morning street. 'I'm still trippin.'

We let our legs carry us, hiding the cans in our pockets between swigs, in case the police were around. We walked down Dame Street and crossed the Liffey, then followed the river past the long, imposing hulk of the Custom House, which now seemed to have a face and a real personality – it struck me that the building only looked so stern and intimidating because it was insecure about who it really was. It was all a front. The thought triggered another fit of giggles.

Town was silent and still like the land before time. We followed the river, past the spindly, sinister figures of the Famine Memorial and the docked yachts, to the port. There, we turned north into the city and kept walking, drinking, tripping, smoking, eventually re-meeting the coast out at Fairview. We walked along the Clontarf Road, by the sea that churned grey foam in a perpetually descending hiss, the sound of the world collapsing in on itself.

Out past the city centre, where the edges frayed into coastal suburb, we climbed over the low wall separating the road from the sea. We clambered down the rocks until we reached a meagre strip of grey, stony beach. Towers and chimneys of industry fumed in the distance along the coast, while cargo ships hulked in and out of Dublin Port. I looked behind us and couldn't see over the wall, couldn't see the road or the cars.

Scag sat down on the pebbles and rolled a joint with a bit of grass we'd been given at the party. When we smoked it, it seemed to rekindle the acid in my system so that once again I was tripping at full intensity.

For a while we stared out at the murky sea under a heavy, dismal sky, saying nothing. The foamy low tide hissed at our feet.

Then Scag pointed forward – at the grey sea and the grey sky that were coupled, almost one thing, one void – and said, 'That's the abyss, Matthew. That's the abyss at the edge of the world.'

And when he said it, something astonishing happened: out on the horizon, behind the sullen murk of the sky, I began to make out the shifting, restless contours of a great void that was opening up, as wide as the horizon itself. I became terrified, I couldn't look away.

'Do ye see it?' I heard him whisper, urgent and reverential.

The abyss was expanding, a great heaving vortex, spreading out across the sky like the Aurora Borealis, wider than the city. And then I could see that the light, the sea, the dead sun and the cargo ships, the seagulls and the city itself – all of it was being sucked in, slowly and inexorably, lurching forward to be swallowed up in the great void.

'Do ye see it?' he whispered.

I fell backwards on the ground, shielding my face with my arms and elbows in a useless instinct of self-protection. I screamed. Then Scag rose to his feet. He started to speak in a thundering voice: 'How were we able to drink up the sea? Who gave us the sponge to wipe away the entire fuckin horizon? What did we do when we unchained the earth from its sun? Where is it movin now? Where are we movin now? Away from all suns? Are we not perpetually fallin? Backward, sideward, forward, in all fuckin directions? Is there any up or down left? Are we not strayin as through an infinite nothin? Do we not feel the breath of empty space? Has it not become colder? Is it not more and more night comin on all the time? Must not lanterns be lit in the mornin?'

As he spoke these words, Scag tore the clothes from his body so that by the end he stood completely naked, his shaded skin like the bark of a tree sprouting from the grey shingle. Black tattoos snaked up the lines of his body. He stepped forward and plunged into the grey sea. After he went under, I watched the surface undulating in its vast indifference, thinking he would never come up again. I felt a desolating loneliness, deeper and colder than anything I had ever experienced.

Then I saw him resurface, thirty metres out, head bobbing on the waves. He called to me and there was laughter in his voice. 'Come on in, Matthew, the water's lovely!'

I stood up, took off all my clothes, and stepped down into the cold sea, wading out until it was waist-high. I dove and swam, holding my breath, kicking with all my energy away from the shore, along the murky floor and out into the cold, deep greyness.

PART THREE

ORGASM OF HATE

Everything is evil.

—Giacomo Leopardi, *Zibaldone*

31 | **Kearney**

**Problems with Reality: What Kearney Brought Back
from America**

The red-eye flight was only sparsely booked. Kearney sat, alone in his row, watching the lights of the Eastern Seaboard recede far below, overwhelmed by the creep of Atlantic Ocean darkness.

What a trip it had been, he reflected. A month in the Great Satan. Dwayne was still back there, in Boston. Kearney had left him in the airport bar after beers, whiskey, spliffs and a couple of lines of coke left over from the night when Stu had called around. Kearney partly envied his brother for staying on in the States, but mainly he was keen to get back home, where he could boast to the lads about his adventures, and show them how fucking clueless they were. And, more importantly, when he returned to Dublin, he could begin to put his plan into motion.

As the plane penetrated the cloud cover and his view was clogged with darkly uniform grey, Kearney closed his eyes and basked in the pride of his newfound confidence and life experience. Through a low electronic shimmer he heard Fallen Henry the Titan's paternal purr: *You done good back there, nigga. I got my eye on you and listen here, we be expectin big things from you, G, real big things.*

Kearney opened his eyes. A blonde, idiotically smiling air hostess was coming down the aisle towards him, from the direction of the cockpit. She was pushing a refreshments trolley and had a firm, luscious pair of tits on her. Kearney waited till she was beside him: then he rammed his hand up her skirt. Next came the rape-squeals in the tiny toilet, the grunts and gasps as he pressed her face into the sink, impaling her from behind with his straining teenage sex …

Ever since that night with Stu, Kearney's fantasies had reached a new pitch of intensity. He felt he was becoming an artist of inner butchery. I am the Beethoven of Brutality, he told himself. Then, admitting that he didn't actually know any of Beethoven's paintings, he revised his self-bestowed nickname: I am the Aphex Twin of Cutting Motherfuckers Open. That was more like it.

He was still refining the syllabic rhythm of his new moniker when he realized that the air hostess had stopped in the aisle beside him and was turned his way. She smiled brightly and said, 'And look at *you*, flying across the world all on your lonesome. My oh my.' She chuckled a little.

Kearney's eyes were wide and happy. He returned her grin.

'Is there anything I can get you, honey?' said the hostess with what Kearney thought to be a flirtatious inflection. Warm and fuzzy from the hash and whiskey, he felt his groin heating up with delicious blood throbs, like red flashes of light.

'Bloody Mary,' he said.

The woman gave another fluttery little laugh. 'Well now I'm afraid I'd have to see some proof that you are old enough for liquor. How about a soft drink? Now I'm not saying you're not a man, but …' She chuckled again. 'How about you show me your passport?' She was finding it all very charming.

Kearney grinned back at her. Then he said, 'How about I show ye me manhood?'

The woman's imprecation was loud enough to turn several near-sleeping heads in the back end of the economy section. She stared with an open mouth for a moment, but then some instinct of shame or professionalism kicked in and she turned away, gazing straight ahead as she pushed her trolley down the aisle, not stopping until she vanished into the rear of the plane.

Kearney overflowed with giggles, charmed by his own devilish wit. He imagined what his friends would say if they had witnessed his antics, and wished especially that Dwayne had been there to see that last display. 'Fallen Henry,' he heard himself whisper a moment later, 'am I a bad motherfucker?'

And Fallen Henry's voice was rich with solemn pride as he replied: *You a BAD motherfucker, Kearney. Ain't NO motherfuckin doubt.*

Kearney sighed in deep contentment and put in his earphones. The hard-tech thump began battering his brain. Things could hardly be better. There was only one way to round off this perfect night flight …

Kearney took a deep breath and then stood up in the aisle. 'ALLAHU AKBAR!' he roared, his confidence feeding on the belligerent surge of his own voice. He brought his blade down on the neck of the bald businessman sitting in front of him, delighted by the fount of blood that gushed forth, spraying the seats and window, painting Kearney's T-shirt. With rising glee he heard the panic-screams of doomed families. He marked the faces stretched in terror as he walked calmly up the aisle, blowing the brains out of any motherfucker who might even consider trying to stop him. He screamed and shot a baby, not giving a fuck if a stray bullet punctured the plane's side. Now he kicked down the door of the cockpit and cut the throat of the pale and whimpering pilot, and shot the co-pilot through the face, feeling the wank-spurt of hot blood on his gun-hand and wrist. He locked the cockpit door and, wearing a lusty slash of a grin, took the controls. Seeing the expanse of city lights come rushing beneath him, he pitched the plane forward to a fresh surge of screaming from the carriage behind. 'ALLLAHH!' he bellowed, and sent the plane missiling into the heart of Dublin city like a great bolt of holy fire. 'AALLLAAHHH!'

32 | Matthew

It was on a Tuesday, two days after I got home from the weekend with Scag, that Rez didn't kill himself.

I was downcast, irritable, still wading through the debris of that prolonged, wrecking bender. I stayed in my room in fading light, lying on my bed and looking at the ceiling, thinking about the abyss at the edge of the world. I was thinking about Scag, too, wondering if he was the kind of person I would become, years down the line. Of all the older people I knew, it was with the likes of Scag that I felt the clearest affinity. It was kind of scary.

Music had been playing but the album finished and I didn't bother putting anything else on. The room was silent.

My ma walked in. I creaked my neck to look at her. I waited for her to say something. She just stood there, watching me. It struck me how vulnerable she looked, how small and frightened. These days I was having the recurrent insight that the adults around me were really still children, in grown-up bodies. They were not, as I had assumed, in possession of the answers about life, some kind of grand truth that everyone was gifted with on reaching a certain age. They were about as lost as I was, maybe more so.

'What is it?' I snapped, irritated by everything and wanting to be left alone.

She kept standing there, still far away. Then she said softly, 'There's bad news, Matthew. Rez has tried to kill himself.'

'What?'

'He's okay, his brother found him, he's alive.'

'Jesus Christ.'

'He's in hospital. He's okay, he's fine.'

I had stumbled out of the bed, reaching pointlessly to put on my shoes. My ma was crying. It struck me that she believed I was distraught. And maybe there was a part of me that was. Mostly though, what I felt was excitement.

———

I wasn't able to see him until the following day. I walked to the hospital with Cocker, bringing fruit and sweets from my ma, and a music magazine that I'd bought.

The corridors and wards of the hospital were painted in that dulled, turquoise colour that they always are, a tone with all the cheer drained from it, as if any vibrancy might aggravate the patients' conditions. Rez was in a ward with two other men, a pale-blue curtain hanging down to screen him off from them. A single, square window let in dull sunlight, only heightening the depressed pallor of everything.

'Heya Rez,' we said, stepping into the ward. His mother was out in the waiting area, dry of tears, staring at the ground and rocking back and forth. She had gone outside so Rez's friends could have a few moments with him. Maybe it would do him some good, the doctors had said.

He gazed at us for a few seconds, then muttered a hello. He didn't smile. Why would he?

I cleared my throat. I had no idea what to say, how to act. Already this was excruciating. Cocker was dealing with it a little better, though. 'Fuckin hell, man, what were ye up to?' he said, sounding close to anger, as if he had been personally insulted, or judged, which was probably the truth. Maybe we had all been judged.

Rez seemed dazed by whatever medication they were pumping into him. His responses were delayed, like an internet phone call to a far-off country. He spoke in a throaty kind of drawl, which, I weirdly found myself imagining, would probably be seductive to girls.

Propped up by a wad of puffy white pillows, Rez shifted a bit on the bed, as if he wanted to kindle a flicker of life in himself. But all he said was, 'What do yis want?'

'What do we want? Fuckin hell, Rez, we came to see ye, that's what we want,' I said.

'Really?'

I thought that because of all the sedatives, or something, he was being sincere. 'Yeah, really. Jesus, Rez. Your ma is out there, destroyed she is. You're killin her.'

While I was speaking, I began to grow uneasy; I had the feeling, as I did so often with Rez, that he could see right into me, and what he saw in there was next to nothing. Under his gaze I felt insubstantial, meagre. Everything I might have said would have sounded like a cliché, what you were supposed to say in these circumstances, devoid of feeling.

As if to confirm these notions, Rez looked right at me and said, 'Matthew, do ye actually care?'

There was silence. Cocker turned to look at me, his brow all furrowed like an upset child's.

'Of course I care. What do ye mean do I care? Of course I care.'

A defensive edge had crept into my voice. As if sensing he had found a sore spot, Rez reared up further from his tranquillized torpor and struck again.

'Are ye sure ye really care, or is it not that it excites ye? Cos that's how I'd feel, if a mate of mine had tried to kill himself. I'd be dead excited about all the drama and glamour and all. A bit of serious reality. Is that not it?'

'No! I …'

No more words came out. Cocker looked at the ground, his mouth open, brow still creased. He couldn't handle this and neither could I.

'I bet you couldn't really give a fuck. You're like a pack of fuckin hyenas, loomin over the bed. I bet yis can't wait to tell all the lads about it. Piss off, would yis? Yis are nothin but a pack of hypocrites.'

I struggled to respond, stunned by his outburst. All I could manage was: 'Jesus, Rez. I can't believe this. We worry about ye, even if ye don't believe it.' I couldn't meet his eyes. They were huge, a pair of moons in his skull.

Then he started roaring: 'Piss off out of here, would yis! Such fuckin hypocrisy. Go on back home and don't be so full of shit. Just get lost.'

'Jesus, man.'

'Piss off. I mean it. I don't want yis in here. Fuck off and leave me alone.'

I'd never heard him like this before – the weird thought came to me that he was like the little girl in *The Exorcist*, possessed by the devil, growling obscenities at priests and women. But it wasn't the devil, it was only Rez.

I resented his reaction and wanted to retaliate, but I couldn't. It was out of bounds, laying into someone who was hospitalized after trying to kill himself.

'Okay Rez, fair enough man, we're goin. C'mon, Cocker. Sorry ye feel this way, Rez. Mind yourself.'

'Off yis go,' he sneered as we walked out the door. One of the men in the ward with Rez groaned. I didn't see his face.

That evening I was sitting in front of the TV with my parents and Fiona, scarcely aware of what was on. Fiona kept looking at me from the corner of her eye. I glowered at her to make her stop. The phone rang. My da went out to get it.

I heard him talk in the soft, appeasing tone that everyone seemed to adopt as they got older, as if all they wanted now was to let the world know they meant no harm, they would agree to anything, sign any paper, as long as they were left alone and not tormented. *Eastenders* came on. It was all grey and sombre, as if they were trying to rub the working classes' noses in how drab and joyless their lives were.

My da was standing in the door, still talking into the phone. 'Okay, Trisha. We'll be thinking of ye. Just keep an eye on yer ma now, okay?' He trailed off in a flutter of byes.

'That was Trisha Tooley,' he said. 'She says Richard really wanted to say sorry to ye for today. He said ye'd know what it's about.'

They all looked at me with blatant curiosity, but I just nodded and said, 'Okay,' and nothing else.

33 | Matthew

On Saturday afternoon, after I'd come home from work, I was called to the phone. I knew who was waiting on the other end: Kearney had got back from the States the day before, after a month away. Reaching for the phone, I felt heavy, listless. I wished Kearney had stayed away for even a while longer.

'Alright Matthew.'

'Alright Kearney.'

'How's things, man?'

'Not bad. How was America?'

'Fuckin great. Jesus, some mental shit happened. Come out and have a smoke with me and I'll tell ye all about it.'

The suggestion wearied me. At the same time, I was curious about what he'd gotten up to. Maybe a bit of a laugh would be good for me. Besides, there was nothing else to do. I hadn't heard any more from Jen and nor had I called her. It was two weeks now since the night in her house. I thought she'd have gotten in touch with me since what happened to Rez, but she hadn't. My ma told me that when she was entering the hospital to visit Rez, Jen had been on her way out. 'She looked devastated,' she said. I had my doubts about this.

I told Kearney I'd meet him at the industrial estate by the school in half an hour. Then I said, 'Listen, Kearney, something's happened with Rez.'

'Yeah, I already knew,' Kearney said.

There was a silence, only the static hiss of the receiver in my ear.

'Anyway, see ye in a little while,' I said. 'I haven't got any hash, so bring enough for a few spliffs, okay?'

———

The factories and yards of the industrial estate were as deserted as ever. Once or twice we'd seen a truck roll in and men shuffle out to conduct gruffly voiced business outside factory entrances. But usually there was no one here. You always had the feeling you were going to be mugged, but not even muggers hung around this place. Only teenagers drinking and getting stoned. It was a graffiti free-for-all. We had personally sprayed slogans like *Don't Be Such a Fucking Sheep to the Slaughter* and *Say No to Everything, Even to This*, but soon got bored and stopped bothering. There seemed little point writing graffiti where no one would see it.

When I hopped over the wall and stepped through the rubble of litter, chalky stone and broken glass, I saw Kearney standing fifty metres ahead, silhouetted against the hulk of two warehouses. As I came closer, I could see that he had a leather jacket on, which made him seem bulkier, not scrawny like he had been before. He was smoking a cigarette, watching me as I approached. He flashed his devil-grin and waved.

'Alright Connelly.'

'Alright.'

Now that I was standing beside him, the change in his stature was even more apparent. He had a kind of presence now; he was very still and somehow he unnerved me, maybe because of that stillness. I had always been a little uneasy around Kearney and now the feeling was intensified. There was something in him that hadn't been there before, a kind of magnetism. I realized then that Kearney fascinated me. I put my hands in my pockets and looked away.

'So Rez tried to do himself in,' he announced. 'That's fuckin mental.'

I resented his tone. 'He nearly died,' I said. 'It was only a fluke that his brother came in when he did. He came home on his lunch break to pick up some document he'd forgotten to bring to work.'

'I hadn't heard that part of it. So he really meant it?'

'It seems like he did. It wasn't one of those cries for help.'

Kearney said nothing for a moment. Then: 'In that case he must feel like a real failure: he couldn't even kill himself properly.'

I looked away, across the warehouses and yards, into the copse of dark trees past the high steel fencing at the far periphery. There was a sewerish little stream out there where we used to look for radioactive fish, which we never found, and frogs, which we did. Kearney had delighted in finding ever more inventive ways to mutilate and kill them.

'That's a fuckin horrible thing to say, Kearney.'

He put his hands up, grinning. 'Relax man, it was only a joke. Ye can't be takin all these things so fuckin seriously.'

'What do ye mean, can't take it seriously. He tried to fuckin kill himself. What's not serious about that?'

'I know he did. But he only did it cos *he* was takin things too seriously. Himself, for example. He needs to tone it down a bit, that's all I'm sayin.'

'Do ye even have any idea what yer talkin about? Do ye know why he did it, even?'

'Yeah, I do. Because he's too into himself and he can't deal with real life.'

Surely the irony was blatant: Kearney, who tolerated reality only because it allowed him to play *Medal of Honour* and *Grand Theft Auto*, criticizing someone else for being out of touch with the real world. But he jabbered away as if oblivious.

'I went in to see him yesterday, did ye know that? His ma was there ballin cryin, but she left when I arrived. She sat out in the waitin area. But Rez wouldn't speak to me. He just sat there on the bed like a fuckin zombie, starin at me, like I was behind dark glass and I couldn't see him. I tried to talk to him but he totally ignored me. I didn't care at first, but then it really fuckin pissed me off. Cos I was tryin to be nice, I really was. I was doin all the normal stuff. I would've just said a few things and left. But he started actin like that, so I goes fuck it. And I started tryin to get a rise out of him.'

'What did ye do?'

'I says to him, "Listen, Rez, I only came here cos I was expected to. I know ye don't like me, and I've never liked you either. In fact, nobody really likes ye." I says, "Most people think yer a fuckin knob-jockey. The only one who can make herself cry about ye is yer ma. If anyone else does any cryin, it's because ye didn't manage to do yerself in."'

I stared at him, astonished. 'Are ye takin the piss?' I asked, genuinely unable to tell.

'Nope. I said all that to him, and more. But he just kept sittin there, just fuckin gawkin at me. I was gettin really angry with him at this point. I says to him, "Rez ye fuckin spa, ye should do both yerself and the whole fuckin world a big favour and give it another shot as soon as ye get the chance. It'd be a much better world without ye."'

Kearney laughed. I stared at him, still wondering whether he was making it up.

'You're fuckin sick, Kearney.'

'Do ye reckon?'

Suddenly I felt deflated. It was no use. Kearney stood there chuckling away beside me, sparking up a joint.

He watched me for a while. Then he said, quietly, 'I'm only buzzin with ye, Connelly. Yer so fuckin gullible. I made all that up. I didn't even go in to see him yet. I've to go in tomorrow. I wouldn't say any of that stuff to him. Do ye think I'm totally fuckin sick in the head? I wouldn't say that stuff. He tried to kill himself. He's me friend.'

I stayed till the joint was finished, neither of us saying much. Then I climbed out of the industrial estate and went home.

34 | Kearney

He spent even more time in his attic bedroom. Sometimes his ma shrieked up at him and he would lie there, stoned, hearing her hateful noise, wanting to slice her face up till it looked like mince. After he had been back a few days she gave up trying to call him. No one bothered him any more.

Rez and his suicide attempt was only a sideshow, a diversion. Kearney had other things on his mind. He had a plan now; he knew what he had to do.

The idea had come to him in Boston, after the night Stu had called around. It had been suggested to him by a video they'd watched.

Throughout his stay with Dwayne, Kearney had slept on the floor of the apartment, with only a pungent, multi-stained sheet between his body and the bare and dusty boards. His brother was one of eleven young Irishmen sharing the ghetto-zone flat for the summer, and space was at a premium: they slept three or four to a room, like refugees, laid out close enough to smell each others' bodies and emissions, hear each others' heat-fever gasps and moans.

There had been an infestation: cockroaches. By night they'd seemed to multiply, appearing in hordes to maraud with nocturnal arrogance, scuttling over every surface and over Kearney's sticky, skinny limbs as he contorted and jerked in the throes of heat-insomnia. And it had been hot: maddeningly, feverishly hot. Kearney and the others could do nothing but endure this relentless heat alongside the hosts of glistening bugs that had occupied their crowded home.

The night of the video, they were sitting in the dark room on cushionless armchairs and couches with springs sticking out of them, or on plastic stools or the grimy floorboards. All twelve of them huddled around the sickly flicker of a TV that, like every item of furniture in the apartment, had been dragged in from the street after anonymous neighbours dumped it as they fled this ghetto full of crackhead blacks and drunken young Irish.

Stu came just after midnight. Dwayne stood up to greet him at the door with a hip-hop-style slapping handshake. He flicked the light switch and Kearney recoiled from the sudden glare. Stu, Dwayne had assured his younger brother, could not only get the best drugs in Boston, but was 'heavily connected with some really hardcore motherfuckers'. (Dwayne had started using words like motherfucker and asshole since coming to America.)

Certainly, Stu's hardcore credentials were confirmed that night; he was the one who brought along the video they watched, as well as the weed, coke and speed the lads had ordered from him.

'Gedda loada this shit, man,' Stu said, waving the video in the air as he stepped into the room and commanded the group's complete attention. He wore a sleeveless basketball shirt and baggy jeans, with a faceful of stubble, peakless cap and eyebrow piercing – full hip-hop regalia, only he wasn't black. He did look like the kind of person you wouldn't want to fuck with, though.

Lankily he sat on the edge of the least tattered armchair, dishing out little plastic bags of drugs as he said, 'I got this video from a buddy in LA. I ain't never seen shit like this, man. It's real, ain't no doubt. Fuckin heavy West Coast shit. You gonna see what I mean, dog. Here.' He chucked the tape to Dwayne and ordered him to turn off the single, bare lightbulb and the shitty stereo. Dwayne complied, and Stu cut out a line of coke for everyone from his personal stash. 'This one's on me,' he said.

They snorted the coke and Stu said, 'Shit, someone gonna roll a J?' Kearney was thinking that Stu talked a bit like Fallen Henry the Titan.

Dwayne got the video player going and retreated quietly to a spot on the floor, Stu having taken his place on the armchair.

The cockroaches kept pouring into the room, big oily things with scuttling legs. Kearney watched them crawl over the feet and legs of the lads on the ground – no one even bothered crushing them any more. He felt a tingle on the back of his neck and flinched, brushing nervously at his collar. But there was nothing there, it was all in his mind.

Kearney was stoned. Very stoned. This grass they smoked here, it was ferocious, completely unlike the stuff they got back home, which he now realized really was just 'crap Dublin hash'; something he had long declared but without any real basis for comparison. As the stoned murmurings in the room died down and the spasms of static resolved themselves on-screen, Kearney reflected that this US skunk was as far advanced over Dublin hash as the Xbox was over the Amstrad he'd played as a kid. He liked this analogy, and hoped he'd remember to use it when he got back home to tell those queer little fuckers how clueless they were about life in general and dope in particular.

But now the film was starting. It began conventionally enough, with two brawny, crewcut guys fucking a trashy, hard-faced slut. They fucked her in the arse and fisted her cunt at the same time. Then she played with her tits while one of them fucked her cunt and the other tongued her arsehole. Next she sucked them both off at once, then let one fuck her from behind while the other pulled himself off and sneered down at her. Eventually they both came in her face.

Kearney was starting to wonder what all the fuss was about, why Stu would get so worked up about a fairly standard porno.

But then, very rapidly, it all changed. Right after the pair of men had come, one of them punched the woman in the face. It was a hard, driving, downward punch, pounding her to the floor. Kearney flinched at it, tensing up all over – there was no way that could have been faked. And the woman clearly hadn't expected it; now she was crying, shrieking, between panic and shock.

The men slung her up from the doorframe, wrists bound by a black leather strap, the first of numerous macabre props that now started appearing on-screen in quick proliferation. The men worked quickly, looking tense and concentrated but managing to turn several times to the camera to flash conspiratorial grins.

For the next twenty minutes Kearney watched the nameless woman being tortured and dismembered. Throughout, she emitted a prolonged, almost unbroken scream and, increasingly bloodied and mutilated, she remained conscious right up to the very end. Her face a gory pulp, teeth smashed in or ripped out, nipples sliced off and hair set on fire, the gapless scream – now more a shrill gurgling – was silenced when the man who had punched her at the beginning drove a screwdriver through her wide-opened eye, impaling her brain.

The screen went black, then buzzed static.

There was no other sound in the room.

'Whaddaya think? Hardcore shit, huh,' said Stu, still gazing into the dead television.

There was a silence. The only things that moved were the cockroaches scuttling across the floor, and the static on-screen. Then Dwayne said, 'Yeah man, hardcore. Hard*core.*'

Mumbles and grunts of vague endorsement rose up around the darkened room like the yeas in a house of parliament; there were no nays.

Kearney remained quiet, pensive. When the torturing had commenced, there was a moment when something in him had recoiled from it. Momentarily he'd wanted to stand up and walk out of the room, run down the stairs and out on the streets, jump into the Atlantic and let the ocean swallow him up.

But he had looked around him as the film played on: a roomful of impassive faces, dull with interest, condoning through inaction. Kearney told himself that it made him fierce, edgy, strong; watching this stuff and, what's more, liking it. And he *did* like it, in a hesitant way at first, but more and more as he willed himself to embrace the horror of what he was seeing.

Then the quiver of protest in him died out, like the SOS of a forgotten submarine going down in cold, black waters.

Very clearly, right before the woman on the screen died, it had come to him: he could do this. He could watch this stuff and enjoy it, and no one was going to stop him.

The next day, the images from the snuff movie were still fresh and bloody, superimposing themselves over Kearney's mundane American reality. That was when the idea surfaced. It was a logical progression, like that which he'd gone through after first watching porno: the viewing, then the wanting to do it for himself.

The woman's death fascinated him: it was the moment it happened, the precise instant when the life force – whatever it was that made the body move, speak, fear, think, know – when whatever it was that did all that, vanished, was snuffed out. It was there, and then it wasn't. And when it wasn't there, all you had was what the woman in the film had become at the end, when the screaming stopped: a heap of meat, an inert sack of mess that was something, but that wasn't human. It fascinated Kearney. He needed to explore this. He needed to know how it felt.

35 | Matthew

I visited Rez in hospital only once more. This time I went there on my own. He looked the same as he had the first time; pale, gaunt, wasted – it was a look that suited him. When I entered the ward, one of the other beds was empty.

'What happened to him?' I asked, nodding at the wafer of absence under fresh, straight covers, by way of breaking the ice.

Rez shrugged his shoulders, managing to make the gesture look like it cost him worlds of effort. 'He got out.'

'What, you mean he's better?' I was surprised; Rez's brother had told me that the man was on his death bed, about to be dragged under by some terminal illness.

'No, he's not better. He's dead.'

'Oh.'

So much for breaking the ice. The bulk in the third bed shifted and groaned at the mention of death. Maybe in his fever he believed I was the Grim Reaper, come to collect him. I saw his face; a grizzled, ugly man with a terrible complexion and worse teeth. He peered at me with wet-eyed suspicion, then turned over and started coughing.

I looked at Rez in his bed. Lately I'd grown depressed at the thought – which not long ago would have felt exciting – that most of my friends were twisted, volatile outsiders. You started out playing with this stuff – the extremism, the chaos – and it felt vital and exhilarating; but then suddenly you couldn't control it, you'd gone too far and it wasn't exciting any more, only frightening.

'How are ye doin, Rez?' I asked, exhausted already by being here, but wanting at least to try and fix things.

'Not bad, considerin I recently tried to commit suicide.'

That was fairly dark, but at least there was a spark of humour in it, something he'd been devoid of last time.

'My ma's worried about them lettin me out. She's afraid I'm goin to do it again.'

'And are ye?'

He shook his head. 'No. It was stupid. I can't believe what I almost did. It terrifies me, especially when I think it was only a fluke that I was found. I wake up sweatin, nearly in panic.'

I wondered if this was the propaganda he was putting out, to lure those around him into a false sense of security while he made another bid for self-annihilation. Rez and what went on in his mind were beyond me. He had drifted out too far, into weird fog: I couldn't see who he was any more.

'Why did ye do it, Rez? Is there somethin ye … somethin that happened to ye?'

'No.' His voice had hardened; he looked ready to lash out again, tense and defensive. 'There's nothin that happened. I just… I've just been seein things clearly, too clearly. And not lookin away.' He shook his head. 'I can't seem to look away, the same way ordinary people do. And when ye can't look away it's impossible to …' He paused; each word seemed a strain. 'To keep livin, doin normal things.'

He looked like he was going to continue, but then he exhaled in a huge sigh, exhausted by the effort. I sensed that he wanted me to leave. But now I realized I had a kind of power over him, something I'd never had before. Rez was vulnerable and I wanted to push him, partly out of curiosity, but also for some other, shadowy reason that wasn't clear to me.

'What do ye mean, though?' I said. 'I mean, what is it ye say ye see about the world that makes ye want to, to go and do what ye did?'

He watched me for a few long moments, making me feel like a faecal germ under a microscope. Then he said, 'You, for instance.'

I waited.

'Me?' I said eventually.

'Yeah. You, the way ye are. And you here now, for example. I know what it's all about. I –'

'Ye what?' I snapped. 'Ye know what about me? Ye always think ye fuckin know about me, and about everyone. What do ye know?'

I was suddenly sick of how everything he said, even every look he gave, was one of accusation.

He said, 'You're enjoyin it, seein me here like this. It doesn't really make ye feel anything to know that I was miserable enough to try and hang meself. All ye really feel is the buzz of it, the drama. I don't even blame ye.'

'Here we go again,' I sneered. 'This same old shit.' I shook my head, exhaled in irritation, and shifted like I was about to get up and leave.

'It's true, though. Even now, the way you're pressin me for information, it's just cos ye want a bit of a buzz from hearin me.'

I looked away. I felt exposed. I tried pleading, hoping for a truce. 'Look,' I said in a softer tone. 'I know it's true that there are horrible, really fuckin horrible things out there in the world. But it's not all bad, there are some good things as well that ye don't have to analyse. Ye have to take things more at face value, not just see the, the ulterior motives all the time.'

'But I can't!' It came out as a terrible screech. His eyes were frantic, like he was looking out at me from a burning room. 'I can't,

Matthew. I don't know how to. I really don't. I just can't turn me mind off. I don't know how to walk down a fuckin street any more. I can't even sit on a bus without thinkin about it from a million different angles at the same time. I keep seein the *reasons* behind things, why people do what they do. It's horrible, it's fuckin shameful. I'm fuckin ashamed of meself. I don't know what to do.'

The medication seemed to have lost all effect, if he was even still taking it. He was definitely not tranquilized, not sedated – he looked like the only thing he wanted now was to try again to kill himself and this time get it right.

'I know, Rez, it's bad, I know. But there's more to it than that, there are some good, valuable things ...' I said this even more softly, trying to put some warmth and emotion into it. But the words floated from my mouth like feeble things, dying on the air. I hated Rez for hearing my useless words and knowing they were useless. I hated him for seeing everything so clearly, especially me. I met his gaze, just as the furtive thought escaped, like noxious gas from the bowels, that it would be better for everyone if he did kill himself. People who saw the truth all the time, and insisted on telling you about it, were no good for anyone.

'Oh Jesus,' he whimpered, as if he'd heard my thought.

I closed my eyes and directed them away from Rez's locked stare before opening them again.

'I'll see ye, Rez,' I said, standing up.

He didn't answer. Still avoiding his eyes, I pulled up my hood and left the room.

'Wait,' I heard him croak as I stepped out the door, letting it close behind me.

———

I had no energy these days. At work I just got stoned and spoke to no one, sluggishly washing cars and filling tanks, coming to life only when my manager gave out to me. I wouldn't have cared if he'd fired me. When I wasn't working, I hardly left my room unless I was going to get wasted with Kearney or Cocker. I hadn't heard anything from Jen. I thought about calling her; maybe we could patch things up and make it like it was before, at the start of the summer. I missed her. But then I would remember what had happened and tell myself that she could be dead for all I cared. Because of what my ma had started referring to as 'the Richard situation' I was left alone, not hassled about anything. That was a relief.

Then Rez got out of hospital. He'd been in there ten days. His ma said maybe it was best that his friends gave him some space for a little while, till things were back to normal.

36 | Kearney

He kept to himself after meeting Matthew at the industrial estate. Now that the intention was there – the intention to kill somebody – he found that his mind was whirring away below decks, doing the creative work while he played *Grand Theft Auto* or smoked on his bed. Ideas would pop into his mind at random moments. For instance, there was the thought that he could push some old fucker down the stairs. Or he could leave the gas on in his grandmother's house, causing a tragic accident that was no accident at all. Or he could go all out and accost someone on the street, or down a dark lane, and bludgeon them to death. When he thought of that one in particular his mind whirled and he experienced a great dizziness, akin to vertigo: there was no limit to what he might achieve if he put his mind to it.

But the idea of bludgeoning, stabbing or beating someone to death, though thrilling, seemed too far-fetched, too outrageous. He would end up getting caught and having to go to Mountjoy for the rest of his life. No fucking way.

When the idea appeared, he knew straight off that it was the right one.

He told no one about his plan. He brooded on it for two days, getting the details just right. Then he awoke on a midweek morning and he knew: it was time to climax.

When his ma had gone out to work – she was a cleaner, Monday to Friday, nine to five, much to Kearney's inner derision – Kearney lifted open the portal in the garage and climbed down the sturdy wooden ladder into the basement. He was wearing rubber gloves. He stuffed what he needed into a Dunnes Stores bag inside a SuperValu bag, and left the house.

He took a bus into town, on his own. He sat on the top deck and looked at no one.

He had a victim in mind. And if he wasn't there, that was no matter; Kearney would transfer his intentions to another of his preferred victim's mangy, stinking kind. They were all the same, all as worthless as one another. Fuck the lot of them.

Kearney got off the bus at the Central Bank. He stepped off Dame Street and down the cobblestoned laneway that sloped through Temple Bar towards the Liffey – a run-off sewer of vomit, fast-food cartons and half-digested burgers.

And there he was, the pitiful cunt, slouched in his usual place, all on his own. There he was, where he always was.

The tramp sat in the shadowy staff doorway of the Hot Chick takeaway, wheezing and splayed like he'd been stabbed, only he sucked on a can of cheap cider every few seconds, ruining the effect. Kearney approached the tramp and stood above him, looking down and feeling like the Angel of Death. He took in the tramp's grey, matted hair that spilled out under an ancient baseball cap with *Remember the Alamo* printed across it, and the shitty grey crust of clothing that swaddled him. Kearney's lip twitched in revulsion.

'There's a smell of piss here,' he said coldly, his eyes on the tramp.

He imagined a camera filming him, someone looking on.

The tramp mumbled something and continued to stare vacantly, vagrantly ahead, at the opposite wall of the laneway. He slurped again on his can, either unaware of Kearney, or just not giving a fuck that he was there, looming above him.

Kearney sniffed, leaning in a little over the tramp and his dank, stinking doorway.

'Fuckin hell man, that really reeks. Does it not bother ye, sittin there in the filth like that? Do ye just not give a fuck, like?'

The tramp mumbled again. This time Kearney discerned the words 'cunt' and 'fuckers', fishing them out of the slur of babble like boots or soiled condoms in the drift of a filthy river. He grinned.

'Ah, it can't be that bad, pal. Shift up a bit there and let me sit down. If ye don't mind, like.'

The tramp didn't respond, so Kearney gave him a hard shove with the toe of his boot, almost a kick. 'Get up, would ye. Jaysus Christ.'

Finally the tramp lurched into a greater awareness of Kearney. He looked up at him in glazed perplexity, like someone who'd just woken up.

'What do ye fuckin want?' he rasped.

'Nothin. Move up a bit and let me sit down.'

'Ye little faggot …' The tramp began to mumble a string of insults at Kearney, but then cut himself short. Dimly scenting opportunity, he said, 'Gis a smoke.'

'What?'

'Gis a smoke, I said.'

'What do you say?'

'I say give us a fuckin smoke. Or FUCK OFF!'

The tramp tried to swipe at Kearney with his can-hand, but succeeded only in spilling cider over his chapped yellow fingers and wrists.

Kearney laughed, but pulled his pack of twenty John Player Blue from a back pocket and opened it. 'There ye go. Have two. Now let us sit down.' He nudged the tramp again with his foot and squeezed into the doorway beside him. He put his faded green knapsack resting between his knees. He lit the tramp's smoke, then lit one of his own. He said, 'I just thought I'd have a bit of a drink.'

The tramp's sullen contemptuousness gave way to fascination as Kearney pulled a can of Oranjeboom lager from the knapsack. Kearney cracked open the can and glugged down a quarter of it, then exhaled loud and slow in theatrical satisfaction. He passed the can to the tramp and said, 'Have a sup, go on.' But he needn't have bothered, for the tramp had already tipped the can back and was pouring the drink down his throat. Kearney tingled in loathing as foamy yellow lager spilled over the thicket of filthy beard that clung to the tramp's flaking face.

The tramp emptied the can, belched in a way that surely signalled grave inner disarray, and flung the can at the opposite wall, where it clanked and fell to the ground, rolling to a stop against an overturned burger carton and a crushed Pepsi cup.

'Do ye want me to say thanks?' hissed the tramp, energized by the sudden inpour, all drunk down hastier than his usual rationing would allow for.

'Yeah, go on,' said Kearney.

'FUCK OFF!' barked the tramp. 'That's what I say to ye. Go and shite. Or else gis another can, ye little fuckin prick.'

Kearney laughed, highly amused.

'Jesus Christ, ye don't really have what ye'd call the social graces, do ye? And ye can't have much of a clue about actin in yer own best interests, cos ye can see that I've got loads more cans here, and I'm probably willin to share them. But then ye go and insult me! To be honest with ye, I'm amazed that ye've reached the level of achievement in life that ye obviously have done, with that kind of attitude.'

Kearney chortled again, this time at his own cutting irony. He pictured the TV audiences, sitting at home and chuckling in sophisticated appreciation of his pitch-black wit. The tramp merely grunted, his zest for insult already spent.

'However, I'm the mellow sort,' continued Kearney. 'And I don't like drinkin on me own. So I'll stay with ye for a while. Only if ye don't mind, though.' He raised his hands and put on a look like he was worried about offending the tramp. 'Seriously, will I stay and have a drink with ye? I've plenty here. Or will I leave ye alone? Tell me seriously, like. I don't mind which, but ye have to tell me.'

The tramp's face had glazed over; he was baffled into mental paralysis by Kearney's head-games. Kearney chuckled a little, thinking the haggard old bastard might live to drink another day. But then the tramp's watery eyes fell again on the bulging green knapsack between Kearney's legs. The greed took over and he said, 'Gis a can.'

'What?'

'Gis a can.'

'You want a can, correct?'

'Yes a can.'

'Yes a can. Is that yer final answer?'

'Fuck off, youth. Gis a can or piss off.'

Kearney laughed again. He pulled out another can just as two teenage girls with tumours of lipstick, clutching pink and white mobile phones, came up the alley from the direction of the Liffey. Their chatter died away when they saw Kearney and the tramp, and their pace quickened, hurrying them away to the many-eyed safety of Dame Street.

Kearney watched them trotting off. He whistled. Then he turned to the tramp and said, 'See the hole on that blonde one? Fuckin Jaysus. I'd say it's been a while since ye had a bit of minge like that, am I right? Sure I doubt ye've even got it up in the last twenty years. Am I right or wha?'

'Gerrup the fuck,' slurred the tramp. 'Open yer can or fuck off back home to mammy.'

Kearney opened the can. He took a swig, then handed it to the tramp, but not before deliberately tilting it so that a puddle of beer fell into the tramp's encrusted lap. Despite being thus insulted, the tramp took the can and guzzled on it, so degraded was he. Kearney thought he might take it even further, get the tramp to dance for him, or have him wave his mickey at some oul one, or make retard noises at the crowds up on Dame Street, or strip naked and roll on the ground, barking like a dog. Or put his finger through his own fucking eye. Kearney's mind blackened, his loathing for this worthless life form flaring up beyond control.

'Yer like me da,' he spat, though the tramp, absorbed in draining the can as quickly as he could before it was snatched back off him, wasn't listening. 'Yer a filthy, sickenin fuckin insect, a piece of shite, a total fuckin disease. I'd kick yer fuckin head in right now if I could get away with it. I'd stamp on yer face till ye were fuckin dead.'

The tramp didn't hear a word of it, or didn't care either way. Finished, he hurled the can against the wall, belched even more violently than before and gestured for more booze. Kearney obliged.

Four cans later, Kearney looked at his watch. He didn't actually have a watch, but he knew the tramp wouldn't notice. Then he said, 'Shit, I have to go in a minute. Late for business. Ye know how it is.'

He reached into the knapsack, fumbled for a moment, then pulled out the bottle of cheap red wine, which had its cork reinserted into the neck.

'I suppose you could probably hang on to this. I don't need it, there'll be plenty of drink when I meet me mate later. Do ye want it?'

The detail about meeting the friend was superfluous, for the alco didn't care about excuses, only booze, and he snatched the bottle of wine, clutching it to him like it might be taken away at any moment.

'Remember the Alamo!' Kearney called back with a cheery wave as he walked away. The tramp had already taken a couple of hefty swigs before Kearney reached the end of the lane, thrust his hands in his pockets and turned on to Dame Street, blending into the indifferent city-centre crowds. Heading towards Trinity College, he wondered how long it would take for the rat poison to snuff out the tramp's filthy, hilarious life.

37 | Matthew

The Saturday after Rez came out of hospital, there was to be a house party at Grace Madden's, on the northside. None of us would have been able to throw a party then – it wouldn't have looked right – but Grace and her crowd didn't really know Rez, so it was innocent. And we saw no great reason to sit at home and mope. Grace's family was rich – compared to me and my friends' families, at least. I never felt comfortable around Grace or her friends, with their Trinners accents and their smug banter. I didn't care, though: I would go along to her party and get annihilated and who really gave a bollocks.

I knew Jen would be there. She and Grace had been friends for years. I considered calling her to say I'd be there too, but in the end I didn't bother.

I met Cocker and Kearney in town beforehand. We bought cans, vodka and an excess of cigarettes and skins, then hopped on a DART at Pearse Street Station. The summer was past its best – a best that had never come – and it was already getting dark as the train rumbled out of the station in a choral tantrum of hisses and screeches. There weren't many people on board, only a few oul ones with bags of shopping and teenagers silently looking out the window, taking in the grimy fringes of the city with wide, vacant eyes. *Human beings have died out. There are only echoes left. They're not real and neither are we.* Most people were coming into rather than leaving the city centre as we were doing. Trainfuls of them hurtled past, a Saturday-night blitzkrieg on the vomit-splattered streets of Temple Bar and town. I cracked open the first can as we came to Fairview, cutting free of the centre, tracing the coast. I looked at the sea and remembered the abyss that Scag had shown me, and I knew that it was real, that the drugs and exhaustion had only made visible what was already there, what was still there.

'Cheers, lads,' said an excited Cocker, raising his can. 'To Rez.'

I winced; he sounded so corny and sentimental. I knew Kearney would take the piss, and so he did, sneering and raising his can high in the air, with a look of mock-tragic feeling. 'I knew him, Fellatio,' he declared – the only Shakespeare quote he'd remembered from the whole school year, albeit in his own, modified way. He waved Cocker's remark aside and said, 'Look, let's just forget about Rez for tonight, okay? We've been goin on about him all week, and he's grand now, he's out of hospital, that's the end of it. Let's just get fucked and have a laugh.'

For once I was inclined to agree with him. After he spoke, Kearney went quiet again, like there was something he was mulling over. I'd noticed it since meeting him at the station. He was distracted, broody. I wondered what was going on.

The train trundled ahead, past the now-empty beaches as the lights of the city came on in amber clusters to our side. 'Here,' said Cocker with a grin, pulling something from his pocket. 'Look what I've brought.'

'Poppers!' I said, seeing the little brown glass bottle. Any high was welcome tonight, even more than on other nights.

'Shhh,' he warned. 'Some oul one will give us grief. Who's first?'

Kearney went first. He passed me the bottle and I sniffed deeply, letting the brain-zapping vapours obliterate pressure, thought, tension.

The lights were on in every room as we approached the large, coastal house, and music spilled out the doorways and windows, on to the street, disturbing the peace. Neighbours would be knocking to complain; police might even be called. Despite the drinking we'd done I was in a black humour and almost wished I'd stayed home. I hated everyone.

Grace Madden answered the door. She threw her arms up in the air, smiling broadly, and said with an exaggerated cheeriness that irritated me, 'Oh *hi*! You're all here. I'm so glad you've come.'

She insisted on hugging each of us, though I was hardly what you'd call a close friend. She wore a shimmering silver dress that pushed her breasts up; I saw Kearney looking down it when he leaned in to receive her hug. His eyes narrowed with predatory lust; alligator eyes.

There were a lot of people at the party. Some lads from school; Aido the Death Metaller, for some reason, and a gawky, Trenchcoat Mafia friend of his I'd never spoken to. I thought his name was Jonathan. The two of them sat under a cloud of gothic doom, drinking cans and ignoring everyone, even each other.

I didn't know most of the people in the sitting room. They all had these D4 accents and they shouted and laughed loudly, some of them sprawling over beanbags strewn across the floor. Smoke hung in the air but it was bright in the room, the orange wallpaper and bulbous lamp warming everything. A group squatting on the floor were talking about the big rave that was set to take place in a couple of weeks, on the night of the lunar eclipse. It sounded like it was going to be a fairly big deal.

'We should put our cans in the fridge,' said Cocker as I was listening in.

'Here, give us them, I'll do it,' I said.

Jen was standing there when I stepped into the kitchen. Her back was against the counter and she was talking to a guy I didn't know. The first thing I thought was how pretty she looked. I felt like turning around, leaving the house and going home. It was going to be too painful to be here with her, and not able to touch or kiss her. But maybe I could talk to her, see if everything wasn't completely wrecked between us.

'Oh, hi,' she said, coldly, when she saw me.

'Hi,' I replied. But she had already turned away, back to the guy she was chatting with, breezy and cheerful as anything. So much for trying to fix things. I flung the cans in the fridge and walked out, cursing to myself and resolving not to say a word to her, not even to look at her, all night.

In the green-carpeted room between the kitchen and sitting room Kearney had already found the games and was absorbed in *Manhunt*, breaking out of his trance only to swig from his can and accept a joint. Cocker came in and sat with me on the couch. We drank our cans and talked, but my attention wasn't on what either of us said; I was wondering where Jen was, who she was talking to, what she was doing at every moment. I watched the girls that came and went, giggling and calling back over their shoulders. Mostly they ignored me.

Jen entered the room. She smiled at Cocker, who beamed up at her and asked her how she was. She ignored me.

After her pleasantries with Cocker, Jen sat down on the floor beside Kearney. What the fuck was this all about? She was talking to him, smiling, looking at his face while he hammered on the joypad. Kearney seemed confused, suspicious of why Jen was lavishing her attention on him. I simmered with hate. It was like she was trying her best to hurt me. She was laughing at Kearney's jokes; he was making her laugh. Sickened, I remembered something he had said once, while we were smoking with Rez in the industrial estate: making a girl laugh, he'd said, is a symbolic way of making her come. You started by making her laugh – or by dancing with her, that was symbolic too – and it went from that to fucking. If you could make a girl laugh, he'd said, you could be fairly sure she was going to gush for you when you got her clothes off.

And Jen was laughing hard at his jokes.

Straining to act cool, I inched forward, trying to make out what was being said now in more hushed tones, accompanied by intimate-sounding laughter. She was asking him about his time in the States.

'… amazin. It pisses all over this fuckin city. Ye can do whatever ye like over there. Everyone is on drugs all the time. Nobody takes anything seriously – work and all that shite. Dublin is full of wankers, I'm goin to save up for a while and get the fuck out of here, go back over there to stay. Only pricks would stay in a fuckin shithole like this. What a load of fuckin cunts.'

A faint smile was fixed on Jen's face. She looked at Kearney with complete attention, leaning in as if fascinated by every word. Kearney was still managing to play *Manhunt* while talking to her. Jen was laughing a lot. Then Kearney stopped playing and turned to face her. He just looked at her for a moment. 'Hold on a sec, Jen,' I heard him say. 'Let me get ye a drink. I learned to make some deadly cocktails in the States. Here, take this. Keep slammin yer man with the cosh.' He handed her the joypad, then stood up and darted into the kitchen. I couldn't believe this crap – I'd never seen Kearney do anything for anybody. Sitting on the floor, holding the joypad, Jen finally turned to look up at me.

I got up and walked out of the room. Cocker stayed where he was, grinning and content with everything like a total imbecile. I decided I would drink as much as I possibly could, as quickly as I possibly could, just for the hell of it.

I was already pissed as I veered towards the living room, where a group of laughing strangers were pouring shots of absinthe at a low glass table. Grace was there. 'Matthew, come and have a shot with us,' she called, and I decided she was alright after all. I got on my hunkers with them, six of us on the carpet crouched around the table, while Aido and Jonathan or whoever sat on the couch, looking on in morose, contemptuous silence.

We all downed a shot together. I started coughing, spluttering. My throat was blazing like I'd swallowed petrol and thrown in a match. 'Jesus Christ,' I rasped, only to trigger another fit of coughing.

'It's *real* absinthe,' said some goon to my side, a pure D4 head. 'The last time I drank this it literally blew my head off.'

'Literally?' I barked.

Grace was at my left side. Her breasts jiggled and pressed against me, warm and full and soft. I envisioned sticking my face into them. Suddenly euphoric, I turned and started leeringly trying it on with her.

'Grace, fair play to ye for havin the party. Yer amazin. Yer a lovely-lookin girl as well, did ye know that? I mean it, yer *gor*geous.'

She laughed, not in an embarrassed way. 'Ah thanks, Matthew. But are you sure you're not just a bit drunk? You look like it. I think you are.'

'No! I'm not drunk, I swear,' I slurred, wobbling forward slightly. 'Yer just gorgeous, that's all.' I raised my hand in an attempt to touch the hair behind her ear, but either she drew deftly away, or I completely missed her. Either way I was all-in by now, and too fucked to be embarrassed. I was considering another swipe at her hair but one of the voices from around the table shouted, 'Another shot goys, let's go!'

Glasses were refilled. Faces swam. I felt all-powerful, though it was getting hard to remain upright as I squatted at the tableside. I downed a shot. Then I slammed my glass on the table and turned to face Grace again. She was laughing at what someone across from her was saying. I reached out and pulled her shoulder. 'C'mere, Grace.'

'Stop it, would you?' she said with an uneasy little laugh, then turned back to the one she was chatting with.

I put my hand on the back of her neck, caressing her hair.

'What are you doing?' she said, clearly irritated now. But I had it in my head that what was needed here, what girls respected, was persistence – barbarian persistence. So I simply leered at her. I stroked the hair above her ear.

'Seriously, what are you doing?' she said.

'Nothin. Just touchin yer hair. Yer gorgeous,' I said. Surely that was the clincher.

'Right. Well, would you stop doing it, please?'

She seemed to be saying it more for the benefit of the others than for mine. She'd crumble yet. I thought of Mick Jagger and all the posh girls who were allegedly crazy about him – I'd seen a documentary. Not to mention the Gallaghers, though they were cunts. There were sniggers from around the table.

'Yer gorgeous, that's all. C'mere would ye,' I said again, and this time I leaned in to kiss her. She gasped and hissed something, trying to pull away, but I dragged her face towards mine with my hand on the back of her neck. I succeeded in finding her lips, or the part of her face just above them, with my own lips – and immediately felt myself being smacked in the side of the head.

Recoiling, numb from the drink, I assumed one of the males present had walloped me, but soon realized it had been her.

'You fucking prick,' she hissed.

'I'm not a prick,' I said.

'You are, you're a fucking prick. Get lost. Jesus Christ.' She turned to her friends. 'Did you see that? God, you'd swear he'd never seen a woman in his life.' There was a chorus of mocking laughter, which at least meant I probably wouldn't be getting my head kicked in by an irate, macho mob.

'Look I'm very sorry, I just thought ye were a bit of a ride,' I said as I clambered to my feet – maybe a compliment would take the sting out of the situation and save me some face.

'Do you hear him? Get *lost*, will you.'

'Fair enough.' I left the swirl of mocking faces, along with Grace's low-cut silver dress and the possibility of sticking my face in her tits. My concerns now were elsewhere; namely with my head, which was swimming badly. I stumbled upstairs, towards where I thought the bathroom might be. I thought I'd fallen over but I hadn't. I needed to get sick. I barged ahead, shoving randomers out of the way, falling up the steps, mostly on my knees.

I shoved against the door to the bathroom. It opened and I fell into blackness, one hand held out, feeling for the bowl, the other slapping my mouth, holding in the upsurging puke. It was past the tipping point, already halfway up my oesophagus, when I realized that I wasn't in the bathroom at all, that there was a bed in front of me, half-lit from the doorway behind. And I realized that Jen was on the bed, with Kearney on top of her, pushing her knees back behind her head, both of their faces turned towards me.

I fell to my knees and spewed. Some of it spurted on to the bed, splashing over the pair of them; the rest splattered into a big puddle on the carpet beneath me. I remained on my knees for a moment, wobbling. I could hear Kearney shrieking with laughter, and he was still fucking her, fucking Jen – he hadn't even slowed down. Then my momentum caught up with me and I fell forward, my hands rising up too late to stop me toppling right into a puddle of my own vomit, as Kearney cackled and Jen moaned and moaned and moaned.

38 | Kearney

Sex, he felt, was never only about the sex. Sex was revenge, aggression, a terrorist attack on the world, on women, and on men as well. Every time he fucked a girl – not so many as of yet, but he was young – he knew that he was taking a little bit of her soul away, stealing it from her and locking it deep inside, to nourish himself with. Whenever he had sex, and could make the girl come, and make her remember it, Kearney knew he was planting himself in the girl's heart and soul like a seed, and he would be there forever, in the background, watching and sneering, controlling. Even if a girl he fucked eventually married someone, and was really in love, he would still have that piece of her, that part she could never take back. It was power: over the woman, and over every man she'd ever be involved with, for Kearney would look on with cruel, gloating eyes at the girls he'd fucked as their decent, kind, weakling lovers tried to give them what he hoped they knew they never could.

The night after the party, he lay in bed with a faint smile on his face, reliving his still-fresh memories of Jen, Jen, Jennifer. That lovely red hair, those pale and bouncing tits; how she had giggled and murmured as he'd laid her out on the bed, her eyes half-closed; how she'd grown confused and scared but he had whispered shhh, it would all be okay, whilst sliding off her knickers, and then he'd laughed and she'd laughed too and from that point on she was eager, pliant, his. Languidly he pulled himself off, stroke after stroke, until he came across his belly, feeling it trickle over his knuckles. A cool night breeze from the skylight caressed his skin, drying his come to a delicate crust. Moments later, Kearney was asleep.

He went back into town a few times to look for the tramp. He wasn't there, where he always was. There were only shadows, and rubbish blowing down the lane like dead leaves in a world after nature, and a whiff of piss in the empty space where the tramp used to sit.

Each day he carefully scanned all the papers in the newsagents, looking for stories of a dead wino. But there was nothing; that, he knew, was because nobody really gave a fuck. It was like the tramp had disappeared, silently fading from existence down a litter-strewn lane.

Kearney didn't hear from Matthew after the party. He didn't expect to. Obviously he was hurt, angry, betrayed. But boredom was boredom, and both of them needed someone to smoke and drink with, and none of the other lads were around.

Kearney waited until Tuesday, then called him.

'Alright Matthew.'

'Alright Kearney.'

' … '

'So what are you up to?'

'Nothing.'

'Fair enough.'

' … '

Kearney sighed: Matthew was playing hard to get. He couldn't be bothered humouring him and decided to cut the crap. 'Are you pissed off with me cos I shagged Jen?'

'...'

'I take that as a yes.'

'...'

Kearney made his voice sound aggrieved. 'Fuck's sake, Matthew, she was the one who was all over me. Anyway, it's only a fuckin shag, man. Yis had broken up, hadn't yis? Jesus, get over it, will ye?'

'Yeah well. Ye could have waited a while.'

'What, half an hour more? Three days? How long? It was a party. I was pissed, she came on to me and we had a screw. Jesus, Matthew. Get over it, would ye. Don't be a hypocrite. Or have ye forgotten about the time I walked in on you and Rachel, in me own fuckin house? At least you and Jen had broken up when I did it. Fuck's sake. I won't be doin it again, anyway.'

'Yeah, whatever, man.'

'What are ye up to today?'

'Fuck all. Watchin telly.'

'Me ma's in work. I've got a half-ounce here that I bought off Bowser.'

A pause. 'Yeah?'

'Yeah. Ye comin around for a smoke?'

'I dunno.' Another pause. 'I was goin to stay here and watch a film.'

'Stall it. I've got the new *Kill-Tech* game, I borrowed it off Decko Byrne.'

'Is it any good?'

'Yeah, it's deadly. Stall it.'

A final, longer pause.

Then: 'Right, I'll be around in a while.'

Kearney hung up.

39 | Matthew

We sat in the dimness of Kearney's room, the shutter pulled, his shit techno like a coma-pulse on the stereo.

Already we were on the third joint. I lay back into the beanbag, half closing my eyes. It was a weird feeling, being stoned off your head in the middle of the afternoon. There was no way back, you had to deal with it for the rest of the day. I would have to sit there and eat dinner with my ma and da later that evening, tense with concentration, trying hard not to look stoned.

Through the haze of smoke I studied the strips of paper sellotaped randomly across the bedroom walls. It was the same sentence, over and over: *'You will never defeat us, because you love life and we love death.'*

The quote came from some Al-Qaeda warrior. Kearney had talked about getting it done as a tattoo that ran up his bicep, with *death* on the neck, but he couldn't afford it. We played *Kill-Tech: Obliteration* for a while, not talking much. Kearney was already an expert. The triangular hover-fighter responded deftly to every flick of his thumbs and fingers: launching missiles through narrow cracks, obliterating command posts, incinerating enemy personnel. I flew clumsily, bouncing off walls, narrowly avoiding collisions with huge, floating Battlehulks as Kearney pursued me – toyed with me – above an elegant future city.

After some time I flung down my joypad and said: 'Fuck this, let's play something else.'

He didn't respond at first, still fused with the game, the screen. 'Hah?' he eventually said, turning around. I had stood up and walked to the window, pulling aside the curtain and looking out over grey suburban nothing. You could see the girls' school across the road. Kearney had boasted before of how he liked to wank while looking out at the girls, even though it was a primary school and the oldest of them no more than eleven or twelve. I didn't know if he was making it up.

Kearney changed the techno CD for one that sounded exactly the same, then started rolling another joint.

'Guess what?' he said as he twisted the end of the finished spliff. 'What?'

'Can ye keep a secret?'

'Yeah.'

'Don't just say "yeah". Can ye seriously keep a secret? If I tell ye this, ye can't tell anyone, okay?'

'What is it? Yeah, okay.'

I took the spliff from Kearney, getting curious.

He paused for dramatic effect. 'I killed someone,' he said.

Stoned, I burst into laughter. 'Fuck off,' I said, ashing out the window. 'Don't give me that bollocks. Ye didn't kill anyone. Who did ye kill?'

'Seriously, I did, I killed someone.' He grinned, dispelling any notion that he was offering a confession.

'Okay, who did ye kill, then?' I said, making it obvious I was only humouring him.

'I murdered this old wino in town. Have ye ever seen the oul lad who sits in that lane in Temple Bar, just off Dame Street? Ye know, the one in behind the Hot Chick?'

'Oh yeah.' I pictured the laneway, but not the tramp.

'The oul lad in there, do ye know him? He's always in the same spot, total wino, like.'

'Yeah, I think I know the one ye mean,' I said, stoned and lazy, to hurry things along. Town was full of alcos and tramps. How was I to know which one Kearney was on about?

'Well, go into town then, and go down the lane to his place, ye know that doorway he always sits in. And tell me what ye find there. I'll tell you what ye'll find: fuck all.'

'Yeah, deadly,' I said. I wasn't in the mood to indulge Kearney – the image of him riding an eager Jen kept intruding on my mind, more so as my stone deepened. I wanted to butcher him. I decided that I'd fuck Kearney up. I didn't know how, but I would do it. Meanwhile, I said, 'Fair play to ye, ye killed him. How did ye do it, then?'

'Ye don't believe me. But I did. I poisoned his drink. He's not there any more. I've been in to check a few times. The fucker's dead.'

He sounded triumphant. I began to consider that, just possibly, he wasn't making it up. 'Wait, so tell me: you're sayin ye went into town and put poison in this guy's drink, and now he's dead?'

'No, I brought the drink in meself, with the poison already in it. Rat poison. I gave him a few cans first, to get his trust and make sure his judgment was cloudy, then I gave him the poisoned bottle of wine. Not that I had to do that: the fucker would've drunk a carton of AIDS piss if I'd told him there was a shot of whiskey mixed in.'

'And then he died?'

'I'm fairly sure he did, yeah. I didn't stick around to see it happen, it would've been too dodgy. But he was gone the next day.'

I said nothing. I puffed on the joint and watched him. 'Jesus,' I said, experimentally.

Kearney laughed. 'Now don't say a fuckin thing, okay?'

I kept looking at him. Suddenly I felt way too stoned.

'I mean it. Don't say a word. Jesus, it was some rush, though. Nobody's goin to give a fuck. Who cares if some old wino is off the streets? People would be delighted if someone wiped out all the alcos and junkies and all the rest of them.'

'I don't know.'

'Well I do know. At the very least, nobody gives a fuck. So I'm goin to do it again. I'm goin to kill a junkie.'

I stared, amazed that this was the conversation we were having. I tried to read Kearney's face for signs of a joke. I could decipher nothing. I said, 'Are ye serious, Kearney?'

'Yeah. I'm serious.'

Abruptly, I shook my head. I exhaled smoke, waved a hand and said, 'Cop on, Kearney. You're talkin bollocks. Ye didn't kill anyone. But leave it before ye really do go off and do something stupid.'

The words sounded unnatural in my mouth, like they only belonged on telly or in films.

'It's a buzz like ye wouldn't believe,' said Kearney. 'I'm telling ye. Ye don't have to believe me. I'm goin to kill a junkie scumbag. They're better off dead. They *are* dead. *Dawn of the Dead*, it's like, when ye see them in town. I'm doin it in a few days, after I get the plan sorted out. Stall it in with me.'

I shook my head. 'I don't think so.'

'Why not? Ye don't have to do anything, just come along for the craic. Look, let me just show ye how easy it is. We don't actually have to do anything. If ye think it's goin too far, I'll stop and that'll be that. It'll be more of a recon mission, just to show ye. Alright?'

I wanted to say something, say no, but I couldn't bring myself to speak. What was this magnetism Kearney had, this weird new power? I felt like I should go along with it, even if only to impress him. For some reason, that was important now. But also there was the excitement, the wanting to see how far it could go, how deranged it could get.

While I was wavering, Kearney said again, 'Stall it. I'm tellin ye, it's only a bit of a buzz. Ye don't have to do anything. We don't actually have to, like, execute him. We can go right to the very edge and stop there, if ye want to stop there. I just want to show ye what it's like. I'm tellin ye, the buzz is like nothing ye've done before.'

We were silent for a few moments. Then I said, 'Alright. Fair enough. I'll stall it in. Just to see. I know you're talkin rubbish, though.'

Satisfied, Kearney turned back to *Kill-Tech: Obliteration*, picking up the joypad from the carpet. I looked out the window again, over at the darkening red-brick walls and fences of the girls' school, and the rows of houses and chimneys behind it, sullen and identical.

40 | Rez

**Problems with Reality: Rez is on Drugs and they're
Messing with his Head!**

In his rare moments of lucidity, Rez saw that the medication the
doctors had put him on, the way it affected his outlook, was yet
another falsity, an airbrush job on the true face of things.

He liked how the drugs made him feel, though: warm, satisfied, oblivious. This must be what it's like to be a junkie or a cow,
he thought dozily, sitting at home bathed in the amiable glow of
the TV, his mother hovering ever-near, watching him even when
it seemed she wasn't. Or it was as if he was enlightened, like the
Buddhist monks he read about, as if he had attained a state of pure
acceptance of the world. The medication made everything benign,
friendly; it rendered all the razor-blade thoughts that cut into Rez's
in-growing brain soft as butter. In fact, he didn't think very much
on the medication at all. He was content to sit there in the softly lit
living room, passively hearing the anxious whispers and murmurs of
his parents, sister and brother.

Days passed. Rez convalesced, if that was what you could call his state of drug-zapped torpor. Nourishing meals were prepared for him at regular hours. Films were rented, books bought and a PlayStation 2 borrowed from one of Michael's friends, all for Rez's amusement. I should have done this sooner, he told himself during one of the intervals of clarity that briefly appeared, only to be swallowed up again by the dreamy water-world of Xanax and diazepam, annulling all sardonic thought, all humour in general. The medicated world was a humourless one, like a totalitarian state. But Rez didn't mind; he accepted everything. Everybody's happy nowadays, he thought wryly, when he was capable of wryness and bothered enough to think.

Nothing happened. Time flowed on, the great lazy river. This, too, was fine with Rez, who, medication notwithstanding, remained convinced that the causes of his despair were fundamental and insurmountable. He kept this conviction to himself.

'You're not goin to do it again,' his mother said.

They were sitting at the kitchen table. A bowl of barely touched cream-of-vegetable soup steamed its heat away between Rez's elbows. Rez didn't know if he was being asked a question or given an order.

She repeated, 'You're not goin to try it again.'

Rez decided it was a question. 'No,' he answered; even such a succinct response cost him tremendous effort. He wanted to be extricated from this conversation, planted back down in front of the Enlightenment Box, left alone to bask in its stupid radiance.

His mother was silent, looking probingly at him. He noted that there were lines around her eyes. Crow's feet – he recalled that that was the name for them: the results of age and decay and therefore not Rez's fault. She was in her pale-green dressing gown, makeup washed off. She seemed withered with anguish, helpless and perplexed. That was how she seemed. Rez was not taken in.

Rez thought, No doubt she thinks she's worried about me.

Rez thought, No doubt she believes that she really cares about me.

Rez knew better. He knew she was merely playing the part of someone who loved another person. It was a decent performance, he conceded, probably enough to move someone who bought into all that shit, someone more naive than him. It didn't touch Rez. Love was not something that existed any more. Love was the dodo or the velociraptor or the Mayan civilization.

His mother was crying now, sobbing and shaking her head, not knowing what to say. A fluttering something – pity, anguish – arose from inside Rez and floated for a moment in the space between them. It was faint, tremulous and delicate, and lasted only for a moment; then Rez snuffed out the sentiment and denied it had ever been there.

With the flicker of feeling eliminated, the null state resumed. Rez was stable again.

It was his pride that had rebelled: if his feelings weren't his own, Rez didn't want them. This left him very little indeed. It left him nothing but pain. Rez had once seen a piece of anarchist street art: a stark, scratchy drawing of a morose little girl against a blackened, polluted cityscape. The girl had looked into Rez's eyes, her predicament given eloquence in a question scrawled at the bottom of the picture: 'If I Cleaned Away All the Filth, Would There Be Anything Left?'

Rez could relate.

He repeated to his mother that he wouldn't do it again. Then he planted himself in front of the telly and thought about nothing.

41 | Matthew

I called around to Kearney's at eleven o'clock that Thursday morning, as he had instructed. It was yet another moody, overcast day, the last of July. It felt like the sun hadn't been out in months. Jen had started trying to call me again, since the party at Grace's, but there was no way I would so much as talk to her now. It was wrecked forever. Cocker had called me as well but I ignored him too. I decided I had no real friends. I might just save up for a while and go away, travel or live abroad or something, maybe drink myself to death in Mexico, like some French novel that Rez would read – I would cut this whole crowd out of my life. But first I wanted to see if this shit that Kearney said was true. Kearney was the worst of the lot, but at least he wasn't a hypocrite.

When I reached his house, Kearney opened the door before I rang and met me with an eager grin.

'Ready to go?' he said with a clap of the hands, like we were setting off on a camping trip.

All the way into town, Kearney was in high spirits. He chattered away about games, porno, telly, drugs and drug dealers we both knew. I considered that maybe it was the excitement of what we were about to do that had him so worked up, and I grew uneasy. Over the past couple of days, I had more or less convinced myself that this was all just one of Kearney's fantasies, entertaining but unreal, and I was going along with it as a kind of joke. Now, I wasn't so sure.

We got off the bus and walked across O'Connell Bridge to the north side of the river, turning on to the Liffey walkway and heading towards Liberty Hall. This was the part of town where junkies usually congregated the most. And sure enough, here they were. Scagged out of it in broad daylight, in dirty shell suits and baseball caps, the junkies clustered and whined. They smoked cigarettes, snarled and hissed amongst themselves, insulted passers-by who didn't give them money. The women were doglike, ravaged things, teeth all crooked or not there at all. The men were nicotine-coloured skeletons with sunken eyes, dried up and lustreless. Maybe Kearney was right: everyone would be secretly delighted if the junkies, winos and knackers were wiped out.

'These are no good,' said Kearney, gesturing towards the clustered junkies. 'They're all together, we'd only get noticed. We have to find one that's on its own.'

We smoked cigarettes as we walked on, getting off the boardwalk and crossing the street, heading down a foul-smelling laneway leading through to Abbey Street. There were a few winos in pairs but no junkies. We came to Abbey Street, sidetracked up O'Connell Street and turned in again, on to Talbot Street. A pair of gypsy types played a flute and fiddle by the James Joyce statue, with tourists and the idle clustered around to watch.

'I'd kill every busker in Dublin as well if I had the chance,' muttered Kearney as we passed.

We turned down a quieter street, more rundown and away from the mid-week shoppers. A group of maybe twenty chattering Spanish teenagers approached. They passed us by and the street was all but empty. Graffitied shutters lined one side, bracketed by shady passages and doorways. On the other side a high metal fence closed off an area of overgrown wasteland, with the rubble of a collapsed wall half hidden among the weeds and grass.

Up ahead, staggering along towards us, was the wiry, scruffy figure of what I immediately recognized to be a junkie, on his own. I could feel the excitement coming off Kearney, whose pace quickened as he said, 'Here we go. This is our man.'

The junkie slumped against the fence several times as we approached. He didn't look up till we were standing right in front of him. For a moment I thought it was the junkie who had insulted us back on the night of the Primal Scream gig. But it was just some other anonymous smackhead.

'Hello there,' said Kearney.

The junkie gazed at us with smacked-out indifference. He mumbled something and tried to walk on. Kearney put up his hand and stopped him.

'Hang on a minute,' he said.

The junkie looked up again, managing a frown, wondering what the hell we wanted of him. He looked youngish, in his twenties or thirties, it was hard to tell. His face had the yellow sheen they always had, his colourless hair and sallow skin merging into one coating of greasy lifelessness.

'Wha?' he said.

'Wha?' Kearney aped, as if he couldn't disguise his loathing, or wasn't bothered to.

I stood slightly behind Kearney, to his side. He was staring at the junkie in what looked like concentration, not saying anything.

I looked around. An old man was crossing the road further down, and behind him was a mother with an old-fashioned shopping trolley, cursing at her young daughter in a heavy inner-city accent. The sight of the people reassured me: Kearney had no plan – unless he was willing to murder someone in broad daylight and spend the next forty years in prison, there was no way he was going to kill this junkie, who was now whining at us.

'Spare us some change for a hostel, lads. I swear I've been robbed, me bird robbed all me stuff and me money. Lads, a hostel, I swear.' He whined with the shrill accent of all the city's junkies.

Kearney's voice seemed to gush with sympathy: 'Aw I'm really sorry, pal, but we don't have any change. I gave me last five euro to a homeless fella around the corner. If I did have money I'd absolutely give it to ye, no doubt about it. I'd love to help ye, I really would, I know what it's like.'

Confused, but thinking he had probably found a true sap, some bleeding heart who would believe anything, the junkie pushed his luck.

'Yer a star, bud, yer a fuckin genuine man. Listen bud, I'm really in a bad way, I swear man, it's cos of me bird. I'm broke I am, I have a baby to feed and everythin, but how can I if I haven't got any money? I swear to ye I amn't a scabby cunt, I hate to have to ask ye this pal, but will ye go and get some money for me out of the bank machine? I swear bud, you'd be really doin me a big favour. God bless ye bud.'

Kearney rubbed his chin as if seriously considering the junkie's request. I said nothing.

'I'd love to help ye like that, but I'm sorry to say it's just impossible,' said Kearney. 'I've only got twenty quid in there and I really need it cos I promised I'd give it to the blind mongo babies in Africa. Ye know what I mean?'

The junkie dropped the pretence of interest and was about to step between us and stagger on down the street, but Kearney held him back with his hand again and said, 'Hold on, there's no rush now, bud.' His voice had lost the false, schmaltzy compassion; it was cold and serious. 'I can't give ye money, but I have something else for ye.'

The junkie waited suspiciously, and I looked on as Kearney pulled down the zip on his leather jacket and reached into the inside pocket. He looked up and down the street before taking his hand out, then spoke in a low, urgent voice: 'Look. I found this in me brother's room. I don't want him messin with this stuff. I don't mind what other people do with their lives, but he's only a kid, basically, and he's too young to be foolin with this crap. I was goin to throw it in the bin, but I feel bad that I can't give ye any money, and I reckon ye like this stuff. Do ye? Or am I totally wrong? I don't mean to be makin assumptions, like, ye just looked like the kind of man who likes this stuff.'

The junkie's face was lit up with reverence. He seemed to have stopped breathing, entranced by what was in Kearney's hand. It was a small plastic bag with about two grammes of light-brown powder in it. I had never seen heroin before and wouldn't have been sure if it really was that. But the junkie's expression confirmed it.

His hand darted out for the package, but Kearney withdrew it easily in time.

'Hold yer horses, boss,' he said. 'Are ye sure ye want this? Don't ye know that it's fuckin yer life up?'

The junkie whined and moaned, reduced to a pathetic state, like a child crying for sweets.

'Do ye hear me? I asked ye are ye sure you want it. This shite will fuckin kill ye.'

Realizing an answer was necessary to get to the smack, the junkie mustered his attention enough to look into Kearney's eyes and whine: 'Ah man, don't worry about it, bud, give me that gear and that'll be the last of the stuff I'll ever touch. I just want to have a little bit, man, ye know what I mean. It's been a shite day … me bird … normally I wouldn't take it off ye but me bird, I was robbed … ah man just give us the gear will ye.'

'I'll give it to ye if you want it. Are ye sure, then?'
'Yeah bud.'
'Fair enough. There ye go.' Kearney handed the incredulous junkie the bag. I watched it change hands.

'Off ye go and enjoy it, now!' he called as the junkie hurried away in the opposite direction, hand clamped around the package, newly energized.

Kearney started to cackle, watching the scampering addict turn off the quiet street.

'What the fuck was that?' I said. It was like I'd broken out of a trance.

'Relax, man.'

'What was in the bag?'

'What do ye think was in it? Gear. Smack. Think I'm a liar?'

'Where did you get heroin from?'

He shrugged, turning to give me his attention for the first time. 'I got it. Doesn't matter where. Ask me no secrets and I'll tell ye no lies.'

'Is it poisonous? Is he goin to die?'

He giggled. 'Affirmative. Yes. That's correct, Matthew.'

'Jesus!' I put my hands to my head, started pacing up and down.

'Ah, give it a rest, would ye. Give over the bleedin melodrama. Ye knew what we were goin to do.'

'What *you* were goin to do. But no, I didn't know ye were goin to give him poisoned fuckin heroin.'

He was serious now, his voice hardened: 'No Matthew, not just me – *we*. You knew what we were doin. *You* said you were up for it. Are ye denyin it now?'

'No. Yeah. I *am* denyin it. I thought ye were havin a laugh. I didn't believe ye.'

'Well ye can believe me now. But think, what are ye goin to do about it? Cos ye know, I've got ye recorded at home, saying ye were up for killin a junkie with me. So yer fucked.'

I looked at him, standing there, not smiling, watching me. I started to panic.

'Oh Jesus, Kearney, what the fuck? Give it a rest, stop yer messin. I didn't say that, I didn't mean it. Leave it out, will ye?'

'It's not too late to help him, ye know. If you want to, ye can run after him and try and find him and tell him –'

I didn't hear the rest of the sentence: I had already started running, fast as I could, through the alleys past Talbot Street, looking for a solitary junkie among the afternoon crowds in the city centre.

Two hours later I sat on the bus home, on my own.

Rain pelted down on the city. I looked out the window; the faces I saw were sinister; the laughter all sounded wrong, full of menace and mockery. It all sounded like Kearney's laughter.

I hadn't found the junkie. I had looked and looked but he was gone, vanished.

I couldn't eat my dinner that evening. I heard my ma whisper something to my da in the sitting room behind me. He lowered his *Evening Herald* to watch me through the door, while I sat in silence at the kitchen table.

He came in and shut the door behind him. Then he sat down, folded his arms on the table and said, 'Tell me straight, Matthew. Have you been takin drugs?'

42 | Kearney

The buzz was extreme, even better the second time. All that night he couldn't sleep, his mind fizzing with ideas and visions. The next morning, frazzled and jerky but still ecstatic, he decided to go back in for another shot. He sensed that his discipline was slipping and he had to rein it in or he'd be undone. But then he thought, Fuck it. He bounded down into the basement to reef up another helping of rat poison, and took the bus into town.

It was a grey morning. Deciding he should probably chop and change the locations to avoid any kind of pattern forming, Kearney let his legs take him through the dull weekday murmur of the city centre, along Harcourt Street, all the way to the canal. There, he stepped down to the quiet, grassy bank and walked alongside the water. And, soon enough, he came upon what he was after: another wizened, babbling old drunk, slouched on a bench by the archway of a bridge. Kearney gulped on the Red Bull he'd bought to keep himself perky, and approached. This would be easy as fuck, just like the first time. And this time he was going to take a souvenier.

'Shift on up a bit there, boss,' he said when he reached the bench. 'Here, I've a few cans with me, perhaps you'd like to share them.'

He was a pro by now. He sat with the scruffy tramp and plied him with booze. Feeding him the second can Kearney said, 'Listen now, Padre Pio. There's only one thing I ask of ye on this fine mornin. Ye can have all the drink ye like from me, but I hope ye won't mind if I make a little film of ye. Just for, like … the Church. To show them the good work or whatever. Alright?'

The tramp was indifferent. Kearney took out his mobile and started filming. This smelly fuckhead wasn't as manic or embittered as the first one. He didn't say much at all, just supped on the can with quiet gratitude. Kearney giggled freely, not bothering to mask his derision. The alco had an innocent-looking face, which made it all the more hilarious. Kearney poked his cheek with his finger, pushing in the skin and making noises like you'd do for a baby, gurgling at him. The alco didn't give a fuck.

When the tramp had finished his third can of Devil's Bit, it was time to cut the banter. Time for a little vino.

Kearney gave him the bottle and made him wave for the camera. He laughed and slapped him in the head, eliciting a low, tremulous whine. Then he went for a walk.

The lack of sleep was starting to catch up on him. He stopped off at Insomnia for two double espressos – a tip Dwayne had given him in Boston, useful for getting to work when there was no speed or coke around. Wired anew, he marched back into the centre, crossed O'Connell Bridge and stopped in at Dr Quirkey's arcade. He played *House of the Dead* for a spell, exhilarated by the exploding faces of zombies and chainsaw-motherfuckers as he shot them repeatedly at close range. The crossfire thrills – caffeine, guns, blood and noise – coupled with the awareness of what was waiting for him back on the canal bank, fused into an intense and indiscriminate eroticism. As Kearney unloaded again and again into the screen, his cock pulsed in his jeans, his jaw fell open and his eyelids fluttered. During a pause in the game action, he scanned the teeming din of the arcade: everywhere, eager little sluts, moaning to be defiled, pouting for the rape.

He couldn't take it any longer. Killed by a chainsaw stuck into his face, he jammed the blue plastic gun back in the metal holster and paced into the toilets. Barely had he slammed the cubicle door behind him than he'd pulled his cock out and was pumping frantically. Images hurtled through his mind, relentless filth. Everything was porno, everyone a victim. Within seconds, groaning at high volume and biting his lip till a hot trickle of blood ran through his saliva, Kearney jizzed all over the place. It pumped out of him in violent spasms, splattering his chin, his hands, his chest, the door and the partition. The spasms didn't abate for many seconds, the spunk gushing out of him like he'd struck milky oil. Kearney continued to moan, overpowered by bliss, not in control of himself. His legs gave way and he crashed backwards on to the toilet seat, falling off and sliding down the partition wall. As the waves of rapture slowly subsided, Kearney started to giggle, then laugh uproariously at the state of himself. He'd never seen anything like it.

He may have passed out for a moment. He blinked awake. His mind was blank. Then he remembered: it was time to go back to the drunken cunt. He gave himself a hasty clean-up and hurried back out of the arcade. He half-ran down O'Connell Street, over the bridge, up Grafton Street, through the Green and down along Leeson Street till he was back at the quiet, sheltered bank of the canal. The water calmly gurgled through the black crescent of the archway, beside which Kearney had left the alco perched on his bench.

And there he was, still in exactly the same place. Kearney glanced behind him to make sure no one was around. All clear. He took out his phone and started filming as he approached the tramp, then stood at the bench beside him. The tramp still reeked of piss and fuck knew what else; he still had dribble or pus or something leaking from the cracked corners of his mouth; he was still a laughable human wreck. Only this time, he wasn't breathing.

You pathetic old fuck, Kearney thought, standing over him and looking down. You pitiful old man, you fucking wretched, disgusting old bastard. Sickened by the sight of the alco even in death, Kearney stepped forward and delivered a forceful kick to the corpse's ribs. The body jolted on impact. Then it lurched to the side, teetered for a moment and fell over, rolling down the bank to fall with a plop into the canal's flow, as Kearney's camera phone drank it all in.

You pitiful fucking wreck. You dirty stinking cunt.

43 | Rez

He didn't go out much. His parents felt that he probably should, but at the same time they were reluctant to let him out of their sight, in case he 'tried it again', as they always referred to the possibility of another suicide attempt.

A little over a week into his convalescence, Rez's ma deemed it time for him to start seeing his friends. For a few days no one came. Then, as Rez was watching a mid-afternoon omnibus of US talk shows, the doorbell rang. The doorbell in the Tooley household was one of those old-fashioned ones that actually went *ding-dong*. Rez heard his ma going to get it.

It was Matthew.

Matthew stayed for less than twenty minutes, during which time he clutched a teacup and looked at the floor or into the telly, swaying faintly in his chair. It seemed to Rez that Matthew's sentences were slurred.

They talked for a while: awkward, stilted questions, and barefaced platitudes in response. As they sipped their tea and stared at an ad for Power City on the telly Matthew said, 'So you're watchin a lot of telly?'

'That's right, I am yeah,' replied Rez.

'That's good, telly's good,' said Matthew, nodding slowly, staring into the screen. 'It's good for ye to watch a bit of telly.'

'Yeah,' mumbled Rez. 'I think it is. It's good to watch a bit of telly.'

They watched telly for a bit.

Somewhat later, Rez said, 'How's Cocker? Alright?'

'He's not bad, not bad,' came Matthew's response, followed by another sip of tea.

Cruising on Xanaxed autopilot, beginning vaguely to enjoy this series of exchanges, Rez asked, 'And how's Kearney?'

On being asked this simple question, Matthew became weirdly nervous. He stuttered and fidgeted, looking away from Rez, first at the wall, then at the floor. He gave no intelligible reply.

Why was he being like this, Rez wondered. But the effort of thinking about it was too great. He had just turned away to face the telly again, when Matthew, in a strange, desperate voice, blurted out: 'Rez, Kearney is gettin all messed up.'

Rez turned back to stare at him.

Matthew said nothing else.

'Matt, you're sayin that like it's a surprise,' said Rez.

Now Matthew looked straight at him: his eyes were pink; he seemed almost frantic. 'No Rez, I mean he's gettin really messed up. He's doin weird things, he's ...'

He trailed off. They looked at each other, the mid-volume chatter of the TV filling the silence between them. Rez waited. Then he said, 'What do ye mean? What's he doin?'

Matthew didn't answer. He appeared to sink into himself. Eventually he muttered, 'Nothing, never mind. He's just mad, ye know yerself. He just keeps goin on about his games all the time. It's wreckin me head. There's nothing goin on.'

Rez turned away and stared at the telly. There was a rocket launch being broadcast live on the news. Distractedly, Rez noted the eager tone of the reporter's voice as the rocket took off: you could tell she was hoping it would malfunction, combust in mid-air like the *Colombia* a few months ago. After the countdown, as the shiny spacecraft corkscrewed moonward and all seemed to be going well, the disappointment in the reporter's voice was blatant. Why else would they bother showing a rocket launch in this day and age, if not for the possibility that it would blow up live on air?

Sluggish with drugs, Rez's thoughts were entangled in the weird insinuations of the televized launch. Matthew's puzzling behaviour receded from consciousness.

And then Matthew was standing up, saying he had better get going, telling Rez to take care. Rez nodded like a businessman, forgetting briefly the exact nature and purpose of Matthew's visit.

Then Matthew left and Rez turned again to gaze into the lively colour-dance of telly.

Telly, he noted, is really great.

44 | Kearney

He kept a close check: there was still nothing in the papers about a dead junkie or dead winos. Or next to nothing: there were two short reports of a 'bad batch' of heroin that was going around, one in the *Herald* and one in the *Independent*, but neither of them mentioned any slaughtered humans.

You needed to see it happen, thought Kearney. You needed to be there at the precise instant when the body passed from life to death – like in Stu's video. He felt like telling Dwayne what he had done, but it was too risky. Instead, he emailed him about the video: '*i jus keep thinkin of it over and over i never seen anyting like it hehe fuckin MENTAL. moddern art!! but hush hush cos we be fucked if anyone ever fund out we seen sumting like dat.*'

The next day, Dwayne replied: '*wot de fuck u talkin about joe?? u mean dat porno with yer 1 who looked like cristina agillerra? r de video wit all de yungfellas tormentin de homeless lad? dat shit is wide spred over here nigga. y wud we b in trubble for watchin dat? wot de fuck u on about joe???*'

Kearney was puzzled and unnerved by this response. What the fuck did it mean? Thinking it over, he found he was starting to get a headache. Better, then, not to think of it at all. He smoked a big fuck-off cone and that helped. Dwayne was a dickhead. All Kearney wanted now was to go back into town and fucking decimate another random cunt. But he knew it was best to cool off for a while. The buzz he was on reminded Kearney of what Dwayne had said once about tattoos: as soon as you get one, all you can think about is the next. You want one that's bigger, brasher, bloodier, and there's no end to it till your body is a mass of pouting sluts, flaming swastikas and blackened landscapes. With effort, Kearney suppressed the impulse to find some other wheezing alco, maybe gouge out his eye or break all his fingers, or pull his tongue out with a pliers. He had to be clever, treat it like a game and not lose control. Otherwise he'd be fucked, end up in Mountjoy.

He holed up in his room for a few days, getting stoned and investigating the online world of hentai, a new Japanese fascination of his. When he ran out of hash on Friday morning, he decided to pay a visit to Mick, a dealer he knew through Dwayne. There was a drought on, but Mick always had his sources. Kearney had enough money for a quarter that would last him a few days, a period in which he intended to stay home, till he felt confident about taking the next step.

He got on a bus and headed into town. It was another grey and sullen morning. No one was around; it was as if the city had been evacuated. Mick's flat was on Parnell Street, down where town starts feeling dodgy and faintly lawless. Kearney rang the bell, waited to be buzzed through, then ascended the stairs. He sat quietly while Mick took his time rolling a spliff and telling supposedly funny anecdotes to three older lads, who laughed obsequiously. Slow, spacey reggae played on massive, bass-heavy speakers stacked on a chest of drawers. 'Dub', Mick called it. Kearney pretended to like it, impatient to get the dope and leave.

After twenty minutes of dub and forced laughter, Kearney left with the hash. Instead of going straight home, he walked to the Garden of Remembrance to roll a spliff. He wanted to be nice and stoned on the bus journey home, before spending the rest of the day in his attic, getting blitzed out of it. He sat down on a bench, noticing that the place was nearly empty, and took out his book, *Naked Lunch*. He had never read it, and never intended to. Reading, clearly, was for faggots. The book had belonged to Rez until Kearney borrowed it one day – not to read, but to roll joints on in public places. It worked brilliantly. Rez was never getting his book back.

He had rolled the spliff and started smoking it when the boy appeared. Kearney watched him entering the garden through the main gates. Even at a distance, he had no trouble discerning it: the boy was handicapped, your classic Down's-syndrome pre-adolescent. His big, round, baby face was stupid and trusting – stupid and trusting and weak. He wore some kind of uniform, a dark-green affair with a yellow and grey striped tie. He was alone. That surprised Kearney; he had thought they never let them out on their own.

Down the steps the boy waddled. At the opposite end from the gate stood the swan statue, and between them was the long central fountain with Celtic weapons painted on the tiled floor.

Kearney kept his eyes on the handicapped boy who misted through the cloud of hash smoke Kearney billowed from his nostrils, a technique he had styled on Snoop Dogg. The boy reached the foot of the steps and came shuffling around the right-hand side of the fountain, approaching the bench where Kearney was sitting.

Kearney had been watching without any agenda in mind, but now, with the boy right beside him, instinct took over: he darted a quick glance up and down the length of the garden. There was nobody around. Kearney thrust out his long, scrawny leg and adroitly tripped the boy up. He fell forward, landing on his face and palms with a groan of incomprehension and pain.

Kearney was up and on his feet immediately. 'Jesus, man, I'm sorry!'

'Uuggh,' said the boy.

Kearney helped him to his feet, brushed him off, made sympathetic noises until the boy was upright and recomposed. He had no plan, no clear idea of what he was doing, what he would do.

'Jesus, I'm sorry about that, pal. I should keep me long legs to meself. Are ye alright?'

'Am alright. You tripped me,' said the boy in a predictable drawl.

'I know, I know. Come on now, I'll walk ye out. Yer on yer way home, I suppose.'

'I have to get home to me mammy, she says don't talk to strangers. They might be sex perverts.'

'I'm not a stranger. I know yer mammy. She's far more of a sex pervert than I am.'

The boy flung Kearney's arm aside with surprising force.

'Don't say that! She's a good mammy, she's my mammy, she's not a sex pervert!'

'I know, I know! I was only jokin. Come on, ye mad thing ye.'

Kearney lightly took the boy's arm again and led him along the length of the rectangular, enclosed garden. They came to the steeper, narrower steps, leading up to the side entrance.

'This my shortcut,' said the boy.

'That's right. Up we go,' said Kearney reassuringly.

They began the ascent, the steps partly hidden by the overhanging branches of the trees around the periphery of the garden. Still Kearney had no thought of where this was leading. But his heart was going like fuck.

When they were almost at the top, near the black iron gate and Parnell Square beyond, Kearney looked back. The garden was still almost empty but a middle-aged, tourist-looking couple had just stepped through the front gateway, absorbed in chat, the man emphasizing a point with open-handed gestures. They were far away.

Kearney didn't hesitate, nor did he think about what he was doing. He shot his leg in behind the boy's calves, then turned and simultaneously gave him a forceful shove. Arms swimming in the air, clawing at nothing, the boy fell slowly backwards like a felled tree. Incomprehension stole over his face, his chubby brow creasing in fright and bewilderment. *Weakness!* thought Kearney. *Weakness!* The boy free-fell in an inexorable arc. He just had time to cry out, and then the back of his head cracked on the sharp edge of the lowest step.

It was a horrible sound even to Kearney, who had now turned and was walking hastily up the remaining pair of steps, out through the black, leaf-shrouded gate. He heard a shout from behind as he came on to Parnell Square and fled into the city with his head down, hands in his pockets, turning here, turning there, losing himself, getting the hell away, heart pounding like some mad fucking thing.

45 | Rez

Late on Saturday morning, the Tooley doorbell rang. Rez's mother went to get it.

Rez was watching television: he was watching *The Weakest Link*. Not fully lucid because of the drugs, Rez wondered if he were the Weakest Link. Was that what she was saying, the stern-looking woman on-screen? If he were the Weakest Link, it would probably be better to not be here at all.

Cocker stepped into the room, smiling shyly, cheeks rosy – maybe Cocker was the Weakest Link. Jen followed behind him. Rez's mother peeked in anxiously, over their heads, then left them to it.

'Alright,' said Rez, already exhausted by the affair.

'Alright Rez,' they said. Jen sat on the armchair and Cocker sat on the smaller couch. Everyone faced the television. For a while no one spoke, all watching *The Weakest Link*.

Then Rez turned to Cocker. 'You are … the Weakest Link?' he said. No one responded. Jen coughed and looked at the carpet.

Eventually, Cocker cleared his throat and said, 'So how are ye doin, Rez?'

'Great, Cocker,' Rez replied. Cocker nodded vigorously, relieved at this response; it made things easier for him. Rez reasoned that he was smarter than Cocker; therefore he, Rez, probably was not the Weakest Link.

Conversation spluttered on for a while, not taking off, not going anywhere. Jen tried to talk about books.

'I'm reading this great one,' she said. 'By Albert Camus. *The Fall*, it's called. It keeps reminding me of you.'

She had pronounced the author's first name like the English version, and the surname as Cam-Uss. Rez's awareness of these errors provoked searing mental pain. 'What's it about?' he muttered. Then he lapsed into staring at the screen. Friendship, he mused, was something you probably had in the nineteenth century, for example.

A few minutes later Jen quietly said, 'I'm goin away soon, Rez.'

He turned to her. 'Are you?' She nodded. 'How soon? What about college? The exam results will be out in …'

'Around three weeks' time,' said Cocker.

Jen said, 'Yeah I know, but I'm goin to go away even if I get into college. You can take a year out, sometimes even two years. But you never know: if I really like it over there, I mightn't even come back. Things here are … it's not the same.'

Rez considered this. Everyone was drifting apart. 'Where are ye goin?' he asked.

'India. I fly to Mumbai this day two weeks.'

'So soon,' said Rez. Something was coming to an end; something was breaking that could never be fixed again. 'Who are ye goin with?'

Jen gave a sad, quiet laugh. 'No one,' she said.

What about Matthew, Rez wondered. But then the news came on RTÉ. Cocker and Jen turned to watch the headlines. For once, the main story wasn't about the Iraq invasion: it was about something foul that had taken place the day before in the Garden of

Remembrance. A camera conveyed from the middle distance the grim-faced forensic squad, the police tape, the sky of solemn grey that seemed to acknowledge the gravity of what had been perpetrated beneath it. Gardaí, said the newsreader, wanted for questioning a young male who had been spotted at the scene, wearing a black leather jacket and black woolly hat.

'Jesus,' said Cocker.

'Oh God,' said Jen.

Rez was gazing at the screen, transfixed not by the atrocity it depicted but by his own pristine indifference. He closed his eyes and craved relief from his thoughts, craved medication, craved being left alone – and right at that very instant, the fogged landscape of his mind lit up in a flash of intense lucidity. Rez was seized by a powerful certainty: he saw it all; the sneer, the surge of reckless malevolence, the gleeful fascination – this was the madness that Matthew had been talking about.

'Jesus,' he rasped. The others assumed he was shocked by the news report and didn't respond. Together they gazed at the screen. Already Rez was doubting himself. Could it really be true? Maybe it was just the drugs tampering with his reality filter, or maybe he was going mad. He knew his logical capacity had fallen into turmoil. He really needed to think this through …

Just then, Rez's mother stuck her head in the door. She smiled wanly at Jen and Cocker; then she scrutinized Rez with her anxious gaze and said, 'It's time for your medicine, love.'

46 | Matthew

On Saturday afternoon it was screaming from the front pages of all the papers on sale at the garage. I stared at the headlines and photos without picking up a paper. I got back to work and talked to no one, and when I was standing out on the forecourt I put my headphones in and played the music at maximum volume.

By the time I got home that night, it was as if the only subject of conversation in Dublin was the killing of James Appleton, or 'Baby James' as they were already calling him. Two German tourists had seen it happen in the Garden of Remembrance. Everywhere you looked – in the papers, on telly, the radio, the net – his round, calm, unjudging face peered out at you. I heard the name repeated over and over: *James Appleton, James Appleton, James Appleton*. That was when the headaches started.

The next day at work, I read *The Sunday Independent*. In the front-page article it said that the 'sickening, barbaric and incomprehensible' killing of 'Baby James' was 'a symbol of the nation's ravaged innocence, and if James' death goes unpunished, the sin will stain all our souls'. By now I was having to take two Paracetamol every couple of hours to dull the glare of pain in the top half of my skull.

On Monday I tried to just get on with things. For the past week I'd taken to secretly drinking vodka in my room. I was drunk that evening as I watched the news, with my untouched dinner on a tray across my lap. My ma was in the room too. That was when the interview was shown – the one that became so famous. My ma was in tears as we sat together before the screen. James Appleton's mother looked straight into the camera, her face all gnarled in agony and madness. She just kept saying, 'How could you do it? How could you do it? How could you?'

Tuesday's editorial in *The Irish Times* described it as 'a shocking, traumatic interview which gave a terrible eloquence to our nation's corrupted soul, to the ravages of the moral plague that has assailed us, and to our collective horror and incomprehension in the face of it'.

The headaches went on all week. I drank in my room, starting each afternoon, with my computer on and music playing, washing down painkillers with vodka or wine. But there were moments that burned through, and I was fully aware.

I woke up with dull light filtering into the room through the pale-blue curtains. I heard a dog bark in the distance, and even further away the music from an ice-cream van, so faint I wasn't even sure it was real. A sad, beautiful feeling came over me, like I was a child again and everything was familiar and okay. There were no thoughts in my head. I lay there for maybe a minute, not worried about anything. Then I tilted my head a fraction and it all came back: the grinding in my skull, the parched mouth, the feeling like maggots squirming under my skin.

I lifted my head to look beside the bed. There was vodka left in the bottle, and a glass with some flat 7Up in the bottom. I poured the rest of the vodka into the glass. I drank it standing with my hand resting on the windowsill, washing down two Paracetamol. Then I phoned in sick.

Half an hour later I cycled away from the house, towards the Phoenix Park. I stopped off on the way to buy another bottle of vodka. When I got to the park I cycled to an empty, flat stretch that was raised slightly, almost a hill. It was near where the Wellington Monument rose towards the clouds. For more than an hour I sat in the grass and drank vodka and smoked many cigarettes. I was miserable, but now and then I had these surges of euphoria, and it seemed that none of it really mattered. There was no heaven, no hell, so why worry about anything at all? Even death was just a natural process, a twig going over a waterfall. Also it was a state of rest, which seemed like bliss. If it did come to that, to killing myself, I would have to do it quickly, not think of my ma and da or Fiona, just get it done before guilt or thinking made me weak.

It was nearly three o'clock. I took out my phone and dialled Jen's number – I had deleted her, but the number was still in my head. I pressed the call button before I had a chance to stop myself.

It rang twice and then she picked up. There was a silence. 'Matthew,' she said eventually.

'Jen,' I said. I blinked hard. I dug the fingernails of one hand into the skin on my face, just under the eye. Neither of us said anything. I tried to speak but my voice had vanished.

'Matthew …' she said after a few moments. 'Matthew, are you … crying?' She paused again. 'Look, I really wanted to –'

'Jen!' I blurted out. 'Jen. There's stuff goin on, Jen. Something's really wrong, I …'

I gasped into the phone. Jen was quiet for a moment, waiting for me to continue. When I didn't, she said, 'Matthew, are you okay? You're really freakin me out here. Tell me what's wrong. You sound –'

'I HATE YE!' I roared. 'I totally fuckin *hate* ye, Jen, I wish we'd never met, I wish I'd never even spoke to ye in me life, I …'

I couldn't say more because now I was sobbing into the phone. I heard her whispering my name. Then she was talking quickly: 'I'm sorry, Matthew, I'm sorry, I only wanted to make you jealous, it was only meant to be a bit of flirtin. Oh Jesus. I was just so hurt at how you'd disappeared after we slept together. I don't know how I could have done that, I –'

'JUST FUCK OFF JEN! I CAN'T FUCKIN STAND YE!'

I pressed the red button and she was gone. I waited for her to call back, ready to hang up again. But the phone didn't ring. I turned it off.

There was nobody around this part of the park, only a few families having picnics over by the monument. The children shrieked and laughed as they chased each other up the stone steps around the base. We used to come here when Fiona was little. I used to like it. The clouds had blown over and now the sun shone down on where I sat, alone in the Phoenix Park. I unscrewed the bottle and drank.

47 | Kearney

He stayed in his attic bedroom, smoking hash, afraid of the outside world. He had found a Stanley knife in his da's old toolkit and he kept it with him at all times, determined to slash his arteries at the first sign that they were on to him. On Monday evening he had watched with the rest of the nation as Baby James's mother wailed into a camera on the RTÉ news. His appetite had disappeared. He couldn't think straight. He lay awake each night that week until dawn or after, waiting for the doorbell to ring, or the door to be simply knocked down. When he did sleep, he sank into a feverish realm of capture, torment, retribution. His ma seemed to notice that something was wrong, but she said nothing. Whenever she looked at him oddly, he scowled back at her, silently warning her not to try anything, to shut up and leave him alone.

'Are you on drugs?' she asked on Thursday evening nonetheless, almost a week after it had happened. She had stepped into the living room after the late-evening news to find Kearney muttering to himself in the armchair.

'Yeah, I am,' he grunted, and reverted to staring at the television, seeing nothing.

She didn't say anything else. Her heart wasn't in it.

By the end of the week the news and the papers still wouldn't leave it alone. Kearney needed to get out of the house. He'd smoked the last of his hash that afternoon and needed more. Perhaps the drought was over and the lads on the estate had something to sell. He didn't want to get stoned on his own, though. He took out his mobile and dialled.

'Alright man,' he said when it was answered.

'Alright,' came Matthew's mumbled response.

'Listen, do ye fancy a smoke? I'm goin out now to try and pick some up, ye should stall it out for a few joints with me.'

'No, I don't think so. I think I'm goin to stay in tonight.' Matthew didn't sound sober. 'Listen, I think I'm just goin to hang around here. These days, like. I don't, I mean, I'm just sayin –'

'What are ye just sayin?'

'Nothin. I'm just sayin –'

'Wha?'

'For fuck's sake, let me finish. I'm just sayin that you probably shouldn't ring me any more.'

'Don't give me that fuckin shit,' said Kearney. 'Jesus, man, relax. I'm only callin ye to ask ye to meet up for a smoke, like. Just a friendly smoke. Don't be gettin all weird on me. We're good mates after all, aren't we?'

'Yeah, but …'

'So what the fuck is yer problem?'

'Ye know what the problem is, Kearney.'

'Oh do I now? Listen Matthew, I'm just bein fuckin friendly and tellin ye I want to meet up with ye for a smoke. We're *old mates*. I'm bein friendly. Don't start pissin me off, or I won't be so fuckin friendly.'

'I've been watchin the news, I –'

'So what? What do I give a fuck about the news? Jesus Christ, do ye think I give a bollocks about Bertie Ahern or the fuckin war in Kazakhstan?'

'No, but –'

'Well then cop the fuck on. Listen, I'm goin around to the estate for a smoke after I pick some up. I'll be there in half an hour. Stall it around. I'll see ye then.'

Beep, beep, beep.

No lights were on in the industrial estate except for one coldly glaring floodlight. It was already dark, and just gone half eight. There was a chill in the air, as if winter was right around the corner. Kearney swigged on the naggin of gin he'd bought on the way over, feeling the trickle of heat in his belly, the relief it gave him.

He sat on a wooden pallet, rubbing his knees. He pulled up his hood. He'd shoved his black jacket and hat into the bottom of his wardrobe after the first news report. Maybe he should burn them, he thought. He lit a cigarette and waited. Soon a hesitant, frail silhouette appeared at the side of the warehouse further on down.

'How's a goin, Matthew,' Kearney called into the gloom.

'Alright,' Matthew muttered back, hands thrust into his pockets as he shuffled through the murk.

'Here, get some of that into ye,' Kearney said, pushing the naggin of gin at him when they were standing together. Matthew took it, unscrewed the top and tilted it back. 'So what's new, man? I haven't seen ye in a while,' Kearney said. 'Not since that day ye came into town with me, am I right?'

Matthew shrugged and looked away.

'What, do ye not remember?' said Kearney. Then he raised his voice, almost shouting: 'The day we went into town and murdered that junkie bastard, remember? The heroin addict. We put the fuckin poison in the heroin and killed the filthy useless cunt. The dead fuckin junkie cunt. Don't ye remember?'

'Jesus, be quiet will ye!' hissed Matthew. He looked close to tears. 'There could be someone around.'

'Okay Matthew, relax.' Kearney laughed, swiping the gin and taking a generous slug. He felt like the crime boss in some Scorsese film. Matthew was shifting, wincing, miserable. Kearney began taking control of the situation, reining it in.

'Listen, don't worry about what we did, okay? Nobody's ever goin to find out. It was a weird thing to do, fair enough. But I don't regret it at all. I can see yer worried we're goin to get caught, but relax man, nobody's goin to know. Anyway, listen to me. I'm fairly sure yer man is grand. I seriously doubt that he actually died. In fact I was in town the other day and I'm nearly positive I saw him, the same fella. It was definitely him. He looked grand, there was nothin even wrong with him. So calm down, okay?'

Matthew looked him in the eye for as long as he could – not very long. Then, eyes to the ground, he said, 'Kearney, you've lost it.'

Kearney waited. Eventually he replied, softly, 'What do ye mean I've lost it? What's that supposed to mean?'

'I watched the news, I –'

'So? What did ye see on the news?'

Matthew looked sat him once more. He said, 'Kearney, was it you who killed that handicapped boy?'

A silence hovered between them. Then Kearney burst out laughing: 'Are ye kiddin? Ye mean that capper who fell down the stairs in the Garden of Remembrance? James fuckin what's-his-name? Are ye fuckin mad? Why would ye even think that?'

Matthew tried to adopt a look of grim resolution. 'It was you, Kearney. Just fuckin admit it. Ye started out with an alco, then –'

Kearney grabbed him by the throat. 'Listen Matthew, I'm tellin ye now to shut yer fuckin mouth. I don't know what yer on about. But if ye want to keep talkin about it, fair enough. But then ye better be ready to talk about that other day as well, when we went into town and KILLED A JUNKIE! WE KILLED A FUCKIN JUNKIE!'

Kearney's roar reverberated around the desolate industrial estate, through the warehouse alleys, across the yards, over fences. Matthew wondered if anyone had heard it, a night security man or something.

'Be quiet, Kearney! Please!'

Matthew was sobbing. He muttered pitiful regrets, tears streaming down his cheeks.

Kearney let go of him and stepped away. He turned his back on Matthew and breathed slowly a few times, calming himself down. He could hear Matthew weeping behind him.

Still facing the other way Kearney said, 'Listen Matthew, I know ye don't feel good about what's been goin on. Fair enough, it is a bit weird, I can see what ye mean. But just let it pass. That's the end of it. Seriously. I promise ye it is. I just wanted to try something like that and see how it felt, but it's over and done with, time to move on. I admit I got a bit carried away. I'm goin to start lookin for a job, just in a supermarket or whatever's goin. And I'm thinkin of goin on to study, something related to games, designin them or something. I don't know, I haven't looked into it yet. Not this year cos it's probably too late, but maybe next year.'

He turned to face Matthew: he had stopped sobbing. Kearney thought it was over. But then Matthew muttered, 'Kearney, just tell me – ye did it, didn't ye?'

Kearney looked him in the eye. He shook his head and said gently, 'Listen Matthew, it wasn't me. I swear to God. I swear on me ma's life. If I'm lyin to ye, then I hope me own ma gets cancer. Okay? Jesus, Matthew, why would ye even believe that?'

Matthew said nothing, sniffling, not really believing, but wanting it enough to lie to himself; so Kearney hoped.

'So how's Rez?' Kearney said after some moments of silence. 'I haven't heard much about him.'

Matthew sniffled. 'He's alright. He still seems a bit zoned out, they still have him on medication. But ye can have a chat with him, like. He's not too far gone for that.'

'Good. He's a decent skin, Rez. I'm sure he'll pull through.'

Matthew looked away. Kearney burst into nervous giggles.

They didn't talk much after that. They smoked in silence, warming the evening cold, the smoke billowing out in wisps and spirals to dissolve in the night.

———————

A second weekend passed. Kearney stayed in his room, smoking, playing games and watching hentai clips, keeping an eye on the news. The Stanley knife was never out of reach.

By Sunday night, very tentatively, the worst of his terror had begun to subside. The incident had happened ten days ago now, and no one had come to drag him from his attic bedroom into the jaws of public vengeance. The media frenzy had raged, peaked, and was finally beginning to abate, the interest in Baby James's murder going cold along with the gardaí's leads. Kearney realized he just might come through this, eventually to reinsert himself, unnoticed, into the human world, into official reality.

48 | Rez

The medication had some peculiar side effects. For one thing, it fucked with Rez's memory.

In the agreeable mist of his serotonin-enhanced sedation, it became difficult to distinguish between, say, memories of real events and memories of imagined ones. Or between dreams and reality. Or between something he had seen on TV and something he had experienced first-hand – but then, that had been the case for Rez even before he tried to hang himself.

Ten days after the James Appleton killing he was talking to his brother, who had come in from work. Michael spoke awkwardly, humourlessly, with a trace of unwitting condescension – the way you spoke to someone who had recently tried to kill himself. Normally, this pissed Rez off, but today he was feeling expansive, the result of a chemical high tide in his drug-flooded brain. He was telling Michael about the new Radiohead album, which he had partly listened to online. It was called *Jupiter Fell and We Saw it Happen*. Both brothers were committed Radiohead fans. Michael was surprised and excited to hear that a new album was imminent, and so soon after *Hail to the Thief*. Rez assured him that it was the finest thing the band had done since *OK Computer*. Pleased by this show of enthusiasm on the part of his brother, Michael left Rez in front of the telly and went off to do his own thing.

Later that evening, after dinner, Michael sat back down in the sitting room, where Rez was watching telly. Iraqi politics were being discussed, as well as the chemical, biological and nuclear weapons that no one could find. Rez had protested before the invasion, like everybody else. But daily now he observed, with sickened fascination, how entertained he was, how satisfied it made him to think the war could last for years and years, generating untold carnage and slaughter.

Michael cleared his throat and said, 'Where did ye say ye heard those new Radiohead tracks, Rez?'

'Online. I can't remember the site. Google it. They're really good. There's actually a song on it about these daisy-cutter bombs they're usin over there.'

'I did Google it. I couldn't find it anywhere. What did you say the album was called again?'

'*Jupiter Fell and We Saw it Happen.*'

'Are ye sure? That's what I typed. There was nothing about it at all.'

'Yeah I am,' said Rez. But not even the second of these three syllables had elapsed before Rez realized that no, he was not sure.

That was only one instance of the side effects the drugs were having on Rez's memory. Far more significant was something Rez hadn't unwittingly invented, but, rather, had completely forgotten about.

He had completely forgotten his realization that Kearney was the one who had pushed 'Baby' James Appleton down the steps in the Garden of Remembrance.

The days passed. Summer was ending and soon autumn would be here. You noticed it in the little things, thought Rez foggily. For instance, the fact that it wasn't as warm any more and the days were getting shorter, and the calendar said nearly September.

Jen called him two days before she was due to fly away, to say that she would miss him and would be thinking of him. Rez thanked her. He believed her. 'When do ye think ye'll be back?'

Jen sighed. 'I don't know, Rez. I really don't. I've enough money to last me a good while. I might see if I can do some kind of volunteer work, or get a job out there, or something like that.'

'You probably shouldn't do the volunteer work,' Rez began mechanically, 'It's only Christian pity, a sort of disease … injustice is the natural order, ye shouldn't fight it.' Suddenly hearing himself, he cut himself short. His heart wasn't in it. 'No, that's good,' he said. 'It's really good. Fair play to ye.'

'Yeah. Thanks Rez,' she said, her voice strained; she was trying not to cry. She said again that she'd miss him, that she'd have no one to talk to about books, but that she'd write to him and tell him everything that was going on with her. 'I hope you take care of yourself, Rez.'

They said goodbye. Then they hung up.

That same evening Rez's mother said, 'Don't ye think it's time ye went out again and spent time with your friends? We think it would be good for ye. Don't we?'

Rez's da mumbled his agreement. Trisha, who had called in for a cup of tea, smiled supportively. She too looked older now, more dried out.

'What do ye think of that?' his ma said.

Rez didn't think anything of it. He watched his mother with calm, dozy eyes. *The poor thing*, he thought, then smiled at this funny phrase that had come from nowhere, the kind of thing an old woman would say. 'Okay,' he said.

The following day, Thursday, he was called to the phone. It was Matthew. 'I got a call from your ma yesterday,' he said. 'She was sayin she thought it would be a good idea if we brought ye out or something.' There was an embarrassed pause. 'Yeah. So, em, there's this secret rave on Saturday we were goin to go to. I've been hearin about it for ages. It's to coincide with the lunar eclipse.'

'Who's we?'

'Me and Cocker. We're meetin in the field at the school. Probably not Kearney. I don't think he knows about it. I mean, he's …' Matthew trailed off. Rez felt something then, a shadowy form lurking just out of view. 'So are ye up for it?' said Matthew.

Rez said he would go.

They hung up.

49 | **Kearney**

– Dwayne Kearney
To: Joseph Kearney
Email received at 14:00
21/08/2003

arite queer!!

stil havin a mad 1 hear in U S of muddafuken A

lissen fag u heard about de rave in greystones dis saturday?? its de EEE-KKLIPSZZ!!! man id fucken LUV 2 b der. me mates r DJn--- seerious fucken techno. hard az fuck. BLOW YR FUCKIN MIND OUT!!! :-> trust me joe itll be fuckin DEADly.

just a heds up 4 me little bro. now den off 2 get me mickey suckt!!!

later fag!!

dwayne IN-Sane

50 | Matthew

Jen left Ireland on the Saturday morning. I knew she was going then because Cocker had told me. Around ten o'clock my phone rang – it was her. I lay on my bed and waited till it stopped ringing. That was the last time Jen tried to call me.

In less than a week's time, on the last Friday in August, the exam results would be out, and then I'd learn whether I'd be going to college to study English. I doubted it; even on the slim chance that I did get in, I wasn't sure that I wanted to study. I didn't know what I wanted. By now, the Future looked even murkier, even colder than it had before. I wished I could talk about it to someone – about everything that had happened – but the weight of it all was too much. Jen was gone, Rez was at an all-time low, and I'd never felt less close to Cocker. I was sure that, from now on, our lives would only diverge further. Soon we would have nothing in common, nothing but a past. I felt more lost than ever. Maybe I could hang around with

Scag more, drop out of the mainstream altogether. At least that was a direction, a way in which to drift.

Near to six o'clock that evening, I headed over to the school. Kearney was waiting for me in the field, hands in the pockets of his leather jacket, an Aphex Twin grin on his face. Erratic against the murky twilight, he reminded me of one of the obelisks in *2001: A Space Odyssey*. There was a rucksack at his feet, bulging with what I assumed to be drink. The faint sound of traffic reached me from behind, past the railings. Again Kearney had that aura, that strange charisma, standing dead still in the field.

'Alright Kearney.'

'Alright Matthew. Haven't seen each other in a while, have we. All set for a serious onslaught?'

'Yeah.'

'Have ye bought drink already?'

I unshouldered my rucksack and shook it.

'What is it?'

'Two bottles of Buckfast and six cans of Dutch Gold.'

Kearney gestured at the field behind me. 'Here's Cocker.'

I looked over my shoulder, saw Cocker folding himself over the railings and dropping ungracefully into the ditch. He emerged and came trotting towards us.

'Howayis lads,' he said when he reached us, out of breath and grinning his usual cheery grin.

'Alright Cocker,' said Kearney, cracking open a can of Dutch Gold. 'Up for gettin monged out of it tonight?'

'Definitely. Do yis reckon we'll be able to get some pills?'

'Yeah, easy. It's a rave after all. Everyone there is going to be yoked off their tits.'

None of us had ever been to a rave before. I didn't imagine I'd care much for the music, but I was curious to see what it was like. By all accounts, tonight's was going to be one of the biggest raves the city had ever seen.

'Did ye talk to Jen before she left?' Cocker asked me.

'No. I'm not with Jen any more, don't forget.' I didn't want to hear about her.

'I know that. I just thought ye might have been speakin to her. She ... she really wanted to talk to ye.' He looked like he wanted to say more, but he glanced up at Kearney and was quiet.

'There wouldn't have been much point,' I said. 'She's probably right, though, doin what she's doin and gettin away from here. It's not the same as it used to be. I'd almost go away myself.'

Kearney pointed towards the fence and said, 'Here's our man. Here's the tragic hero.' Rez was lowering himself down from the railings with slow, exaggerated care. We watched him crossing the field towards us, like an alien; strange to everything.

'Alright Rez,' said Cocker.

'Alright Cocker. Howaya lads.'

'And how's young Prince Hamlet?' said Kearney.

'What?' said Rez.

'Give it a rest, Kearney,' I said.

'No, I'm only messin. Yer lookin well, Rez,' said Kearney. 'Good to see yer back in the game. Here, get that into ye.' He passed him a can of Dutch Gold. Rez cracked it open and started to drink.

After an hour in the field, drunk and eager, we got on a bus to town, smoking and drinking in the upstairs seats. We got off and walked to Tara Street Station and took a DART out along the darkening coast, for the last big night of the summer.

The beach was wide, dark and made of stones. It was past the lights of Greystones, at a distance from the town's few, quiet streets.

Already there were a lot of people arriving, packed in cars or in the carriages of the DART trains that stopped at Greystones before turning back for the city centre. We had taken the second-last train of the night: there was no way of getting home till morning.

Our pace quickened as we walked from the station towards the beach. The pulse of techno drew us in, charging us with anticipation. Kearney passed me the whiskey and I swigged on it. In a rush of euphoria, I reflected how much like old times this was, like it used to feel, before all this shit happened: before Rez tried to hang himself, before Kearney started doing such fucked up things, before I had got with Jen and then lost her in the most painful way possible. But the euphoria vanished when I realized that the old days I was nostalgic for were only a few months ago, lasting up until we finished school. And now there would be no more school. There was only the Future. I almost wished we could all go back to school for just one more year: at least back there things were clear. We knew who we were and what we were against. But that would only have been delaying the inevitable – being spewed up on the shores of the adult world and expected to choose, embrace, belong.

On the beach, rigs of strobe lighting had been set up alongside the sheltered DJ tables. Ravers came in clusters, stationing themselves around the dance area and along the edge of the sea. The grey skies had fallen away in the late evening and the night was clear. Stars shimmered, the moon was big and bright. We sat down to the side of the main dance area, rolling joints and drinking.

Watching the dancers, Rez said, 'It's all just sexual advertising. Look at the males, the way they spread their limbs out and twist like that – they're tryin to show the females how virile they are. It's all so obvious, it's just embarrassin.'

'Rez, yer soundin like yer old self. Good man!' laughed Cocker.

'Yeah man, he's right. It's good to see,' I said. 'Seriously Rez, yer mad to have done what ye tried to do. I hope ye never try it again, or I'll kill ye meself. I mean it, man, ye have yer mates, ye know.'

Sentimental from the drink, I reached across and squeezed Rez's shoulder. But after a slight, embarrassed nod, his expression shadowed over and he pulled away, drinking his can and retreating into himself, thinking thoughts he chose not to share. I wondered again whether there was some kind of awful secret in his past that he had never told us about.

'Lads, it's nearly midnight. It's about time we started lookin for some yokes,' said Kearney.

'Yeah, I suppose so,' I replied. The idea filled me with a vague dread. 'You're not going to take any, Rez, are ye?'

'I think I will, yeah,' he said.

'But … don't ye reckon ye probably shouldn't? I mean, it might not be good for ye at the moment.'

Kearney butted in. 'Ah, give over, will ye, Matthew? Let him make up his own mind, for fuck's sake. It's only a pill or two we're talkin about. Jaysus.'

'Maybe Matthew has a point, though, Rez,' said Cocker weakly, intimidated by Kearney.

Kearney snorted. 'You as well? A bunch of oul ones, yis are like. Jesus Christ, the fella gets out of hospital and he's goin through all this stuff, bad times, like, and all youse want to do is tell him not to have any fun.'

I wanted to challenge Kearney, ask him in front of the others why he was so keen for Rez to drop some pills. I knew the answer: the possibility that Rez would get badly depressed after them and try to kill himself again excited Kearney. But I knew too that he would deny this, throw it back at me somehow. You couldn't win with Kearney. I said nothing.

'I'll go look for them,' said Cocker. 'I'm in the mood for a walk. Stall it with us, Matthew.'

'Okay.'

'So how many are we gettin?'

After a brief debate, we decided to get five each – a proper end-of-summer blitzkrieg.

We left Rez and Kearney and set off along the beach. Up ahead was a huge bonfire, its pyramidal blaze animating a stretch of choppy sea. Squatting around the fire in a big circle, bearded, dreadlocked lads and girls with army jackets and hoodies were beating drums. Joints and cans were being passed around.

'It's like some tribal ceremony or something,' I said eagerly. 'We should be able to find some pills over there.'

The fire glowed on our faces as we approached. Tall, slender girls danced near the drum circle, spinning flaming poi in swirls and arcs. We reached the fire and stood there, drinking cans and feeling awkward.

A guy with long red hair who was sitting on a log gestured for us to sit. We did so. The drums throbbed over the crackle of burning wood, and the fire danced. After a while the red-haired guy turned and shouted to me over the beat, 'Are yis on a good one, lads?'

We nodded.

'Cool. Are yis looking for a bit of smoke by any chance?'

'No, we've already got some. But listen, do ye know where we'd be able to get some yokes?'

'How many do yis want?'

We bought twenty pills for eighty euro. When we got back to the lads Kearney said, 'Five each! This is goin to be a quality night.'

'Let's double-drop to start things off with a bang,' said Cocker.

'Yeah, fuck it, let's go for it,' I said, tired of being the sensible one. I took out eight pills and gave two to each person. 'They're speckled Mitsubishis,' I said, peering at the face of one of my pills, seeing the tiny blue crystals glint in the white logo. I rewrapped the remaining pills and slipped the bag into my back pocket, intending to give them to the others later on.

Rez raised one pill above him. 'Body of Christ,' he said.

'Amen,' we replied in chorus.

Ten minutes later I could already feel it coming up on me. I walked out on the dancing area and flung myself against the waves of sound, crashing into the barrage of dancers and strobe lights. Coming up higher and higher, I had the sense of being nothing, no one, fused with the night and the music and the lights, merged with the flux all around me.

Now a girl was smiling at me. I saw her as a fixed point within the swirl of light and noise. She was pretty, with bare arms and shoulders, black hair falling straight down the sides of her face. I smiled back at her. The beat speeded up, the volume intensified. I moved through the crowd, towards the girl, her big round eyes, her smile. Nothing could ever be wrong.

I leaned in closer to her and shouted, 'Hello there, how's a goin. You're not Irish, are ye? Where are ye from?'

'Where I'm from? From Germany. Berlin,' she shouted back, laughing. I lightly took her hand and we began to dance. At that moment, the volume rose even higher and the music raced towards a crescendo. The strobe lights pulsed brighter and faster. Then everyone around me was roaring, a great surge of sound like the earth was being rent open.

The girl was pointing at the sky, tugging on my wrist with her other hand.

I looked up: the shadow of the earth was sweeping across the face of the moon, devouring it. A third, a half, three-quarters of the lunar disc were swallowed up. Then the entire thing had vanished and the world was plunged into darkness. Every light on the beach had been switched off the instant the eclipse began. Now the crowd's roar subdued into an awed, tense hush as eerie ambient sound washed over the scene through the stacked speakers.

Everything stayed that way for a timeless moment, the frozen darkness. Then a curved blade of white light slashed the sky. The moon re-emerged. Another great roar rose up from the beach, like an offering to some weird new god.

The strobe lights flashed and the beats pounded once more. The girl was dancing, arms flung up in an arch above her head. I threw my arms to the sky and roared.

51 | Rez

Something was calling to him. It was like a muffled voice, urgent as the help-cries of someone trapped underground. The ecstasy was infusing him steadily. He sat with Kearney and Cocker, the two of them chatting animatedly but Rez saying nothing. For a while he lay back on the stones, looking up at the night above. The stars were distant and, he knew, dead, non-existent. The universe was vast, unutterably vast, the earth a cold, tiny stone that hurtled through it. There was no grand reason for anything. There was no plan, no purpose, no punishment or reward, no hope and no divine meaning to it all. It was chaos and mad accident, violence and raw energy. There was only the fluke of human life, a tiny flicker in an immense darkness – the darkness that filled Rez's dilating eyeballs, a limitless ocean of night-time.

He got up, leaving the others to their talking. He walked along the beach, away from the sound and lights of the dance area, past the bonfires, out to where no people were. He walked closely alongside the water, and waves broke over his feet, soaking through his runners. It was cold but he liked how it felt, the shiver of cool, the high-energy tingle.

Rez was exhilarated. Everything was humming with life and chaos and thrilling destructiveness. The ecstasy triggered cascades of insight and revelation. He knew, like he had never known before, that the vastness of the universe, the hopelessness he felt, the void of heaven – all of these need not be oppressive, as they usually were for him. Or they need not only be that; they were also cause for elation; rapture, even. Rez was alone in truth. He had nothing to live up to and felt profoundly free, a godless orphan, master of his own fate.

He found he had walked out to where the throb of techno was a low, distant rumble. He clambered over rocks that rose up where the stones of the beach ended, nearly slipping into pools of black water. It was windy out here, darker and colder. But Rez was thrilled by everything, he was happy to be in this place. He followed the rocky outcropping around a bend in the coast and reached a headland. Sparse lights twinkled along the coast. He couldn't hear the music at all from here, nor could he see the rave if he looked behind him – it was obscured by the dark matter of jutting rocks. He sat on the headland with the wind on his face and the crash of the sea against the rocks below. He closed his eyes and inhaled deeply.

He had been a fool, he decided, to have ever wanted to kill himself. It wasn't that it had been untrue, all the terrible things he'd become obsessed by: the end of reality, the impossibility of love, the brutal and pitiless character of existence. It was all true – but that wasn't reason enough for suicide. The challenge was to live in this weird, catastrophic, haywire world and ride it out, create your own pride and meaning within it, to face up to the nihilism and not be crushed by it. You had to keep yourself alive: through hate, through loving whatever there was left to love, through music and art and inspiration, through passion and intensity and feeling.

Out there on the headland, Rez felt like he was perched on the edge of the world, before a great abyss. There were no laws and no limits, everything was possible. He tilted his head back and the stars dived in his eyes. He laughed out loud and assented to all the whims of the chaotic, hurtling planet. If there was nothing to hope for, then there was nothing to fear, either. His life from here on in would be a reckless experiment in discipline, negation and vehemence. He vowed never to try to kill himself again, even after the euphoria faded, no matter how bad things became. He swore he wouldn't.

Then his smile wilted and he became very still. He had just remembered.

52 | Matthew

We kissed in front of the DJ rig as dancers whirled all around. Then we walked out past the rave, towards the sea. I felt like I'd known her for a long time, like this kind of thing was easy to do.

'What's Berlin like?' I asked. 'Tell me, tell me all about Berlin.'

'It's amazing, the best city in the world. You can do anything you want there, it's completely free. Everyone is making art, or the music, or doing something interesting. You can go out to the party every night until the afternoon if you want to. We say Berlin is poor, but sexy.'

'It sounds incredible. I think I want to live there.'

'You should. I think you would like it.'

'I will. That's it, I'll leave tomorrow. I'll leave tonight.'

We made our way to where the beach frayed into raised, uneven rocks. Laughing, we climbed up and sat together, our fingers entwined. Elena – her name was Elena – leaned over and kissed me, running her fingers through my hair. I touched her face. Her tongue tasted of Red Bull. We drew apart and looked into each other's eyes.

'You're so gorgeous,' I said. We kissed and the whole world vanished. I was nothing; I wasn't there.

But then a voice was saying my name. It sounded urgent. I drew apart from Elena, confused.

It was Rez. He was coming towards us slowly, careful not to trip and fall on to the rocks and into the sea. He came not from the direction of the lights and music, but from the other side, out where it was forbiddingly dark.

'Matthew,' he was saying. 'Is that you?'

'Yeah, Rez. Are ye alright?'

He slowed as he stepped over the final rock to arrive at where we sat, cross-legged and facing one another.

'Matthew, listen, I've to talk to ye for a second.'

'Em, yeah, okay. Hang on a sec. This is Elena, by the way.'

'Heya,' he said, not even looking at her.

I turned to Elena and said, 'Sorry about this, but I think it's something important. Just hang on here, okay? I'll be back in just a minute or two.'

She smiled. 'Okay, sure.'

'I'll just be a sec.'

'Don't worry.'

I clambered down from the rocks ahead of Rez and waited for him on the shingle. He hopped down and came over.

'What's up, man?' I said.

I expected him to launch into one of his rants about the techno-apocalypse, how he couldn't live with his mind any more, how it distressed him too much to be a non-voice in a dead world. But instead he said, 'Matthew, listen to me. Kearney is really messed up.'

I laughed. 'Ye mean you're only thinkin of that now? I hope ye didn't walk all the way out there to ponder things on the rocks and then only realize that Kearney is fucked up. He's –'

'No, I don't mean just like normal fucked up. He's –'

'Ye mean the pills? Has he taken too much or something?'

'No! Will ye be quiet for a moment and listen to me: Kearney killed that handicapped boy, the one on the news and in all the papers.'

I stared at him. My reaction must have come across as blank incomprehension, because Rez added, 'That one, James Appleton. Remember? It was Kearney who killed him, the handicapped boy in the Garden of Remembrance, he was pushed down the steps and had his head cracked open.'

I recovered enough to act astonished: 'Rez, what are ye talkin about? What makes ye think that?' I paused, a crazy new possibility emerging: 'Did he tell ye that himself?'

'No, no he didn't. I just, I don't know. I just know he did it. It's the clothes he was wearin, some of the things he said, and there are other reasons, little things, stuff he said to me when I was in hospital. I think I knew it was him the moment I saw it on the news, but … I don't know, I couldn't be sure, or I didn't trust myself. But I know it now, I'm absolutely certain it was him.'

The wind picked up and a cheer rose from behind me – a new DJ must have come on. I tried to meet Rez's gaze and continue to act amazed. But I started to sense that he could see right into me.

I looked down. 'I know. I already knew it was him. I mean, I suspected it. I didn't want to believe it. I think I … I convinced myself it couldn't be true.'

'What!' Rez was astonished. So I'd been wrong: he hadn't suspected me at all. 'Ye mean ye knew all along?'

I nodded, looking down again. 'I think I knew. He didn't tell me but I knew, I put it all together.'

Rez fell silent, considering this. Some time passed. Anything was possible now: Rez could go to the police, tell them that I had known about the killing and hadn't done anything. We were all going to be famous and on the news.

But Rez started speaking, saying words that made no sense at all.

He was saying, 'Matthew, give me the rest of the pills.'

I shook my head in bewilderment. 'What do ye mean?'

'Give me the pills,' he repeated, louder and more firmly.

'What do ye want them for?'

He didn't reply. He stared into my eyes. Then I knew. I took the pills from my pocket and handed them to him.

'Will that be enough?' I asked, amazed by what was happening.

'I don't know. I hope so. But go on back to that girl. Matthew, don't say *anything*. Okay? Not a word!'

'Okay. Not a word. I –'

'Go on,' he urged, shoving me away. 'And act surprised when ye see it later on.' He turned and walked back towards the rave. I watched him walk away, then I climbed back over the rocks, finding my way by the moonlight.

Elena was still sitting on the rock, her arms around her knees. She turned to me as I approached. She put her arm around my hip as I sat down beside her, and the two of us said nothing for a while, gazing out at the dark expanse of the sea.

53 | Rez

Kearney was out of his mind when Rez found him. He was staggering around the dance area with his face craned to the sky, howling like a maniac. The bottle of whiskey teetered in one hand and a can of Dutch Gold in the other.

'Rez ye bender ye!' he yelled when he saw Rez approaching.

Rez smiled and drank from a bottle of Buckfast. Then he held up a second bottle and said to Kearney, 'Here, do ye want this?'

'Yeah I fuckin want it!' Kearney rasped, deflecting the bodies of more stable dancers.

Rez grinned and said, 'Are ye sure ye want it, Kearney? Are ye sure ye want the bottle of Buckfast?'

'For Jaysus sake, just gimme the fuckin thing!' Kearney snatched the bottle out of Rez's hand.

'Fair enough, man. But listen, who are ye callin a faggot? Let's race these bottles down and see who's the dickhead, will we? I betcha I can skull the whole bottle before you can.'

'Lemme see how much yiv already drank,' Kearney slurred,

grabbing Rez's bottle as well. He pushed it back at Rez and shoved a finger into his chest. 'Fair enough, Rez. Lez go.'

'Body of Christ,' Rez said, then started to guzzle his bottle, closing his eyes as the syrupy, sickly-sweet liquid gurgled over his tongue, splashing down his throat. He swallowed it in big gulps, as fast as he could. When it was nearly gone, Kearney shoved Rez on the shoulder so that the bottle slipped and some of the Buckfast spilled on his face.

'I'm finished,' Kearney croaked. 'It tastes like mank – did ye fuckin jip into it or somethin, Rez?'

Rez smiled. 'Well done, man! Fair play! You've done it now, it's all over. You're fuckin finished.'

'Yeah.' Kearney started to say something else, but his wobble took him elsewhere, back to crashing a path through the thicket of bodies.

Rez retreated to the edge of the dance area and watched. Everything in him felt light and free. Ecstasy and Buckfast pulsated through him, imbuing the night with grandeur. He felt like he was at the Coliseum or some ancient human sacrifice. Kearney on the beach, about to fall – a blood offering to the no-God.

Kearney stumbled away. Rez followed him through the crowds, across the bustle of the beach. He was calm; it was only a matter of waiting. The music was getting harder, the beat like the war drums of some demon army howling through the night. Rez watched, enchanted, almost in love with him. Kearney wore a beatific smile as he unconsciously headed towards the drum circle, honing in on the towering bonfire like a moth to the light. Rez imagined the massive quantity of drugs that were right now coursing through Kearney's body, flooding his system, the intensity with which he must have been feeling everything. This was the greatest moment of Kearney's life.

Then Kearney's dance began. First, little quivers started pulsing through him, tingling along his skinny limbs. He began shuffling around on his feet as if he were standing on hot coals. He twitched about all over the place, not in time to any rhythm Rez could hear. He stomped and then leapt into the air with an animal grunt. He threw his head back and started to howl and shriek, his madman dance dragging him in backward circles through the startling crowd.

Rez followed, fascinated. Kearney veered towards the drum circle, then he stumbled through a gap in the ring of a dozen kneeling drummers. He was inside the circle, just Kearney and the looming blaze. The drummers looked up at him, stoney-faced, lit up by the bonfire. As if feeding on Kearney's frenzied energy, their drumming intensified, pounding and pounding, faster and faster. Amazed, Rez fell to his knees on the edge of the circle and watched.

The drumming fused with the beat of the techno and Kearney danced, licked by the flames, a streak of motion, a strip of coiled lightning.

Nobody but Rez could see the changing expression on Kearney's sweat-slick face – the distress that now flooded it. Still he danced. And now he began to emit a noise: a weird, inhuman shriek, unbroken as it rose over the pounding of the drums and the techno beat.

Then Kearney was screaming, clawing at his glistening face with the look of a man on fire. The drums pounded hungrily; it was as if the drummers knew they were present at a dreadful ceremony, a sacrifice.

Kearney leapt up once more, high into the air. When he landed he stood still for a moment, perfectly upright. Then he clenched his fists and roared: 'FALLEN HENRY, DON'T LEAVE ME!'

And with that he spun on his heel, his back now to Rez, facing the flames. His head jerked up and he fell to his knees, eyes rolling and face turned to the sky. He wobbled in front of the fire, and it was unclear which way he would fall. The tottering kept up for a few charged seconds as the murder-drums reached their climax, a frenzy of pounding.

Kearney fell into the flames, his head and torso swallowed up by a surge of fire.

No one reacted. Everyone watched Kearney, face down in the maddened blaze.

Somebody roared. Men scrambled up and dragged him out, hands clutching at each splayed limb. Out of the fire, he was flopped over on to his back. Rez stood up and looked down at Kearney as the drummers crouched around him and cried out for help.

Kearney's entire face was charred black, with pink globs dripping over the singed, smoking mass of flesh. His hair was still ablaze. One of his eyes had burst in the heat, but the other gazed up at the night and all its stars. Overcome by wonder and love, Rez felt he had never seen Kearney looking so beautiful, so serene.

He stepped back, unnoticed but witnessing everything. Commotion had swept across the beach, pulsing out from the charred and smoking centre in concentric waves.

Rez sat down on the sand, his legs crossed beneath him, and contemplated the corpse. He felt magnificently peaceful. He turned his gaze from dead Kearney to the flames that danced on, indifferently; the fierce desire arose in him to stand up and walk into the blaze, to let it consume him. There was no rage or guilt in this impulse, only a wild, effusive joyfulness.

He stayed where he was and the urge to incinerate himself faded. He closed his eyes and inhaled deeply. The universe shimmered in ecstasy. He imagined he could feel the presence of powerful spirits.

The crowds swarmed all around them and there they were, Rez and Kearney, two points of stillness in the heaving techno night.

54 | Matthew

I held Elena's hand as we leapt down from the rocks and walked back towards the rave. There were blue and red flashing lights now, and sounds that weren't part of techno or trance or drum 'n' bass.

'Shit, it's looking like a raid,' said Elena.

'Yeah, maybe that's it,' I said quietly. 'Throw your grass on the stones, just in case.'

When we reached the emptying dance area, the blackened body was sprawled out on the ground like the corpse in an American cop show. I let go of Elena's hand and walked ahead of her, stepping across the stones until I was right above Kearney. It seemed to me that Kearney's expression under the layer of curling black flakes was one of elation. I felt a gushing of affection and tenderness for smouldering, horror-movie Kearney.

Then the medics came and waved me away. They moved slowly because they knew they had no work to do. The police were there too, and everyone at the rave was rounded up, taken in to be searched and questioned. Camera flashes lit up the beach like sheet lightning, reporters already on the scene.

At the police station, through the commotion I caught a glimpse of Rez, who met my gaze and looked serene as we were led past each other in a crowded anteroom. Cocker was in a corridor with his face in his hands, shaking his head and understanding nothing – or maybe he knew it all. Maybe he always knew more than we thought he did.

I didn't see Elena again. I was one of the last to leave the police station, along with Rez and Cocker, after it was established that we were Kearney's friends.

We told the gardaí almost everything of relevance: we were frank in admitting what drugs Kearney had taken, how much he'd drunk, informing them that he hadn't suffered from any heart defects that we knew about. We were helpful in almost every regard. The only important thing we neglected to mention was that we had killed him.

'We'll be contacting you soon, boys,' the kind-of-pretty police-woman said to the three of us in a compassionate voice. It was near dawn and Rez's parents were in the waiting room, ready to drive us all home. Kearney's ma was in another room, screaming till she tore her vocal cords and repeating, 'He's NOT! He's NOT *FUCK*IN DEAD!' to the solemn coppers.

But he was dead. Kearney was as dead as the fucking dodo.

55

DUBLIN DEATH-DRUG SHAME

An illegal rave on the beach at Greystones ended in tragedy late on Saturday night when Joseph Kearney, an eighteen-year-old from South Dublin, died as the result of an ecstasy overdose. He had also sustained severe burns after falling on to a bonfire in the commotion immediately preceding his death. Police and paramedics were called to the scene but the victim was already dead when the first ambulance arrived. The state pathologist told the press after the autopsy that 'a substantial quantity' of the illegal drug had been consumed, adding that Mr Kearney's heart had become overworked before rupturing in his chest, causing a heart attack.

Mr Kearney had attended the rave in the company of three friends: Gary Cocker (17), Matthew Connelly (17) and Richard Tooley (18). The teenagers were said by gardaí and eye-witnesses to be 'devastated', 'incredulous' and 'numbed' by the death of their friend and former classmate.

The lord mayor of Dublin has today expressed his 'deepest condolences' for the victim's family, and called for tougher measures to be adopted in 'our continuing efforts to weed out this scourge that is, as we have once again so painfully seen, a serious and fatal threat to the brightest hope that our nation has, its young'.

I kept that clipping, along with a few others from the tabloids and broadsheets. I put them in the small wooden box, alongside the pictures of Becky. The irony in some of the headlines, articles and editorials was of a kind that Kearney would have appreciated – if only his heart hadn't exploded in his chest.

RAVED TO HIS GRAVE

TRAGIC DEATH OF 'ANGEL' JOSEPH AT TWISTED DRUG ORGY

That cracker was in *The Sun*.

The *Independent* had this to say, heading an opinion piece a few days after the event:

HOW MANY MORE LAMBS TO THE SLAUGHTER?

Pusher Fat Cats Profit While Our Young Perish – And Politicians Do Nothing

Et cetera, et cetera.

I stayed away from Rez for a long while afterwards. The only time I saw him during the period directly following the death was at the funeral, the day before the Leaving Cert results came in. He looked solemn and respectful, handsome in his black funeral clothes, his hair slick and immaculate with gel. His skin had a healthy glow to it – he looked like he'd awoken after a long rest. Everyone there knew what he'd tried to do to himself before Kearney died, and treated him with appropriate awkwardness.

I met him outside, at the bottom of the church steps. It was a crisp, sunny morning. Our parents and others were close so there was no way we could have talked openly, had we wanted to. But beyond the bland, excruciating words we exchanged for the sake of appearances, there was a sole, secret message that passed between us.

I had said, for the benefit of any nearby listeners, 'I just can't believe it. I can't believe he's not here any more.'

'I know,' said Rez, nodding solemnly.

Our eyes met, and then it happened: a smile broke out over his face, triumphant and gleeful, like he couldn't contain his delight. Had anyone looked at him for that moment, while he was smiling, they might have guessed the rest.

Then the smile vanished and the conventional mask of anguish and concern fell back into place. We shook hands, ridiculously. Then we walked away.